MY BROTHER'S KEEPER 2

U. E. Wynn

ISBN-13: 978-1-7320325-3-8
ISBN-10: 1732032538

ABOUT THE AUTHOR

U.E. Wynn

A self-educated, business savvy, humble entrepreneur was counted out at a young age by his peers, teachers, and family members. After enduring life altering events that would destroy and/or diminish any individual, he chose to overcome and excel. He turned what would be deemed a negative into a positive. He reevaluated himself and reclaimed a positive position within society.

U.E. Wynn is the founder of 501C nonprofit, Save a H.O.M.I.E. Inc. and an active activist within the community. He continues to assist disenfranchised youth, feed and clothe the homeless and bring forth literacy to the illiterate. Wynn also helps in providing a positive, productive and social atmosphere for the youth to unwind and enjoy themselves throughout the Carolinas via events, concerts and parties.

This is Wynn's second novel presenting you with a page turning, nail biting, exotic read.

DEDICATIONS

This is dedicated to Kwame A. Thomas and Jessie L. Taylor. It's because of you two guys I can maintain the change!!!

December 2, 2010
Prologue

Two weeks of living on the Bronx notorious streets had finally taken a toll on Koran. No longer did he resemble the cute, twelve year old his mother constantly fussed over. His hair normally braided in neat corn rolls was now tangled and dirty and looked more like a brillo pad. Dark purple rings blotched his red droopy eyes, results of sleeping on the train and from spooky nights he slept in alleys. His filthy clothes hung off his small frame like rags smelling of garlic bread and onions. To make matters worse, he had spent the last of his money the day before on a slice of pizza and a pocket knife for protection.

No, the streets of New York were no place for a twelve year old kid, but Koran was determined to make it because there was no way in hell he was returning home to the Monroe projects. Well, he couldn't call it home anymore Since his mother and sister were moving to North Carolina. It's what forced his decision to move away. Having a stubborn streak like his older brother Jahad, his mind was set on staying in the Bronx. He would rather live on the streets than move to the boondocks around a bunch of sheet wearing rednecks.

What really pissed him off is it had already been agreed that he would stay in New York with Jahad when their mother moved. Then, at the last minute they changed their minds claiming New York wasn't the place for him. It made no difference because he'd showed them both. So what if he went hungry sometimes? So what if he hadn't taken a bath in two weeks? And so what if his home was a cardboard box. He was still in the Bronx and he was there to stay.

Crawling from his cardboard box Koran stretched some the aches from his muscles and then walked out of the alley on Commonwealth Avenue glancing around for an unsuspecting victim. Since running away, he had reverted back to his old ways of scamming and pick pocketing. A skill he picked up when Jahad was locked up in Spofford Detention Center in an effort to bring money home to his mother. Now it was his only means of survival.

For a cold Tuesday morning herds of people crowded the sidewalks, walking purposely to work like ants. Dark puffy clouds painted New York's skyline. A sure sign of snow Since temperatures now hovered at forty degrees. Koran blended in with the crowds, then scanned both sides of the streets to make sure no cops were around. This was something he learned to do his second day on the streets after he was chased by two plain clothes cops for snatching a white woman's pocketbook. From that day on he studied people looking for shifty eyes, bulges under armpits, and tight pants. The sure sign of a cop, he figured.

He walked by a bread bakery and paused for a second, the aroma making his mouth water. He then fell into step with two white men dressed in expensive business suits. His eyes stayed glued to their back pocket while in his mouth, he pictured a plate of fried chicken wings, rice smothered with thick gravy, and a cold glass of cherry cool-aid. Food was his biggest motivator because if he didn't score he didn't eat. Once his belly was full then maybe he would catch a cab to Fordham road and do a little shopping depending on how much he came off with. To lessen his risk of getting caught he tried to stretch his licks out as far as possible and kept a mental note to be careful how he spent his money. Drawing closer to the two men he caught snatches of their conversation, something pertaining to a case they were trying later that afternoon.

"Lawyers!" Koran whispered to himself grinning. If he did this right, he could possibly be set for a whole mouth.

Before making his move he scanned the street once more, then did two things simultaneously. His right hand shot out towards the lawyer in his left back pocket, at the same time he stumbled hard onto him using his index and middle finger to slip the wallet from his back pocket. When he turned Koran ran into the lawyer on the right hugging him tightly.

"Help me! Help me! He's gonna get me!" he screamed, taking wild glances over his shoulder.

Repulsed by the smelly black kid clinging to his two thousand dollar suit the lawyer pried Koran's hands away without a clue that his wallet was no longer in his pocket.

"What's wrong kid? Who's after you?"

"Some man. Some bum back there," Koran pointed behind him with crocodile tears in his eyes. "He tried to pull me in the alley."

Both lawyers glanced over their shoulders confused. "There aren't any bums back there kid," the lawyer on his left said annoyed.

"Un huh! C'mon, I'll show you."

"No, No, that's alright," the lawyer on his right looked at his partner. "You're okay now. Just stay away from that alley."

Dummies. Koran laughed as he Started back towards his cardboard home so he could count his money. "Koran! Koran!" A familiar voice called out behind him just as he was about to turn into the alley. Koran turned around and locked eyes with the closest person he knew to a grandmother. Mrs. Harris.

Dressed in a beige cotton dress, long wool coat and wearing thick bifocals, Emma Harris ran towards him and smothered him with a warm hug. "Boy where you been? Michelle is worried sick about you," she said scowling.

Although he knew trouble was ahead, he couldn't contain the joy he felt. Two weeks was a long time to go without a hug, especially from someone he loved. "I'm a'ight Mrs. Harris. I've got my own little place," he said, pointing down the alley to his cardboard box.

"Humph!" Emma grunted. "You know better than running away like that. Anything could have happened to you out here. And look at you. When's the last time you washed your butt? You should be ashamed of yourself smelling like that. Come on here and let me get you home." She grabbed his arm and walked to the edge of the sidewalk to signal for a cab.

"Mrs. Harris I can't."

Emma cut him off with a sharp look. "You can't what?"

"I can't go home. They trying to make me move down south. I don't wanna leave New York, Mrs. Harris. I can't!" he pleaded on the verge of crying.

Emma's stern look instantly turned sympathetic. "I know baby, but sometimes you have to roll with the flow of things. You know you can't live out here on the streets like this Koran."

"Let me stay with you then. I'll be good, I promise. I'll do good in school and I'll do chores. Please Mrs. Harris?"

His words touched her heart and brought tears to her eyes. "I wish you could stay with me baby, but I doubt Michelle will let you. Hey, you never know, you just might like North Carolina," she said attempting to brighten his spirits.

"No, I won't! I'll hate it. I hate it already," he said pouting.

At that moment a cab pulled up and she ushered him inside before sliding in herself. In the cab Koran stared out at traffic, sidewalks, and store fronts soaking up the scene. He imagined it would probably be one of the last times he saw New York in a while and the thought filled him with dread. Making a quick dash when the cab stopped crossed his mind, but reading his thoughts, Emma took hold of his hand. Fifteen minutes later the cab parked across from Monroe projects and his dread turned into desperation. His face wore a mask of misery when Emma tugged his hand, urging him from the cab. With her grip he knew there was no way he could escape now. On the elevator ride to the tenth floor, he paced in small circles desperately trying to figure a way out. Then, as the elevator came to stop something came to mind. A move he used occasionally when pulling one of his schemes.

"Mrs. Harris, I have to use the bathroom real bad!" He doubled over grabbing his stomach. "It's been almost two weeks."

Emma took in his pained expression and whipped him away to her apartment. Inside Koran dashed to the bathroom holding his stomach with Emma on his heels. For twenty two minutes he made loud grunting noises and flushed the toilet every two minutes until she finally stopped asking if he was okay and left. Now all he had to do was slip from the apartment and he was home free.

When he cracked the bathroom door, he held his breath, praying Emma wasn't waiting for him in the hallway. A deep sigh of relief escaped him when he found it empty. Almost there, he thought as he crept to the end of the short hallway like a cat burglar. He paused when he heard Emma rambling around in the kitchen, then jogged lightly to the front door.

As he eased the door open he froze catching sight of his mother and Latrice stepping from the elevator. The strong urge to run out and hug his mother washed over him, but thoughts of moving down south held him in place. Once they turned the corner he stepped out into the hallway looking around as if he had just escaped from prison. The staircase door was only a few steps away, but he made no move towards it. Since his mother and sister were gone, he figured he could grab some of his clothes and his notebook computer before they returned. His only worry was Jahad, but at ten o'clock in the morning he doubted if he would be home. Jahad had always been an early riser. With that thought, he decided to test his luck and dug in his dirty jean pocket for his key.

Paranoia set in again by the time he reached the apartment door which was only two doors away from Emma's apartment. If Jahad was inside, moving down south most likely would come with a severe ass whipping too. Then he thought of Emma finding him gone and quickly entered the apartment. Silence greeted him as he closed the door, but he still wasn't taking any chances. Remembering a scene he saw once on television, he took off his sneakers and sprinted towards his bedroom on his tiptoes without making a sound.

He felt a rush of homesickness when he opened the door. His bed was neatly made with the thick black comforter and fluffy white pillow making him yearn to sleep in a comfortable bed again, his comfortable bed. All his sneakers were stacked along the front of his bed looking crisp and new. He looked down at the badly scuffed Air Force One's he held and shook his head. This wasn't him at all. He normally was a fly little dude. Now here he was dressed and smelling like a smoked out crack head. A lump formed in his throat thinking of how rough he had been living, but he only had one other option, one he refused to accept.

Pushing the thought aside, he walked to his closet, passing Jahad's messy side of the room when he heard the apartment door open.

"Oh shit!" he whispered and then dived into the closet head first frantically snatching clothes off the hanger to cover himself.

A few seconds later Jahad and Tony entered the bedroom. Tony dressed in a Pelle Pelle jean suit, gray Timberlands, and a gray and white New York Yankee's sweatshirt. He bore a close resemblance to the rapper Methoughd Man. Golden brown skin, a wild mouth, full lips and wide set chinky brown eyes. A sharp nose flared at its nostrils, and long hair that he wore in corn rolls that hung down to his shoulders.

Jahad wore black Roc-A-Wear jeans, Red and white Air Force Ones, a red and white Roc-A-Wear hoodie and a white doo rag on his bald head. His large soulful light brown eyes the color of a Hershey chocolate bar, stood out against his dark complexion. He had facial features that look like they could have been shaped from stone. High cheekbones, a broad, slightly crooked nose, thick lips, and a strong jawline ending at his pointed chin.

"A yo, what's that smell, son?" Tony asked, wrinkling his nose as he sat on Korans' bed. "You got some sour clothes in here or something?"

In the closet Koran bit the inside of his cheeks to keep from giggling. He knew he smelled, but he didn't know he was that funky.

"Nah, I don't think so. Let me open the window though, because I smell it too." Jahad opened the window that sat right above his dresser, then sat on his bed facing Tony and shook his head. This shit is stressing me all the way out Tone, word up. Where in the hell is this little nigga at," he asked, his eyes holding Tony's as if he held the answer. "You know what I'm trying not to think, right? But if Hector…"

Tony held up his hand. "Don't speak it into existence, Jah. You better believe that wherever Koran is he's alright. Lil dude just heated right now. He'll show up sooner than later…watch."

Koran cracked a smile. Tony was his man, he thought.

"It's been two fuckin weeks Tone!" Jahad shouted, pushing himself off his bed. He went to his dresser, opened the bottom drawer and took out a box of Dutch master cigars and a sandwich bag of lime green marijuana before he sat back down. "You know, I can't blame nobody but myself for this shit. I never should have lied to the lil nigga," Koran mumbled, his expression tormented.

"I won't tell you to stop worrying or blaming yourself, but you have a lot of shit on your plate right now, so stay focused, son."

Jahad nodded. "You right. So what's up? You still bouncin' or you gonna fall back and help me blow the M.G.'s out the water?"

Tony sighed. "C'mon Jah. We built on this a hundred times already. As much as I wanna stay up here and help you pop this shit off, I can't. It ain't about me no more, Jah. And it ain't about you, money, bitches, or the game. It's all about your sister and the seed she carrying. I can't afford to be selfish and risk going up North or getting killed for the sake of what I wanna do. My son or daughter, your niece or nephew, won't grow up like we did. I'ma make sure of that. You gotta respect it Son."

Jahad rolled a blunt, lit it, then walked to his window without responding. Although he understood, it didn't change the fact that he played a major role within the M.G. structure. If it wasn't for his help the organization would have never been formed. A month ago, they successfully took out a drug empire and now were in the process of taking total control of the drug trade in the South Bronx.

Tony was needed. He was their financial man. His gifted hustlers mind and money making scheme's always produced money. With this move money would be pouring in and Tony would be the perfect Treasurer. Jahad went to the extent of offering to buy him and his sister a house in New Jersey as a wedding gift to keep him close to New York, but Tony declined the offer. He had found something that held his interest more than drug dealing. Something that demanded his time and loyalty. That something was love and the chance to raise his child.

"What? You gonna take kill the blunt yo self?" Tony asked.

Jahad took a deep pull before passing it. He blew out a cloud of bluish smoke, then gave Tony a pleading look

"Tone, I feel you on what you saying man, but damn! You supposed to be here now that we're eating. Think about it. New York is about to be ours. We taking this shit, and the ill part is, won't nobody know nothing!" he said with feeling.

Tony shook his head. "Nah, Jah. My place is with Trice and my seed. I see where you coming from, but it ain't in me no more! I mean, my love for the game is gone. All I see is death now, Homey."

"C'mon with that bullshit, Tone. It'll always...."

"No, listen man. Nothing lasts forever, Son. Believe dat! So take what I'm about to say to heart. Make your money, then leave this shit alone. I mean fall all the way back."

Jahad screwed up his face. Since the CoCo twins destroyed his dream of owning his own record label, he now craved power and wouldn't be satisfied until he had it. "Fallback? No, you need to get off that Holy Roller shit. You know the drill man. When Sha' comes home, we moving on East New York and Brownsville. The same goes for when Lord, Prince and Star come home. Bed-Stuy, Harlem, and Southside Jamaica Queens is gonna be ours. Shit, it's about to be on my nigga!"

Tony looked at Jahad solemnly. "And like I said, all I see is death."

"So be it," Jahad said and hunched his shoulders.

Holed up in the closet Koran listened awestruck. He half suspected Jahad was behind what police labeled *"The Bronx Drug War"* where thirty-six people had been slain over the course of the month. But now he knew the purpose. Even at the tender age of twelve he understood completely the impact Jahad's plan would have. It amazed him, and at that moment made him more determined to stay in New York. He had no idea what the M.G.'s were, but his sole ambition was to become a part of it.

Jahad and Tony talked for a few more minutes before they left.

Jahad was still trying to persuade Tony to stay and Tony continued to refuse his offer as they eased out the apartment. Koran waited until he heard the front door slam and then scrambled out the closet with their conversation still buzzing in his head. He had to find a way to let his mother and Jahad let him stay in New York. Maybe if he stayed gone another week or two they would realize how serious he was about staying. At least he hoped so or he would have to run away again.

After packing his book bag full of clothes he tossed three pairs of sneakers in a plastic bag and then quietly left the room. At the end of the hallway, he was about to make a left to enter the short hallway that led to the front door when he heard movement in the living room which was directly to his left about five feet away. He flattened himself against the wall, his heart racing trying to figure out what to do. It all boiled down to two choices; sneak back into his bedroom and hide in his closet or make a dash for the door. After a few seconds, he went with his second choice and sprinted off like a track star. In the living room, all Jahad saw was a black streak shoot pass but recognized Koran immediately.

"Koran?... Koran, bring your little ass back here!" he yelled, just as Koran reached the front door.

Driven by fear Koran ran as fast as his short legs would carry him out the apartment to the staircase door. He reached the handle thinking he had escaped when Jahad suddenly snatched him back by his dingy collar.

"Where the hell you been, huh? Where the fuck you been!" Jahad screamed resisting the urge to hug him.

Koran was about to answer, but Emma ran from her apartment scowling, her church hat turned sideways on her head "Koran what in the world are you doing out here? I thought you were using the bathroom."

Jahad whipped his head around. "Bathroom? He's been with you the whole time?" he asked angrily.

"Don't take that tone with me Jahad!" she snapped. "You know doggone well I wouldn't have you or Michelle worried like that. I bumped into him this morning when I was doing my grocery shopping. I was bringing him home until he lied and said he had to go to the bathroom with his slick butt. He must've snuck out while I was in the kitchen."

Koran turned away from Emma's glare.

"What the hell is wrong with you Koran? You know how worried we been man? You got Moms and Trice about to have nervous breakdowns."

Koran held Jahad's stare defiantly. "I ran away and I'ma run away again soon as I get a chance. You said I could stay with you when Mommy moved and I'm staying! I don't care how many times you beat me up or mommy beats me. I ain't leaving!"

Jahad looked back at Emma as if asking What should I do? She responded with a shrug of her shoulders. Feeling like his hand had been forced he turned back to Koran with a sigh. "A'ight man. You got a winner 'cause I did say you could chill with me. But if you ever try some bullshit like this again I'ma beat the breaks off you, word up!"

"I ought to beat the breaks off you now," Emma added, secretly thrilled that he was staying. A smile lit up Koran's face. He was staying. The words replayed over and over in his head like a chant.

"I don't know what you smiling for. You about to be on lockdown for a whole month. No T.V., no video games, no phone, no nothing!" Jahad barked.

Koran didn't care. All that mattered was that he was staying. When he was old enough, some way or another, he would be a M.G. What he couldn't possibly grasp, and what none of them could foresee, was what he would become.

Chapter One
Saturday, April 5, 2005

A spectrum of colorful lights lit up Harlems 125th street. The Apollo Theater had just let out so the sidewalks were crowded. People dressed in their finest clothes were walking shoulder to shoulder to Lincoln Town Car Cabs. Some were hanging out along the busy street trying to decide what night spot to hit next. The congested traffic looked more like a car show as drivers inched by in their Benz's, BMW's, Range Rovers, and Hummers with the music blasting.

Stalled at a stoplight on Adam Clayton Powell, a sleek black Bentley G.T. idled quietly drawing second glances from pedestrians. The driver, a man on the brink of stirring up madness, smiled out at a group of pretty young women crossing the street before he reached for his cell phone. He looked down at the number written down on a Macy department store receipt, a number he'd spent months searching for. A number that would set in motion a stream of mistrust and murder.

So much time, years in fact had been spent orchestrating what he considered would be the perfect revenge, but also the ultimate game. A game in which he would be calling all shots, pushing all buttons and controlling all the players, therefore making him the Operator. Though who lost, well, they died. That was the main objective of the game. The prize, total control of New York's most secretive and deadliest organizations. The number he now dialed started the clock.

"Hola?" His party answered in Spanish just as the light turned green.

"Hector?"

"Speaking... Who's calling and how did you get this number?" Hector, Jahad's arch enemy asked sounding paranoid. Since his drug empire came crashing down nearly five years ago, he had been slowly rebuilding his team. During the process he was extremely careful to keep his name from circulating on the street due to numerous attempts made to end his life. Somehow, no matter how safe and secluded he felt, he was always found. However, before each attack, he was miraculously notified in advance. So he stayed on the move never laying in one spot longer than a month. What he failed to realize was any involvements he had with the streets in the four boroughs the M.G's were active in, would sooner or later filter back to Jahad. The M.G.'s had long arms and very good ears.

"Who I am ain't important. What I can do for you is all that matters," the man said with a satisfied smile as he made a right on 130th and Lenox.

"Listen, whoever you are, I'm not interested in buying anything and I have no time for riddles…Goodbye."

"Yo!" The man shouted, but Hector had already hung up. "Stupid Bitch!" he cursed quickly before dialing again and spoke as soon as Hector answered. "Don't hang up again! Now I'ma say one name and then you tell me, do you have time for riddles…Jah."

The hairs on Hector's arms stood erect. "I'm listening"

"Got your attention now, huh? Hear this then, I'm the dude to help you get your face back. We…"

"Who are you? What do you mean by getting my face back? How did you get this number?" Hector spat rapidly, his Spanish accent thickening.

"Whoa Poppi, you speeding. Now who I am like I said, ain't important. I'm the dude to put you in a position to merk Jah though if you're interested. I ain't feeling dude either. I just can't merk him. Well, I can, but I choose not to. What I want you to do is give it some thought. I'll get back at you through some of your people."

Click.

Chapter Two

Over a five year span the M.G.'s grew enormously in numbers and strength, and dominated 60% of the drug trade in South Bronx, Harlem, Brownsville, East New York, Bed Stuy, and Jamaica Queens right under the noses of New York's underworld, the N.Y.P.D. and the F.B.I. This was accomplished by an ingenious system put together by the Heads (Jahad, Sha', Star, Lord, and Prince), while locked up on Riker's Island. Their birth caused the name M.G. to be whispered among drug dealers, gangsters, and stick up kids the way children spoke of the boogie man; in a quiet spooky manner. And just as children feared the boogie man, grown men feared the M.G.s mainly because no one knew who they were or if the organization even existed.

In 2004 after an off and on two week heated debate, a cap was put on the M.G. membership list. Sha' and Star, both believers that numbers produced strength, voted to keep the numbers open. Jahad, Lord, and Prince agreed, but were also believers that too many numbers produced weak links. Already each head supervised a 60 man crew, for a total of 300 extremely dangerous, money oriented brothers recruited straight from Riker's Island. As a whole, the M.G. had two main objectives, money and murder. If anyone was foolish enough to stand between their money making operation, they were found a few days later floating in the Hudson River or stinking up an abandoned building. It was never personal, always business. Big Business.

Jahad played the role of a small time businessman to cover the secret life he led. A year after the M.G.s were in full operation, he approached Joe Collins, his former boss and owner of Joe's moving company, with a huge offer to buy his business. More out of respect than money, Joe sold his twenty year business for pennies on the books, but a small fortune under the table. Enough so he could never have to lift another couch or dresser again in his life. Since then, Jahad turned the already established business into a money washing gold mine.

While the M.G.s thrived, Koran grew into a man. At seventeen he graduated from Theodore Roosevelt at the top of his class earning a full scholarship to St. Johns University with an astounding 1400 S.A.T. score. Jahad, like a proud father, went out and bought him a brand new 2005 smoke gray Range Rover thinking he was going to college. He was sadly mistaken. Koran had only one goal in mind and he made his wishes known a week before his classes were to start.

Jahad sat in the living room after putting in ten hours at work that Tuesday afternoon. His feet were propped up on the glass coffee table, a double shot of Hennessey in his hand, and a blunt hanging from the side of his mouth. He had enough money to afford a five million dollar mansion in Long Island, a few hundred thousand dollar cars, a Lear Jet, but chose to live in the projects and play his hard working business man role just to divert attention and the notion that he was fooling Koran.

Only inside his apartment could a hint of his wealth be seen. Plush burgundy carpet covered the living room, hallways, and bedroom floors. The living room held expensive black suede furniture, a 60 inch plasma screen television perched on the wall between two African covered masks, and a Dell computer that sat right beside a red oak wet bar. All three bedrooms had king sized beds, a small dresser, and 42 inch flat screen televisions hanging on the walls. There wasn't much room for anything else except for the computer Koran squeezed inside his room.

Yes, he was rich beyond his wildest dreams. Happy? Well, Joy was emotion Jahad rarely dealt with. Since the M.G's came into existence, he only allowed room for one feeling. A bitter coldness that came straight from the core of his heart. As the years passed, he no longer felt human and could no longer feel the same emotions humans felt. Now he was more like a reptile and no amount of heat could change that he was a cold blooded animal.

Pushing himself off the couch, he walked over to the window behind the bar and Stared out over the South Bronx wondering how his life would have turned out if he never bumped Heads with the CoCo twins. With his eyes closed, he drifted off into the fantasy of his lost music career. He stood on stage at Madison Square Garden, thousands of fans screaming his name, sweat pouring from his face as he belted out slick hardcore lyrics only the streets would relate to, but everybody, black and white could feel.

Beside him to the left, Eric, his best friend and rap partner stood swaying to the beat waiting to rock the mic next. Tony stood to his right moving his hands from side to side hyping up the massive crowd. Then it all disappeared when he heard the front door open and reality came crashing down. Eric was dead, had been dead for years, killed by the CoCo twins. Tony was in North Carolina happily married and working for a radio station in Raleigh. And he was… He was a mass murderer slash drug Lord hiding behind his moving company. The thought left him depressed.

Koran walked in a few seconds later fresh off a date with one of his girlfriends. He had grown into his lanky arms and big feet standing at a slim six feet. If he were a few inches taller and a bit bulkier, he and Jahad could almost go for twins. They both had the same strong facial features with their mothers light brown eyes, but where Jahad was dark Koran was high yellow. He wore lime green Timberland's, Gucci jeans, a white and lime green striped Gucci button up shirt, and Jahad's diamond platinum chain with his own rose gold Cuban link holding a son piece flooded with yellow diamonds. At the time his life revolved solely around clothes, clubs, and women, but this was about to change.

"A yo, I told you about rocking my chain. You could have one if you ain't spend all your money trickin'," Jahad said, turning from the window, his face set in a scowl.

"Whatever." Koran dropped his keys off on the coffee table, then sat down and put out the blunt Jahad had been burning in the ashtray. "We need to talk."

"Whatever?" Jahad started towards him. "Nigga, I'll…"

Koran quickly held up his hands. "Chill Jah. We need to talk for real."

For months he had been trying to figure out the best way to bring up the subject of him becoming a M.G. He already had in mind what Jahad would say. No, followed by a lecture about how important college was, promises he made to their mother, blah, blah, blah.

"What's so important that we need to talk about besides you taking off my chain, right now!"

"The Money Getter's, the M.G.'s, whicheva' you wanna call them."

Jahads' mouth dropped open. No one outside the M.G.s knew their identity besides Tony, or so he thought.

Koran cracked a smile. "Guess you ain't stressing' the chain no more, huh?"

Jahad covered his surprise with a look of annoyance. "I don't know what the hell you talking about. You high or something?"

"No, I ain't high and you know exactly what I'm talking about."

"Yeah, a bunch of meatball shit." He grabbed his glass and poured himself another drink refusing to meet Koran's eyes.

"Was it meatball shit when you came home from the Islands and all though bodies Starting poppin' up? That was meatball shit too, right?"

"What kinda shit you on? You trying to be a detective or something?"

"Nah, just the opposite. I'm gonna be a M.G." he said, fighting to control his temper.

Jahad burst out laughing. "Well, send your application to Superman or Batman. One of them should get back at you."

That did it. Koran snapped. "What you playing stupid for Jah! I know what's poppin'. You remember that conversation you had with Tone back in the day trying to get him to stay so he could help you build the M.G.'s? I was in the closet the whole time, so you can chill with the jokes."

Jahad Stared coldly at Koran for a second. He set his drink down, then crossed the living room and snatched him up by the collar of his shirt. "You nosey lil muthafucka! I'm sending your ass down south on the first plane out. Now who the fuck have you told!" He shook Koran like a rag doll.

Koran struggled in vain to break Jahad's grip. "No fucking body! Who in the fuck did I tell when you and Razor bodied all them people in the park? I don't even know why you asked me some crazy shit like that for."

Sobered by Koran's words Jahad let him go. His thoughts traveled back to the time he and Razor, who had been killed by the N.Y.P.D., murdered sixteen of the CoCo twin's workers in P.S. 100 School Park. By eyewitnesses account, Razor held a man hostage in broad daylight before he killed two police officers. The man's identity was never learned, but from his bedroom window facing the park Koran watched the bloody scene unfold through powered binoculars. Since that day not a word of what he'd seen had been spoken until now.

"You think I would tell somebody about the M.G's? That my brother is the nigga that started it? If so, then yeah, I need to go down south. Anywhere to get the hell away from you."

Jahad grabbed Korans' shoulder before he could walk off. "Hold up yo. Pardon me lil nigga, but you don't understand how serious this shit is."

"Evidently I do. I kept it to myself all these years."

"Yeah. Still, you know I won't... I can't bring you into this shit. You know why, right?"

Koran didn't answer.

"Cause I love your lil ass."

"Look at me Jah." Koran held out his arms. "I ain't little no more and from my S.A.T. scores, I'm damn near a genius."

"Do you know what you're asking for? No! Why you wanna get mixed up in some bullshit when you got the mind to make millions legally?"

"If the M.G.'s eating like I think, y'all be seeing millions. Tax free dough at that."

Jahad sighed and ran a hand across his face. Koran was making this hard. "It ain't about money Koran, well it is, but the price you have to pay ain't worth it. Not when you gotta different way of getting dough. The shit I do not good for the heart and it ain't good for the soul. It'll kill a weak nigga."

Koran frowned. "You trying to say I'm weak or something? I know how weak niggaz get down. They be crackheads, snitches and faggots. None of though labels fit me."

"No, Koran. No!" Jahad shook his head frustrated. "You know the promise I made to mom. Besides, there's better things you can be. You start college next week bro. You wanna throw that away for this?"

"I don't wanna be nothing else Jah. You know how long I had my mind set on this? Five years. Five years of following all your bullshit ass rules so that when this day came you wouldn't deny me. Everything has a price, you just said it. Now it's time to pay up."

"You think it's that easy nigga? That I can just snap my fingers and bang! You're in. It don't work like that man. You don't got no idea what we do, who we really are. This ain't a fade you..."

"I know..."

"Listen!" Jahad shouted bitterly. "We're like fucking vampires Koran, only we don't kill for blood, we kill for money. You get the concept? We don't do it outta greed, it's our nature, what our environment produced. Every last M.G. is a cold hearted killa. Is that what you wanna be? Think you can handle that?"

Koran took the time to think before answering. "I mean, if that's what it takes then yeah. I can handle it."

"Dammit Koran!" Jahad slammed his hand against the wall. "Why you bein' so fucking hard headed. What you think moms would say if she found out?"

"C'mon Jah. Mom don't know a damn thing about the M.G.'s so come with something better than that lame ass excuse. This is what I want. All I'm asking for is one chance. Just one chance and I swear I won't let you down."

Jahad stared at him through slanted eyes for a full minute. "You wanna chance, huh?"

"Just one."

"A'ight," he nodded, thinking of a scheme that would work in his favor. At least he thought it would. "A'ight, this the lick though. If you make it through all this extra shit I throw at you, then you're in. If not…"

"What extra shit?" Koran asked frowning.

"I ain't finished!" Jahad snapped. "If you can't handle it, then you take your ass to college and never mention the M.G.'s to me again. We gotta deal or what?"

"I'm saying, what's this extra shit you talking bout?"

"You'll find out if you agree to the deal."

"It ain't no crazy shit is it?"

Jahad shrugged his shoulders.

Reluctantly Koran nodded. "A'ight, Jah. But don't try to trick me on some bungee jumping fear factor shit."

Jah laughed. "I ain't gonna trick you. It won't be no cake walk though."

"When do I start?"

"As soon as you take off my chain and go to the park."

"The park? What the hell am I suppose to do in the park?"

"Nothing. I want you to sit on one of the hard ass park benches and watch everything moving." He looked at his watch. "It's ten now so I'll only give you two hours tonight. Tomorrow, though from eight to twelve. That's where you'll be. Don't talk to nobody unless you have to. You'll be out there for a reason. Can you guess what?"

"Yeah, but what the hell does sitting in the park have to do with me becoming a M.G?"

"Every fucking thing! Niggaz in this shit are special made niggaz. We been through shit that you couldn't possibly understand. If you gonna be one of us you gonna go through the same shit we went through, know what we know, and think how we think. Just because you my brother don't mean nothing. You gotta prove yourself nigga." He took a deep breath before continuing. "I ain't no M.G. because I wanted to be one. I didn't want this shit, it chose me. Though times I got bagged, bodied nigga's, I didn't want none of that shit to happen. But it's what life dealt me. It's what made me a M.G. That goes for every nigga that's part of this shit. You understand?"

Koran nodded.

"I doubt it," Jahad snorted. "But you will by the time you become a M.G. Until that day, starting right now, all your time belongs to me. In the morning we going to the P.A.L. and I'll plug you in with the old man Jimmy. He's trained a few title holders. That will be five mornings a week; Monday through Friday. When you come home from the gym, I'll have some books I want you to read and memorize. That should keep you busy until it's time for you to hit the park. Weekends we going to the firing range and I'll take you up on the roof and show you some shit I learned when I was at Spofford.

"That partying shit is dead. That shopping shit is dead. All that fucking you were doing is dead. You won't have time for it. No more hanging out. No more…"

"Damn Jah. You saying I can't get no pussy at all? C'mon man!" Koran looked stricken.

Jahad laughed. Koran was juggling six girlfriends all from different parts of the city. "We'll work something out. Listen to what I'm bout to say though. Love and the M.G.s don't mix so don't go falling in love with no bitch."

"Pssss! Me fall in love? Picture that."

"I'm serious Koran. We loyal to only three things. Ourselves, our families and the M.G.'s. Ain't nothing outside those three. I'll give you a little room so you can keep doing what you doing. That's keeping a stable of ho's to choose from so you won't be spending too much time with one chick. Got that?"

"Yeah, is that all?"

"Hell nah. You know me. I'll keep coming up with some new shit just to keep you occupied since you wanna be a M.G. Whatcha' waiting for? Don't you got somewhere you need to be?" Jahad pointed towards the door resisting a smile after seeing look on Koran's face.

Chapter Three

The next morning after Jahad dropped Koran off at the boxing gym, he drove to Harlem for a meeting with the Heads. Koran's knowledge and request to become a M.G. had to be brought to the table. He figured he was about to catch hell for a good reason, since he had voted for the books to be closed. He was against the decision himself. Koran was too young and the last thing he wanted was for his brother to be murdered. There was really no way around it though with Koran knowing their secret. The only option was a thought Jahad couldn't begin to fathom and he wouldn't let the Heads speak of it.

As he made a left on 130th and Lenox driving towards Prince's brownstone he mentally cursed Koran for forcing his hand, something he seemed to be good at. The impression it would make on his comrades bothered him if they didn't understand his reasoning. Maybe they would think he was blatantly disregarding what he had made law just because he could. Or worse, think he was taking a stand as the role leader when all five ran the organization as one. No matter how they took it, he wasn't about to let no harm come to Koran regardless of how they felt.

Nearing Prince's home in his 1979 Rusty brown Delta 88 Oldsmobile he spotted Stars silver 745i BMW parked behind Prince's white CL 55 Mercedes Benz directly in front of the brownstone. Lord's burgundy Yukon Denali was parked slightly on the curb on the other side of the street. He must be high Jahad thought. He saw no signs of Sha's forest green Range Range Rover and figured he rode with Lord. They meant they both were probably high.

Out of all the Heads, Jahad was the only one who did not own a stable of cars. For years they hounded him to get rid of his hoopty, but the car was once his father's and held sentimental value. He would never get rid of it. So when his friends called him an African Cab driver it didn't bother him at all.

Whenever he wanted to stunt, which wasn't often, he drove a 2004 black 600 Mercedes Benz that he kept in an alley behind his moving company. The secret life he had made him cautious about drawing too much attention, something he once stressed to the other Heads. If they didn't have legitimate business to account for their income more than likely they would be driving beat up cars.

After parking behind Lord's truck he got out his rust bucket, took a deep breath, then made his way towards the brownstone scanning the street as he went. He had done so much dirt over the years he was constantly looking over his shoulder. He couldn't get caught slipping. Before he made it up the steps Sha' pulled up in his Range and parked in front of Lords' truck.

He was the tallest of the Heads standing at a slim six three. She hopped out the truck smiling, showing off his hundred thousand dollar platinum diamond grill. He wore a typical Brooklynite outfit. Beef and broccoli Timberlands, army fatigue pants pulled up around his calf muscles, and a plain white tee shirt. His narrow face, long sharp nose, slanted brown eyes, and high cheekbones hinted at a trace of Asian in his blood although his roots were from Antigua.

"A yo, that's a damn shame." He glanced at the Oldsmobile as he crossed the street. "You got all that damn money and still pushing that piece of shit.

Jahad smiled. "That's a classic right there Son. All it needs is a paint job and I probably get few G's for it."

"Shit, you'll have to pay a nigga to take it off your hands. Give me five hundred and I'll do what needs to be done."

"What's that?"

"Blow that muthafucka up." He laughed and gave Jahad hug. "What up with you and how the college boy?"

The smile left Jahad's face. "I'm good, and the college boy is the reason I'm here. I need to holla about something that came up with his stubborn ass."

"He a'ight right?"

"Yeah, he a'ight. It's…."

Jahad was cut off when Prince opened the front door. Years of good living turned his once 190 pound frame into 250 pounds of chubbiness, but he wore it well. Decked out in a white Louis Vuitton velour sweat suit and white Prada sneakers, he was the most flamboyant out of the Heads. It was to be expected being where he was from though. He had a personal garage where he kept his expensive cars and wore thousand dollar outfits every day of the week. The Louis X111 liquor he drunk went for $1300 a bottle. The reefer he smoked was priced at $650 an ounce. His cover was a barbershop he owned on Broadway, a clothing store on 125th, and a night club on the lower east side that catered to the young white people.

"What y'all holding the meeting out here or something? Get your asses in here," he said with a smile spread across his wide face.

The inside of his home showed another reflection of his extravagant lifestyle. Black marble floors, expensive English furniture and built in wall aquariums in the foyer. A huge white bear pelt, its head raised baring sharp teeth, layered the living room floor beneath an octagon shaped black onyx coffee table. Lord sat behind the bar off to the right not far from the 60 inch plasma television that was built into the wall with a gold picture frame boarding the edges. On the love seat Star sat rolling blunts, his head bobbing to Papoose's gritty rhymes playing on a Kay Slay mix tape.

"What up with you niggaz?" Lord asked, glancing up as he poured a drink. The oldest Head, he sported a neatly trimmed full beard and was rarely caught without wearing a black or white Kuffie. He wore a wife beater that looked like it was about to split across his wide barrel chest, gray Roc-A-Wear sweatpants, and a pair of gray and white Air Jordans. Standing at five-eleven, he weighed close to 270 pounds and all muscle. "What y'all drinking?"

"Give me some of that expensive shit Prince be drinking on the rocks." Sha' grabbed one of Star's rolled blunts, lit it, and choked instantly.

"I was gonna smoke that," Star said grilling him, then went back to rolling blunts. He had a box of White Owl Cigars on the table in front of him with two more left to roll. At five-seven, he was the shortest Head, but the deadliest, mainly because of his size and looks. He had the youthful face of a sixteen year old although he was twenty six with long Congo dreads that hung to his waist.

"Nigga you just finish rolling one."

Star gave Sha' a devilish grin. "You know I always try to smoke Prince shit up when I come over here. What up Jah?"

"Ain't shit Homey. I got something I need to spit with y'all about..." He Paused and turned to Prince. "A yo Price, dead the music for a minute, son."

Prince shut the music off by remote control and took a seat in his recliner while Lord passed out the drinks.

"What up, Jah? Everything good on your end right?" Lord asked, handing Jahad his drink before taking a seat on the couch.

"Yeah, ain't no problems. I gotta spit with y'all about something that came up with Koran. Before I get into it, I want y'all to hear me out first and try to understand where I'm coming from before you say anything."

"C'mon with the dramatic shit Jah and say what you gotta say," Star said sitting up in his seat.

Jahad looked at each of his friends. "Koran knows what's up with us. I mean the M.G.'s. He…"

"What!" All four Heads shouted at once.

"A yo! Hear me out… Damn! He knows what's up. I just found out last night. The lil' nigga been knowing since he was a kid."

"Has he told anybody?" Prince asked.

"Nah, he ain't say…"

"You believe him?" Star broke in.

"Hell yeah, I believe him!" Jahad snapped, feeling anger rise in his chest. "When the lil' nigga was only ten he saw me and Razor body sixteen muthafucka's and never said a word to nobody. My brother ain't no muthafucking rat."

"Nobody said he was Jah. It was only a question," Lord said playing the mediator.

"Yeah, so calm the fuck down," Star added.

Jahad Started to bark, but Star was only being Star.

"Okay, so he knows." Sha' looked around at each head. "You know the only logical thing to do right? I mean, Jah I understand he's your brother, but…"

"What the fuck you talking about Sha'?" Jahad stood up ready to pounce.

"I'm saying," Sha' continued unfazed. "He can still go to college or whatever, but we need to bring him in, make him one of us."

"Oh," relief swept over Jahad as he sat back down.

"We can't bring him in. The books are closed, remember." Sha' looked pointedly at Jahad. "And another thing, just because he your brother don't mean he built for the M.G.'s. Shit, he only seventeen. He ain't been through enough to be one of us. I mean, I believe you when you say he can keep his mouth shut, but being able to hold water don't qualify him to be a M.G. It's more to it than that. You know that Jah."

"Yeah, I do. If I didn't, the M.G. wouldn't exist right now," Jahad replied coldly reminding Star whose idea it was to form the organization. "You think I would bring him in without making sure he was built for it first? If he proves himself after I take him through this shit he started last night, then he's in. That's if I get two of you to agree with me."

"What you mean?" Lord asked, sitting his drink down.

"Koran wants to be a M.G. That's the reason he told me he knows about us. So I made a deal with him. For the next year or so I'ma put his ass through training on some military shit. If he can make it through everything, he's in. If not, he goes to college and never mentions the M.G.'s to me again."

"You serious?" Sha' asked, surprised.

"Yeah, and I want y'all to help me."

"How?" Prince and Star asked.

"I told him before he can come in he gotta go through the same shit we went through. We learned most of what we know from the streets so that's where I put his ass. Right now I got him in the Big Park so he can study niggaz. I wanna keep him out there for a few months them send him to one of y'all so he can post up a block somewhere in your hoods. Rain, hail, sleet or snow I want his ass on the streets. By the time he puts in three or four months on one spot send him to another part of the city. Keep doing that shit until he's familiar with everything in each spot. The hustlers, crackheads, dope fiends, beatwalkers, stick up kids, everybody. Then…"

"That shit could take years, Jah," Star cut in.

Jahad smiled. "I know. That's the whole idea. Hopefully he'll get fed up and take his stubborn ass to college. I know you don't think I want him involved in this shit. I tried to talk him out of it, but he claims it's what he wants, so I'ma give it to him the hard way. On the weekends I want him at the firing range until he can use a gun better than a cowboy. Star, your knife game is sick. Teach him that shit. Lord, when he's with you, put his ass on them weights. We all got boxing gyms around our way. I want him in there five days a week. Sooner or later he'll break. If not, he'll be just as dangerous as we are."

No one spoke for a moment, then Lord gave Jahad a solemn look. You sure you wanna do this Jah? I mean, that's your brother man. We might fuck around and turn him into an animal. Koran has a future, you know?"

"Lord, I told him the same shit and he didn't wanna listen. The plan is to break him."

"Why not just tell him no?" asked Prince.

"I did at first. He threw some shit in my face that I won't say forced my hand, but made me consider giving him a chance. Don't worry, he won't make it through this shit. If he do he'll be a bad muthafucka."

~~~~~

After the meeting broke up Jahad and Prince sat in the living room reminiscing over their time spent at Rikers Island once the other Heads left. Jahad was in the process of taking a sip from his third glass of Louis XIII when Prince brought up someone he had been trying to get off his mind for months.

"A yo what happened with you and Candy?"

"Who?" Jahad said playing ignorant.

"Candy nigga. The chick I plugged you in with on V.I. What? The pussy wasn't good or something?"

Jahad laughed. "Oh Candy. Nah, just the opposite. If I woulda kept fucking shorty I'd be fucked up. Why you ask?"

"I saw her a few weeks ago up on Broadway and she asked about you. Said she ain't heard from you in a few months. Thought you was locked up."

A warm feeling filled Jahad's chest like it did every time he thought of Candy. After his relationship with Janet he vowed to never fall in love again and he didn't want to. Then Candy came along and made him feel emotions he thought were dead inside him. She was everything he could ask for in a woman. Beautiful, sexy, street smart, loving and she minded her business. The qualities that had the potential to make him fall in love. So instead of falling victim to his emotions, he backed out of their relationship suddenly without warning. Love was a deceiver. This he learned from Janet.

"Do me a favor. If you bump into her again tell her I got bodied."

"What?" Prince frowned. "C'mon Jah it ain't that serious."

"It is to me."

"That chick Janet fucked it up for everybody, huh?"

"Yeah, she did. I'm on some stick and move shit now and Candy wants more than I can give. I mean, she wasn't putting no pressure on me for commitment, but she was doing lil' shit to draw me in."

"Using pussy power?" Prince laughed.

"Was she! You just don't know. Throwing the pussy on me all crazy, cooking for a nigga, back rubs. Shit a bitch do when she trying to lock a nigga down." Jahad shook his head. "Yeah son, she was trying to get me."

"I'm saying Jah, you don't wanna have kid's some day? A few rugrats to hold your name down."

Jahad sat back on the couch and stared up at the ceiling before answering. "You know, I never really thought about having kids. But yeah, I gotta have a few lil Jah's running around."

"What about the chick then?"

"What chick?"

"Whoever the chick is you gonna have seeds by since you say you not falling in love?"

"Oh, she won't be needed after my seeds are born."

"What? You gonna body the chick!" Prince sat up snapping his head towards Jahad.

"Nah, man. I ain't that cold hearted. I'd throw some dough at her so she'd be a'ight or whatever."

"A yo, let's stop talking about this sucka for love shit. It's depressing."

"Nigga, you brought it up," Jah said laughing.

Chapter Four

During Korans' first year of training, the Heads turned his life into pure hell without throwing an ounce of mercy. He half expected Jahad to show him a little sympathy and give him time off to handle certain small things. He wanted to do a little shopping and hit the Tunnel every now and then for a bit of relaxation. That wasn't the case. In fact, just the opposite.

He was stripped of everything. Jahad kept his Range Rover parked behind the moving company, his money supply was cut off completely, and he only had five hours on Sunday to spend time with his girls. His schedule was so crammed that he barely had time to use the bathroom. Jahad explained that there were three things he had to learn and master before becoming a M.G. Observation; being it would put him in tune with his surroundings. Self- control; because it dealt with controlling his emotions. And the art of killing; because, well, that's what they did. From there, with the help of the other Head's, they proceeded to push him harder than an Army drill sergeant in hopes of breaking him. But Koran was unbreakable. Once he realized what they were up to, everything they came at him with he sucked up and asked for more.

After a year and a half the results were shocking. His grueling boxing lessons advanced his skills to pro level. Every last sparring partner who stood in front him minutes later would be staring up at him from a canvas. That is if he didn't knock them out, which happened often. Time spent working out with Lord turned his once 170 pound boney frame into 190 pounds of rock hard muscles. Star taught him now how to use a knife better than a Ninja. With a handgun he could put a hole right between a person's eyes from nearly 200 feet away.

In spots secretly controlled by the M.G.s, such as Pikin Avenue in East New York, Dumont Avenue in Brownsville, Nostrand Avenue in Bed-Stuy, in the Bronx, Broadway in Harlem, and Queens Boulevard in Queens, he could break down each strip and knew exactly who was who and the roles people played. When he wasn't on the streets or at the gym, he was studying combat tactics, psychology and numerous other books Jahad picked out for him to memorize.

Soon, Lord's prediction became true. Only they weren't creating an animal, they were building a machine. A killing machine! Worn down by Koran's persistence, the Heads gave up trying to break him and were ready to bring him in. But Jahad held back and pushed him even harder clinging to hope of breaking him. In the process, his efforts only added fuel to the fire making Koran sharper, faster, and deadlier.

~~~~

Two months before Christmas going into his second year of training Koran's big break finally came. He sat in the Big Park on a hand stone bench, his shoulder hunched, a mask of boredom on his face while he pretended to watch a group of singing wino's huddled around a burning trash can blowing *Jodeci's, Stay*. His thoughts, although no one could tell, was on Premo. Premo was one of the surviving Puerto Ricans from the CoCo twins old crew turned crackhead who stood a few feet away to Koran's left with his lips wrapped around a crack pipe.

For nearly three weeks Koran noticed Premo lingering in front of his building which really wasn't uncommon being Premo lived in Monroe Projects too. What was uncommon were the days and the times he had chosen to be there. Jahad with his work alcoholic habits could only be seen twice a week during daylight hours in the projects, Saturday and Sunday. The days he and Koran went to the firing range and the same days Premo chose to be posted up by their building.

Sensing something wasn't right Koran took upon himself to follow him whenever possible. On three separate occasions Premo met, always in a different location, with a tall Puerto Rican with long black hair flowing over his shoulders. Koran had no idea who the tall Puerto Rican was, but felt it was time to tell Jahad what he suspected.

Later that night as always Jahad sat at the computer in the living room typing in shipping addresses when Koran walked in. Looking up from the screen he took off his reading glasses and turned in his chair.

"Sha' gonna pick you up tomorrow. You'll be in Brownsville until a week before Christmas, then we're going down south. Mom wants to have Christmas in N.C. this year."

Koran rested a smile. Out of the Heads Sha' was his closest friend. Whenever stuck on the streets in Brownsville or East New York they often snuck off to the strip clubs with Jahad not knowing. Then he thought about going down south and his spirits dampened.

"We always have Christmas up here. What we gotta go down south for?

"Because Moms said so. What? You don't wanna see her or something?"

"Nah, it ain't like that. I just ain't feeling the south. It's boring. But it doesn't matter." Koran sat on the couch and shrugged off his coat. "A yo, you know Premo, right?"

"You talking about crackhead Premo?"

"Yeah, that smoked out Puerto Rican dude."

"Yeah, I know him. Why?"

"Something ain't right with dude. He be lounging in front of our building all crazy every weekend. You ain't peep it?"

"It ain't nothing to peep," Jahad snorted. "In case you don't know, Premo lives in building 1785. You just paranoid."

Koran shook his head. "Nah, you slippin'. The only time you be seen in the projects is on the weekends when we go to the firing range and that's the only time that dude be posted up. I been following him and he been meeting with this tall Puerto Rican dude every Sunday. Why, I don't know, but..."

Jahad shot out his chair. "How this tall Puerto Rican dude look?"

Koran took a moment to picture the face in his mind. "He's about six four, long black hair hanging over his shoulder like a bitch. Pretty ass dude with..."

"Hector!" Jahad shouted venomously.

"Who?"

"Hector, one of the Coco twins. That muthafucka! He just don't know when to sit his ass down."

"Oh word!" Koran had heard stories of the infamous Coco twins over the years, but had no idea that Hector and Jahad were mortal enemies. Or that the Coco twins had brutally murdered his father.

Jahad sat back down and looked at Koran with pride in his eyes. "I don't think you figured it out, but my plan was to string you along until you finally gave up and took your ass to college. I..."

"What! C'mon, Jah. You know that shit ain't right man!" Koran stood as if he was about to jump on Jahad.

"Sit down and let me say what I gotta say." Jahad waited until Koran was seated. He ran a hand over his face, then continued. "You know I don't want you in this shit. You don't really understand the effects it's going have on you. Right now you looking from the outside in and you can't understand. So before you fully commit yourself to something, let me tell you what to expect. This shit gonna change you in ways you won't wanna be changed. Every time you kill somebody you gonna grow colder and colder until eventually you won't be able to feel shit. That's if your conscience don't drive you crazy first. Yeah, you gonna see so much money your eyes might turn green, but that does't mean you'll be able to enjoy it."

"What you in it for then?"

"I told you, I didn't choose this. It chose me."

Koran shook his head. "I can feel that, but you gotta get some sort of satisfaction from it or you wouldn't stay in it."

"You right. I see them psychology books taught you something." Jahad cracked a smile. "The satisfaction I get is being in control and having power. I'm addicted to it. Money is power 'cause a lot of muthafucka's crave it. And when you have money, lots of it, you can control all the muthafucka's trying to get it; feel me?"

Koran nodded astonished. Jahad's explanation clarified the meaning behind the saying *'Money is the root of all evil.'* For though trying to get it, there were no limits to what they could do. And the M.G.'s were a perfect example.

"That's some deep shit Jah."

"Yeah, it is. Now check, tomorrow you can go get your truck. I been putting your allowance money to the side. I was gonna wait until I broke your ass before I gave it to you. Since I didn't, you can get it now. You got about twenty-five thousand to trick with, 'cause I know that's what you gonna do."

"Word? So it's over?"

"Yep. After we handle this situation with Premo, you're in."

Koran jumped from the couch smiling from ear to ear. "Shit, let me get my money then so I can go get me some pussy. I'm baccccckkk!" he yelled, doing a little dance.

~~~~

Since receiving the mysterious phone call nearly a year and a half ago, Hector became overly suspicious of everyone in his crew. There could only be one logical explanation of how the mysterious caller, who now calls himself the Operator, came to have his cell phone number. It had to be someone in his crew. It had to be. Coming to the conclusion not long after receiving the phone call, Hector decided to put on a demonstration to show what happened to though who dared to defy him.

He gathered his whole team together, which only consisted of twenty six people all who hustled outside the Bronx, in an abandoned warehouse out in Mount Vernon. He questioned each one, then picked three random members and put a bullet in their Heads. He figured the act would let the culprit, as well as the rest of his clique, know that the penalty for betrayal was death. His effort was made in vain.

He sat on the couch in his apartment on Stratford Avenue watching ESPN when his cell phone vibrated in his pants pockets. "Hola?" he answered, his eyes glued to the television. The Giants were playing the Cowboys and he had nearly twenty thousand dollars on the Giants placed with different bookies.

"Do you always answer your phone in Spanish 'cause I don't understand that shit. You in America now Poppi, speak English."

"Who is this?!" Hector shouted, waking his four year old son who was asleep on the couch beside him.

"C'mon Hector. You're hurting my feelings. I know you ain't forgot about me already," the Operator said with a smile in his voice.

"Oh, it's you, Mr. Mystery Man. How you keep getting my number?"

The Operator laughed. "I like that, the mystery nigga. Sound kinda...."

"How did you get my number?!" Hector snapped, his patience gone.

"Breathe easy, Duke. You act like you don't wanna talk to me or something."

"Maybe I wouldn't mind if I knew who I was talking to."

"I'm the mystery nigga. You said it yourself." The man chuckled, then grew serious. "Now listen, you been sending a crackhead to spy on Jah. I...."

"How do you know about that?"

"Because the mystery nigga knows everything. Now shut the fuck up and listen. Jah knows what's poppin'. He plans on following this crackhead nigga wherever y'all be meeting at so he can body your ass.

As far…"

"How can you…"

"Didn't I tell you to shut the fuck up! Both of us can't talk at the same time and I'm the only one who needs to be talking. I'm trying to save your sorry ass life and you keep cutting me off. When I say shut the fuck up, you shut the fuck up, a'ight?"

Hector didn't answer. Never in his life had he been so insulted or spoken to like he was a child.

"You hear me nigga!"

Hector willed himself to calm down. The time would come when this fool revealed himself. When he did Hector planned to teach him some manners. "Yeah, I hear you."

"Act like it then." man paused to see if Hector would speak again. "I said I was gonna help you and I am. So stop trying shit on your own before you fuck around and get bodied. You don't know what you're dealing with fucking with Jah. Just chill. Your day is coming."

"How can I trust someone I have never seen?"

"I feel you, but think of me as God. You ain't never seen him and you won't ever see me. It's all about faith Poppi. And from now on you can call me the Operator. See ya." The Operator laughed as he hung up.

Chapter Five

Two weeks from the day Koran informed Jahad what he suspected about Premo, Jahad set up a situation to see just how bad Koran wanted to become a M.G. It was Friday afternoon and Koran had just returned home from a date still making up for his time spent in seclusion. He had another date set later that night with Monica, his freaky Puerto Rican chick. The thought made him smile as he walked to the kitchen to fix a snack. The smile turned into a frown when he saw the note Jahad left for him posted on the refrigerator.

Meet me on the roof at ten, Jah. It was scribbled in Jahad's sloppy handwriting.

"Shit!" Koran cursed, thinking it was another one of Jahad's crazy lessons. "Jah, you fucking my pussy plans up with this bullshit. What is it now? Catch bullets with my fucking teeth!"

He stormed out the apartment pissed off deciding to grab something to eat from the Chinese restaurant right up the street. He stepped out the building dressed for the brittle weather in a thick pair of Roc-A-Wear jeans, brown suede Timberlands, a Gino Green Global hoody and a brown Timberland snorkel coat. His attention was drawn to a beautiful young woman walking with a little girl around six or seven towards building 1790 which was right next to his building. He couldn't say why, but something about the woman seemed oddly familiar.

"A yo shorty!" he called out, but she was too far away to hear him. On impulse, he started jogging towards her then stopped abruptly and shook his head. "I'm buggin'. I don't chase no chicks." Laughing to himself, he turned back to his destination. I got enough women on my hands, but one more wouldn't hurt though, he thought, laughing again.

Back at the apartment after wolfing down an order of beef and broccoli and two egg rolls, he played Madden until it was time to meet Jahad. When he made it to the top of his building, cursing all the way up, a gust of rigid cold wind nearly pushed him back inside when he opened the roof's exit door. Forcing himself out he saw the Head's standing near the ledge with their backs turned slightly towards him.

"What up with you nigga's?" he asked, approaching them. He then froze after catching sight of Premo. He was naked shivering from the cold and fear. His wrist and ankles were bound together with duct tape.

"You see what's up," Jahad said, casting an evil glance at Premo. "This piece of shit right here gotta go. I figured you'd wanna do the honors. If not that's cool too."

This was it, the final test and deep down Jahad prayed Koran would say he couldn't do it. If he took Premo's life there was no way he would be denied.

Koran looked at the Heads who were all studying his face to judge his reaction. He knew what was expected of him. He knew when he first laid eyes on Premo's naked body what the call was. Now his shock was gone and replaced with blood rushing adrenaline.

"Give me a gun or am I supposed to stomp his ass to death? I ain't trying to fuck up my Tim's."

The Head's laughed except for Jahad who began revising his plans for Koran. "Nah, man, it's your choice. You can blast his ass...." Star held out a bulldog 44.

"Or you can choke him the fuck out." Sha' finished the sentence holding out a piece of rope about three feet long.

Another test Koran thought. Without hesitating, he took the rope from Sha', dropped to one knee looping the rope around Premo's neck, and started choking the life out of him. Premo struggled hard, desperately trying to use his weight to roll over until Koran placed his knee in the middle of his back for leverage. He tightened the rope around his neck, pulling upward with all his might until Premo Started to convulse and a foul odor filtered up from his body.

"What the fuck is wrong with this dude?" Koran yelled, jumping up seeing shit run between Premo's legs. He fought to keep from throwing up. Not only from what he was witnessing, but from the act he just committed.

The Head's looked at each other knowingly then Lord burst out laughing. "A yo, you choked the shit outta that nigga Koran. Literally!"

"Word!" Prince added, Shaking his head.

Sha' walked over and threw an arm around Korans' shoulder. He turned to Jahad who was still deep in thought. "Let me get my dough, Jah. I told you he was a natural born killer. I could see it in his eyes."

While Jahad forked over a thousand dollars to Sha', Lord and Prince grabbed Premo's lifeless body and threw him off the roof. Koran watched transfixed as the body grew smaller and smaller until it slammed into the concrete below.

"You official now nigga. All we gotta do now is figure out where to put you," Lord said turning away from the ledge.

"Whatcha' mean?"

"C'mon, let's get the hell off this roof first. It's too damn cold up here. We'll handle all that when we get to the crib." Jahad shoved his hands in his coat pocket and walked towards the exit door leaving the others to follow.

Back at the apartment before they settled down, a ceremony was put on for Koran's initiation. Sha' and Star rolled blunts of Purple Haze. Jahad and Lord were behind the bar placing gold bottles of Cristal on the counter. Prince was at the stereo putting on a new Dip Set underground C.D.

"What you standing over there for?" Jahad asked, looking up. "Grab a bottle."

Koran shook his head. "You know I don't drink Jah."

"You do tonight. Smoke too. We went through the trouble of putting this shit together, so you gonna get fucked up with us."

"That's right nigga." Sha' stood from the couch and grabbed a bottle of Cristal. "C'mon, y'all nigga's gather around so we can make a toast." They made a circle around the coffee table holding their bottles out in front of them. "From this day forth you are one of us. We hold you down, you hold us down. We make you stronger, you make us stronger. It's as simple as that." They clicked bottles together, then took long swigs except for Koran who nearly choked from the first swallow.

"A'ight, let's get down to business. Star, pass me one of the blunts." Jahad took the blunt, lit it, then sat back in his recliner facing Koran. "Before we decide where to put you let me break some shit down for you. You got professional basketball players, football players, and boxers. Professional meaning they're the best at what they do. The M.G.'s, we're professional drug dealers. We ain't no gang like the Bloods and Crips. We don't go around broadcasting who we are. Our sole purpose is getting money and that's the only reason we kill. More than half the niggas in New York moving weight are selling our shit without knowing."

"Now it comes times when other weight moving nigga's try to move in our spots. Nigga's might plug in with the Columbians or Cubans and get hit with mad bricks or whatever and they gotta move them. I mean it's part of the game. But being who we are, we don't go for it. That's where the killing comes in at. To put an end to the competition, we kill off the whole crew including the connect. Once the word gets around the next nigga thinks twice about trying to move on the spot."

"I'm saying, how often does this happen? I mean niggas trying to move in on our spot?"

"Like every four or five months," Star answered. "Understand that we're talking about four boroughs and all our spots do numbers. And when I say spots, I'm not talking about petty ass nickel and dime crack, weed or heroin spots. We supply the weight to the niggas who supply the nickel and dime spots, feel me?"

Koran nodded in awe. "So when other niggas try to supply the niggas who supply the nickel and dime spots, that's when we do what we do?"

"Exactly. That's what the body squad is for," Prince said.

"Body squad?"

"Yeah, the Body Squad," Jahad took over. "Like I told you, we're professionals so everything we do is organized. We have three types of M.G.'s; Workers, Watchers, and the Body Squad. Worker's, they're M.G.'s employed at our local businesses. Besides doing whatever job they're assigned to, their sole purpose is to count money and deliver drugs."

"The watchers do just that, watch shit. Every nigga we supply drugs to has a M.G. watching them around the clock in case they get knocked. It's basically set up like any other job with eight hour shifts. Then we have the body squad. They handle all hits whether individually or as a team. When it's only one or two muthafucka's who gotta get ghosted, names are dropped into a hat and whoever name gets picked, gotta do the hit. If a whole crew has to be taken out, then they form Voltron and get busy. Don't get it twisted though, every M.G. I'm speaking of bust their guns. It's just that niggas on the Body Squad have special talents, you know?" Jahad cracked a smile glancing at Star.

"How many M.G.'s on the Body Squad?" asked Koran.

"Fifty and that's all we do. Body shit!" Star answered, grinning.

"I wanna be on the Body Squad then," Koran blurted out.

"I figured you'd say that, but it ain't up to you," Jahad said frowning. "Why not a worker or a watcher?"

"I'm saying, y'all made me go through all that crazy shit for two years. I wanna try some of that shit out on a muthafucka to see if it works," Koran replied dead serious. The Heads looked at each other, then burst out laughing.

"A yo, Koran, you wild nigga. I feel you though." Star looked at Jahad. "I'm wit it."

Jahad smirked. "I'm sure you are, but it ain't your brother we talking about," he said and turned back to Koran. "Check it, niggas on the Body Squad already got mad bodies under their belts. They veterans when it comes to laying shit down. You think this shit is a game or something? You could fuck around and get bodies lil' bruh."

"I feel you Jah, but I ain't no slouch. Look at the shit y'all took me through. I went through all of it with ease. I feel I'm that nigga for the Body Squad. I mean, I could be that nigga as a watcher too after all that time I spent on the street. But think about it. I know how to blend in with any hood, be on any scene without being seen, you know? With that skill I'll be able to pop tops like beer cans."

Jahad looked away.

"He made a good point Jah," said Sha'.

"So you want him on the Body Squad? How about you Prince, Lord?"

"I think he can handle it," said Lord. "Yeah, me too," Prince agreed.

Jahad nodded. "A'ight, the Body Squad it is. But check this." He faced Star. "You run that shit so I'ma hold you responsible if anything happens to him. That's my word! It's easy for you niggas to say put him on the Body Squad. He ain't y'all brother. I'm the nigga who raised... "

"Whoa! Stop there Jah," Sha' said, holding up his hand. "That shit you screaming is pure bullshit. Koran is our brother just as much as he's yours. Nah, we ain't raise him, but love is love, Son."

"Word up! You gone hold me responsible?" Star mocked angrily. "If I didn't think he was built for it, I'd say no. I can't believe you came at me with some shit like that," he said mumbling something in Creole under his breath.

"A'ight, Star, don't go putting none of that voodoo shit on me," said Jahad laughing. Star glared at him a moment before cracking a smile. "You keep talking that crazy shit I'ma have your ass walking around here thinking you're a chicken."

"So, I'm on the Body Squad?" Koran asked grinning.

"Yeah, that's your position. I still want you at Joe's at least three days a week so I can show you how to freak the books. That'll be your cover. Plus, if I'm ever outta town you'll know how to run the shop."

"A'ight, but you just wanna get some extra work outta me."

"The boys a genius," Jahad laughed, but secretly he had plans for Koran. Plans none of the other Heads were aware of.

Chapter Six

Candy entered Macy's department store pushing her two year old son in his stroller while a face from the past haunted her. A face that tormented her heart as well as her thoughts and refused to let her think straight. A face that made her forget all about being engaged to a man who loved and spoiled her constantly. That face being none other than Jahad's.

For nearly three years, Candy believed him to be dead. Thought her son would never get the chance to know his real father. This was until two weeks ago when she and her fiancée were leaving the Apollo Theater after attending the Amateur night performance. The couple walked from the crowded building arm in arm, deep in conversation. Then all at once it came to a halt and Candy cut her words off mid-sentence. Twenty feet away Jahad stood leaning against a black 600 Mercedes Benz with his arm around a woman pretty enough to be a super model. He was casually dressed in brown slacks, brown Louis Vuitton loafers and wearing a brown chinchilla mink jacket looking good as ever.

Stunned, Candy forgot all about her fiancée and screamed Jahad's name, then started towards him, but her fiancée roughly yanked her back. Hearing his name Jahad whipped his head in her direction while reaching to his waist for his gun preparing for the unexpected until their eyes connected. The effect was like someone had splashed them both in the face with cold water. Time ceased to exist and everyone around them faded to black as a magnetic attraction took over their minds and bodies.

Jahad released his date and started toward her. Candy tried her best to break away from her fiancée who held a firm grip on her waist and a scowl on his face directed at Jahad. Then Jahad's date grabbed his arm and broke the connection.

Candy felt an intense wave of jealousy wash over her although she knew from experience the woman meant nothing to Jahad. He was incapable of love, so she thought. The few years they dated she went out of her way to shower him unconditionally with all the love she could muster.

It didn't matter though. Jahads' love went no further than sex even though he was quite lovable. He was also considerate, funny, generous, and great in bed. He had all the qualities that would make any woman fall head over heels in love, but Candy could never reach his heart. When she finally thought she was making a little progress, he disappeared. A week after his departure she found out she was pregnant and thoughts of them finally having a life together filled her mind.

It all came crashing down a month later when she ran into Prince at a Rucker's Basketball tournament and he told her Jahad was dead. For months afterward she lived with chronic depression, having daily thoughts of suicide. The baby she carried was the only reason she didn't give into temptation. The child was her only connection to Jahad and one she couldn't imagine letting go. Her fiancée came into her life not long afterwards. And even though she still mourned Jahad, she had to move on for the sake of her child.

But Jahad wasn't dead and all her old dreams came rushing back. Once he found out they had a child together, she felt it would bring him back into her life where he belonged. Despite having a fiancée she was going to contact Jahad no matter how long it took. With that thought she smiled down at her son who looked so much like his father.

Chapter Seven

Jahad sat at his office desk trying hard to focus on the stack of shipping addresses he was trying to doctor, but he couldn't concentrate. In the middle of adding up figure's his thoughts kept straying to Candy and he'd have to start all over again. Finally, he gave up. It was obvious he wouldn't be able to get any work done. He reached for his ashtray where half of a blunt sat, lit it, and then let his thoughts drift back to the night of the encounter a week ago.

It surprised him how she had the same effect on him. Only one other woman held the power to evoke the emotions he felt and she was dead. The thought of paying her a visit just to see how she was doing crossed his mind despite the man he saw her with.

Whoever he was, he couldn't mean that much to her. If he did then she wouldn't have tried to break her neck to get to him.

'Yeah, I'm still that nigga,' he said to himself smiling just as someone knocked at his door. "Come in."

The door opened and Vincent Valentino strutted in fashionably dressed in a black Armani suit, white silk shirt, a blue tie, and wearing a pair of black ostrich skin shoes. His glossy black hair speckled with gray was slicked back in a vain attempt to cover a forming bald spot in the middle of his crown. Years of good living transformed his six-four 200 pound frame into 260 pounds of olive colored flesh. Alert ice blue eyes sat back in his meaty face below his bushy black eyebrows. He still possessed his Hollywood good looks though. More like an aging Robert Deniro than a vibrant Brad Pitt. He was still the best dressed lawyer in New York and the best defense lawyer period. That is before he slid from the spotlight to live a more adventurous life.

A full blooded Sicilian, he was once nabbed by the press as being a mob lawyer, which was true to a certain extent. What set him apart was Valentino was his own man and refused to be tied to one crime family, even his own. With Valentino it didn't matter who you were or what was your crime, as long as your money was right. He had morals when it came to winning a case. There was no right or wrong, guilty or innocent. What mattered was winning and he did so by any means. With connections on both sides of the law, he could pull strings to have a certain judges hear a case as easy as he could whisper a witness name in the right ears and make him disappear… for good!

His business relationship with Jahad began shortly after he revealed the shocking truth behind Jahad's father's death. Jahad needed a lawyer to handle his legal affairs when he purchased Joe's moving company. He also needed someone to teach him how to wash his dirty money. Valentino was more than happy to help knowing Jahad's plan for the M.G.'s. Soon he found himself knee deep in all their legal affairs.

Jahads' moving company, Princes' barber shop, clothing store and night club, Sha's detail shop, Lords' sports bar, and Stars' strip club were all products of a massive money laundering machine governed by Valentino. How they made their dirty money was none of his business. What they did with their dirty money was their business.

Valentino's cut of the money he washed meant nothing. He wasn't in it for the money. The thrill of beating the system is where he drew his satisfaction. At fifty-one he was divorced twice, had no kids, and filthy rich. But beneath the five thousand dollar suits and sharp mind was a crook at heart who thrived on the old way of doing things. The M.G.'s reminded him a lot of the old Mafia before John Gotti came along flaunting his power. This above all is what turned him into the fold of the M.G.'s.

"Did I come at a bad time?" he asked, reaching into his crocodile skin briefcase.

"Nah. You caught me getting toasted," Jahad said as Valentino placed a stack of papers on his desk. "What's this?"

"Something I've been doing a little research on. What do you know about prostitution?"

"You talking about selling pussy?"

Valentino smiled. "Exactly. I'll explain why you read," he said, nodding towards the papers. "When I say prostitution I'm not speaking of hookers walking the streets showing off their ass and tit's. I mean escort services. Expensively catered escort services. The type where beautiful women from all over the world are employed to appeal to a man's ultimate fantasy whatever it may be. They are two such businesses in the heart of Manhattan, controlled by two crime

families; the Leopardi's and the Corsello's. Two undeserving families since neither have the protection to secure their holdings."

Jahad glanced up sharply. "What you trying to say Vinny?"

"If you turn to page 12 and look to the bottom of the page you'll see exactly what I'm trying to say."

Jahad turned to the page and slowly his eyes grew wide. "Get the fuck out of here! $200 million selling pussy?!"

"Among other things, yes. Porno movies, porno magazines, and yes phone sex. It's all in the Dossier. I included one for each of your friends."

"These figures, they for both spots?"

"Annually, yes. And the money is as clean as snow. Another 60 million comes under the table from drugs." Jahad grew quiet a moment before speaking. "So you saying you want us to move on the mob?"

Valentino held Jahad's stare. "No. I'm saying I want both families wiped out completely. You remember when I told you about your father and how my family wouldn't allow me to avenge his death because we were in the middle of a war?"

Jahad nodded.

"We were going against the Leopardi family. Not long afterwards they join forces with the Corello's and nearly wiped my family out. Though who survived escaped back to Sicily with my uncle. This was years ago. My uncle has regained some of his power now. That's the reason I'm willing to be so daring. I have his approval as long as he can wet his back."

"Wet his back?" Jahad frowned. "Whose idea is this, yours or your uncles, and how much does he know about us?"

"To answer your first question, it was my idea. Then I ran it by my uncle. If you decide to go through with it not a word can be mentioned when it's over. Ever. Both families are weak, but still have ties in the old country where a vendetta is never forgotten. A move like this will be too big to cover up. That's why my uncle is needed. When we make our move here, a similar one will be made in Sicily in an effort to eliminate all aspects of a threat afterwards. Still, we must be extremely careful to lessen the risk of any identities being revealed. Both companies will be signed over in my name through several dummy corporations. Once everything is completed, you will be given six numbered offshore accounts that will be set up for each of us."

"So you saying you will have complete control over everything I own, including the dough?"

"Yes and with good reason, which will answer your second question. My uncle is aware of my plans to seize both companies. By my going about it this way, he won't have any idea about you. He suspects I have my own muscle, which I do." Valentino pointed at Jahad grinning. "What he doesn't know is that my muscle are young black entrepreneurs. This way your identities will never be known or it'll be all of our asses."

"Why, because were black?"

"No, because you're not Sicilian. It has nothing to do with the color of your skin. The situation would be the same if you were white. It's my families custom to always keep business within the family."

"A'ight. So what's up with these two families? I mean, how strong are they?"

"In your dossier there's a map and full layout of Lenny Leopardi's mansion in Sheepshead Bay along with the number of men he employs. I'm still working on David's Corsello's. He lives out on Long Island. He feels safer in the wilderness."

"You say your uncle gave you the green light as long as he can eat. How much he is talking about?"

"10%. This is only of what's shown on the books. He won't touch a dime of what's made under the table."

Jahad shook his head. "Personally, I don't want to mix the drugs up in this. I'll see what my man's says, though."

"We have to. We're dealing with very wealthy clients that are used to getting what they want at the snap of a finger. In order to satisfy them, if drugs are requested, then the drugs should be provided."

"I'm saying, supplying the drugs won't be a problem. None of my people can be involved, though."

"If you supply the drugs, then I'll make sure they reach the right hands."

"I'm cool with that," Jahad nodded and looked over the papers again. "How soon can you get the information on the other dude?"

"Give me some time. I don't want to move too fast. It may draw attention."

"No doubt. One last question. Once we killed these dudes, what happens to their other businesses. Who gets that?"

Valentino smiled. "Today, prostitution. Tomorrow, who knows?"

~~~~

Later that night a hard stinging rain fell as Jahad road to Harlem for the short notice meeting he set up with the Heads. So many ideas were flowing through his mind, he couldn't sit on them until tomorrow. Valentino's information held so many possibilities and so much power that the implications were overwhelming. The move could transform the M.G.'s into an invincible force with Valentino as the figure head while the rest of them played the shadows like always. The problem, he figured would be convincing the other kids that Valentino should be given total control.

Jahad was the first to arrive. He parked his Oldsmobile in front of Prince's brownstone, grabbed his briefcase, then dashed out the car with his head tucked. Just as he was about to ring the doorbell the door open and Prince stood with a cream silk robe holding a double shot of Hennessy in a clear tumbler.

"Heard that piece of junk pull up," he said, handing Jahad the drink. "The rest of the family should be here in a few minutes. What's up? We got a kill somebody or something?"

"Yeah, something like that," Jahad replied, following Prince into the living room where a fire was blazing in the black marble fireplace. "Valentino got at me today. Got some info I want y'all to check out."

"Oh word?" What he…" Prince was interrupted by the doorbell. "Hold on, son."

While Prince answered the door, Jahad fixed himself another drink. A second later, Prince returned, followed by Sha', Lord, and Star. Star was decked out in a brown pinstripe suit and brown gators.

"Somebody fucked up, right?" Lord asked, taking the soaked kuffie off his head.

"Nah, not this time." Jahad took a sip from his drink, then cut his eyes over at Star. "Where you coming from church?"

"Ha, ha," Star mocked with a scowl. "I'm on my grown man shit. Tell him Prince."

Sha" shook his head as he shrugged off his leather Rock-a-Wear jacket. "Harlem niggaz can get away with that pimp shit. You look like Gary Coleman before he went broke."

The room erupted with laughter.

"A yo chill with the short jokes Sha' before I get on that

aluminum you got in your mouth frontin like its platinum.

Star turned to Jahad. "What's up Jah? It must be important for you to get us together at damn near midnight."

"Yeah, it's important. Valentino got at me today and put me on to something that can take us to the next level." Jahad nodded toward the dossiers he sat on the table. "Read them and tell me what y'all think."

While they read Jahad explained everything Valentino told him, including the need to stay anonymous. There were a few snorts and grunts otherwise no one interrupted. When they finished the dossiers the room was quiet except for the crackle of the fire until they thoroughly processed the information.

"You know, I'm feeling the figures, definitely feeling the figures," Star said, breaking the silence. "What im iffy about is the white boy running shit. I mean, anytime he wants, he can pull some David Copperfield shit and we'll be left holding our dicks."

"True," Jahad nodded. "But if it blows up in his face we still good 'cause it's his show."

"We talking about 260 million-a-year, Jah. A mutherfucka would sneak God for that kind of dough," Sha' said, looking at the other Heads.

"Word!" Star agreed.

"I'm saying, Jah. You think we can trust Valentino enough to put everything in his hands?" Prince asked.

"We trusted him up to this point, so what's the difference now?"

"260 million is the difference," Sha' answered. "Greed is a motherfucka, Son."

"So what you saying, we should fall back and pass up the chance to get this money?"

"Nah. Hell nah! But we do need to have some type of leverage on him in case he tries some funny shit."

"He got kids?" Star asked.

"Nah. No kids, no wife, not even a dog. His only living relative is a sister down in Florida besides his people in Sicily. He has a penthouse apartment on Park Avenue and a crib out in Connecticut he uses sometimes on the weekends. I found all this out when we first Started dealing with him. Personally, I don't got no beef with it. If Valentino wanted he could have fucked us over a long time ago. We've been in the position to do the same to him. So far everybody been keeping it fair and I don't see why it will change now."

Prince nodded. "I feel that. Valentino knows we're not to be fucked with."

Jahad turned to Lord, who had a thoughtful expression on his face. "What you think homey?"

"I see the situation from both sides sort of. I mean, it's a possibility that Valentino could flip, but we really wouldn't be losing nothing."

"What you mean?"

"I mean we ain't really risking shit. Valentino wants us to body a few white boys and from there everything is in his hands. If he fronts, we body his ass too. If he keeps it official we all eat. It's as simple as that."

"You exactly right. So what's up? We all agree or what?" Jahad asked, looking at each head.

Once they all nodded, he continued. "Right now we only got information on this Leopardi dude. Valentino is still working on Corsillo. He also hinted that we go move on the rest of their shit. Y'all cool with that?"

"Shit, when we kill this muthafucka it should be ours anyway," Star said, then added, "Well Valentino's."

Jahad picked up on his sarcastic tone instantly. "We're all one in the same. Valentino can't make no moves without us and we can't make none without him. You know that."

Reluctantly, Star nodded.

"A yo, any of you niggas been hearing about some funny shit going round y'all spots?" Sha' asked.

Prince screwed up his face. "What you mean?"

"Crook told me he heard some outside niggas were moving weight in Crypress, but ain't no word came through our channels."

"It might be bogus then," Star said.

"Probably," Jahad agreed. "But have someone check it out. This ain't the time to have nobody trying to make moves on us when we about to make moves of our own. Now if this meeting is over, let's smoke up Prince's weed and drink his expensive ass liquor like we normally do."

Star grinned. "Shit, you know I'm with that."

U. E. Wynn

Chapter Seven

Within six months Koran's body count grew to seven, excluding Premo. Being the newest member of the body squad with the least amount of kills, Star allowed him to claim most of the solo hits after Koran explained how he needed the experience. It wasn't that he enjoyed killing, he told himself. It was a chance to sharpen his skills.

A gold plated stiletto given to him by Star was his weapon of choice. It was easy to conceal, razor-sharp, and could kill instantly without a sound. His favorite kill zone was a thrust under the left armpit through the tender flesh between the ribs straight into the heart. Five out of his seven kills he'd used the deadly knife. Once on a crowded train without drawing any attention.

As he grew confident in his abilities, it seemed as if he'd picked up a blood lust. Whenever a meeting was called he would get all excited knowing someone had fucked up and he'd get the chance to kill again. Soon the body squad gave up on going through the normal process of drawing names. Why bother when Koran would claim the hit anyway. Someone should have stopped him. Star, Jahad or another one of the Heads, but they figured he would eventually tire himself out. What they didn't consider or grasp was that they had created a monster.

There was a downside to Koran's killing nature; his conscience. Regardless of how well he controlled his emotions, his sub-conscience never let him forget the lives he took. For the first couple of weeks after each kill his dreams were more horrifying than a Wes Craven horror movie. His victims were returning from the grave with gruesome wounds leaking blood and all types of green shit from their eyes, mouth and noses. In one dream, the most frequent, he stood on the roof the night he murdered Premo. Only now when he ran to the ledge to see him fall Premo would be floating in mid air holding hand fulls of shit calling his name repeatedly.

Another downside was the guilt he felt when he awoke from his nightmares. It was almost enough to make him give up the life he led altogether. But the M.G.'s, Jahad mainly, had too much influence over him. The guilt soon pushed him to Start smoking weed. He found that being high was the only way to cope with the nightmares. Still, when it came time to kill again, he jumped at the opportunity. It's what he signed up for when he asked to become a M.G. and there was no turning back now.

When he set up to do his eighth hit, that's when he learned how much of a professional he was. It was also when he learned that his heart wasn't as cold as he thought. Frosty, a well known big time heroin pusher from the Polo Grands unknowingly owed the M.G.'s for three kilo's of heroin. He claimed the work went bad when it came time to pay, although he had just bought a brand new Bentley. Then word on the street was that he was spending money like he had hit the lottery. The M.G.'s weren't into sending threats, so after an hour debate, the Heads decided that Koran would send him to his maker.

For three weeks Koran studied Frosty's every move. Frosty lived with his girlfriend or wife with their infant son. He had followed them on separate occasions in different parts of the city. That's where he ran into problems. Koran had his limitations, and killing women and kids was one of them. But close to a quarter million dollars was involved, so he had to search the apartment. He just prayed they wouldn't be home when he did.

The day of the hit he dressed in some old dirty clothes, smeared some dirt on his face and wore a nappy afro wig, giving him the appearance of a bum. Every night at approximately eight o'clock Frosty returned home and stayed at least an hour before leaving out. At precisely seven thirty Koran followed a group of kids in the building, hung an out of order sign on the elevator, then made his way to the staircase. It was cold and damp with the raunchy odor of stale piss heavy in the air.

In between the fifth and sixth floor he lay sideways across the cold steps as if he were drunk so Frosty would be forced to stop. Like clockwork, a few minutes after eight Frosty came bounding up the stairs carrying a brown grocery bag. He wore a pair of gold addition Timberlands, Red Monkey jeans, and a brown, tan and white Coogi sweater. When he came across Koran, he frowned disgustedly taking him for a heroin addict and kicked him in the side.

"Get your stinking ass out the way man. This ain't no fucking hotel."

Frosty drew back his foot to kick Koran again, but before the blow could land, Koran sprung to his feet, his gun pressed hard into Frosty's jaw.

"You one of those pretty ass Harlem niggaz so I suggest you keep your ass still unless you want your face splattered against the wall."

Koran did a quick pat down finding a .380 in Frosty's back pocket. He grabbed him by the back of his collar and balled it in his fist. "We about to walk to your apartment like we old friends. You fake one move and it will be your last. Now move!"

Frosty glanced over his shoulder as Koran shoved him forward. "Listen man. I got some cash…"

Koran popped him hard upside the head. "We'll talk about all that in a minute. For now, shut the fuck up."

At the staircase door leading to the sixth floor Koran paused to check the hallway. He found it empty, so he guided Frosty to his apartment door. When he lifted his hand to knock, Koran popped him again.

"You think you slick, huh? Use your damn key before I merk your ass right here. Stupid ass!"

With shaky hands Frosty opened the door. The aroma of frying chicken greeted them as Koran reached into his hoodie pocket and took out a pair of handcuffs he'd bought just for the occasion.

"Hold your hands behind your back."

"You a cop?" Frosty asked fearfully.

The question told Koran he had something he wasn't suppose to have inside the apartment. Koran had a pretty good idea what that something was. "Yeah, I'm a cop. Now put your damn hands behind your back before I show you how cops like me get down."

Mary J. Blige's soulful lyrics came from behind the stereo in the living room as they traveled down the short hallway and made a right into the kitchen. The woman Koran assumed was Frosty's wife stood in front of the electric stove with her back to them singing along with Mary. Their son, who was no older than two or three, sat to her left in his high chair playing with an action figure.

"Osty! Osty!" the child yelled, happily bouncing up and down in his seat.

The woman turned, smiling until she saw Koran standing behind

Frosty holding the gun.

"What's going on Frosty? Who is this man?" she asked, glancing at her son who grew still sensing the tension.

Koran flashed a smile wanting to keep her calm. "A yo, everything is cool. We need to have a little chat and I'm out, a'ight. You got somewhere to put your kid while we talk?"

The woman looked at Koran strangely a second, then at Frosty for reassurance. "It's okay love. Just do what he says."

Hesitantly, she turned the stove off, then lifted the child from his chair and led the way out the kitchen. Koran followed closely holding Frosty by the cuffs to a small bedroom off to the left side of the hallway. Toys, a tricycle, and stuffed animals were scattered around a large play pen that sat in the middle of the room. After placing the child in the playpen she turned on a small 18inch television perched on a tv stand across from the playpen. Soon cartoons filled the screen. As if in a trance the child stared at the television and paid no attention to the adult as they left.

Entering the living room Koran noted that everything was new. The black carpet, maroon leather furniture, fifty inch wide screen television, Dell computer, and a Kenwood stereo. Pictures of the child from birth up to his current age, decorated the walls along with a few of his mother in different poses.

Once they were both seated on the couch, Frosty somewhat uncomfortably with his hands behind his back, Koran got straight to the point.

"You might not know why I'm here and you might not have heard of the M.G.s', but that work you got? Well, let's just say you fucked with the wrong niggaz shit. I'm here to fix that problem."

Frosty's eyes flew open. "Hey man, I told Storm that shit went bad. It was packaged wrong. He ain't say nothing about having to pay for it!"

Koran shook his head. "I don't know who in the hell Storm is and I really don't give a fuck. That ain't even the issue anyway. This is." Koran held up his gun. "You have two choices; give up the dough and die fast or stall and die slow. Either way you're a dead muthafucka."

"I thought you said you just wanted to talk!" the woman screamed. "You don't have to kill him. The money is in the closet and the drugs..."

"Shut the fuck up!" Frosty yelled.

Squinting his eyes in annoyance Koran crossed the room in two quick steps and grabbed a throw pillow from the couch using it to cover the barrel of his gun.

"Bluk! Bluk! Bluk!"

The muffled shots slammed Frosty's head back into the cushion before he slid sideways slumped over the couch armrest. Beside him the woman screamed hysterically.

"Shhhhhh!" Koran hissed aiming the gun in between her eyes. "Calm the fuck down. Now!"

Instantly her screams came to a stop, turning to near silent whimpers although her eyes were still terror struck. "That's it shorty, take a few breaths. That's it. Everything is good," he coached, putting the gun away for a show of good faith.

"Are...are...you...you... go...going...to kill...kill me?" she stuttered, looking at him through pleading eyes.

A picture of Michelle and Latrice flashed through Korans' mind. This was someone's mother, possibly someone's sister. Her son was in the next room and his father already lay dead. He couldn't kill her. Yet, he knew this was a witness. Someone to bring him down. Someone to bring the whole organization down since the M.G.'s had been mentioned. He had to kill her. However, the thought of her son alone in his bedroom caused a major conflict. He would not, could not kill a child. Taking a deep breath he met the woman's eyes and came to a life altering decision.

"What's your little man's name? How old is he?"

"Huh?"

"Your kid. What's his name?"

"Oh, Jamel. His name is Jamel."

"Word. His birthday soon?"

"He'll be three in March. March 19th. Why?" she asked, confused.

"Just wondering. Cute kid."

"Listen mister, please don't kill us. I'll tell the police I didn't see your face. That you were wearing a mask or something. On my son's life I swear I will!"

Koran felt a tug at his conscience. "Don't sweat that shorty. Just show me where everything is and I'm out."

Standing on shaky legs, she led him to the kitchen where she took two large rice containers from the refrigerator. Koran dumped the containers in the sink and came up with seven ounces of heroin wrapped individually in plastic.

"This it?" He frowned down at the dirt colored drugs.

"It's all I know about, I swear!" she cried backing away fearfully.

"Chill, shorty. I told you everything is cool. What's up with the dough?"

"It's in the bedroom. C'mon."

As they walked passed her son's room towards the bedroom, Koran glanced at the child who was still engrossed in the cartoon with a crooked grin on his baby face. For a second Koran felt a strong sense of Déjà vu' before he tore his eyes away from the child. In the bedroom the woman went straight to the closet, dug under a pile of new clothes with the tags still on them, and pulled out a brown leather briefcase. She walked over to the bed and was about to open it when Koran stopped her.

"Whoa, Ma. I'll do that." Koran walked to her side and undid the brass latches. Inside were neatly stacked bills held by rubber bands filled to the top. He closed the case and snatched it up. "Come on, walk me to the door. Give me a few minutes before you call the Jakes though, a'ight?"

"You're serious?" she asked, with a spark of hope in her voice.

Koran nodded, dreading what he knew had to be done. Don't do it! Don't do it! Think of your mother, your sister. Imagine if someone murdered them in cold blood for nothing. She's innocent Koran! She's innocent! Frosty was your target. Frosty, not her! He clenched his teeth and fought with his conscience. He fought the softening of his heart and pushed his emotions aside.

"Lead the way, Ma."

She gave him one last look and turned to lead him to the door. Before she could take a step, Koran wrapped an arm around her neck and with one vicious twist killed her instantly. Once her limp body fell to the floor guilt rushed him in waves.

"I had to goddammit! I had to!" he roared, gripping his head. He stared at her a moment and a vision of his mother lying dead before him filled his mind. Kneeling down in front of her he brushed his hand lightly across her smooth chocolate cheek with tears on the brim of his eyes. "I'm sorry shorty. I didn't wanna do it. I swear I didn't," he whispered. He stood up and fought to get his emotions under control again.

When Koran walked into the child's room Jamel looked up, his large brown eyes focusing on the gun tucked in front of Koran's jeans.

"Bang Bang!" Jamel said and pointed the gun.

"Huh?" Koran looked down, then smiled. "Yeah, this my bang, bang," he said, moving the gun to the small of his back.

"Mommy? Where's mommy?"

No amount of self control could keep the anguish from showing on Korans' face. "You like ice cream lil' man?"

Jamel nodded. "I eat ice came."

"How about cheesecake? You like cheesecake?"

"Cake and ice came!" Jamel squealed, holding his arms up, gesturing for Koran to pick him up. "Mommy get ice cream too?"

"Nah, lil' homey. It's me and you now. I'ma hold you down though, a'ight?"

"Alwight."

~~~~

True to his words after leaving with Jamel Koran changed into a clean set of clothes he kept in the stolen black Honda Accord. Once he made it to the Bronx, he and Jamel went to Fun World on Fordham Road for cake and ice cream. From there he took his time driving home knowing a confrontation awaited him once he explained to Jahad that Jamel was now part of the family.

Jahad sat in front of the television, eyes glued to the Madden video game he played. He paid no attention when Koran walked in with Jamel asleep in his arms. Koran placed the briefcase on the coffee table, sat on the loveseat, and lay Jamel beside him.

"Is it done?" Jahad asked, without turning away from the television.

"Yeah, it's a wrap for dude. I ran into some problems though."

"What kind of..." Jahad paused when he saw Jamel, who had curled up into a ball. "Who's that?"

"That's the problem I ran into. His name is Jamel. I had to body dude and his shorty. Lil' dude was at the crib so…"

"What you bring him here for?" Jahad asked, frowning.

Koran looked at Jamel for a moment before answering. "I'm keeping him."

"You what? Have you lost your damn mind? You keeping him! He ain't no fucking puppy, Koran!" Jahad couldn't believe what he was hearing. "Who the hell is suppose to take care of him?"

"I'll handle that. I made the lil' dude a promise. I gotta keep it, Jah!"

"Hell no!" Jahad shook his head. "Think about what you saying, Koran. You bodied the niggas parents. You know the cops gonna be looking for him like crazy. It's too much damn heat. What you gone do is take his ass to the nearest orphanage and leave him on the steps. What the fuck wrong with you?"

"I…"

"Another thing," Jahad went on. "You're nineteen with a lot of shit on your plate. How you figure you can have time to raise the lil' nigga, answer that?"

Koran took the time to think about everything that Jahad said and couldn't deny the truth. For a while Jamel's face would probably be all over the news, which would bring all types of heat. This didn't stop him from keeping his word though. All babies looked alike. It would be nothing to pass Jamel off as a little brother or even his son, he thought, warming to the idea. As far as the other activities, he didn't see Jamel interfering too much. Most of his time was spent at Joe's learning the business. That's when he wasn't out doing what he did best. Emma would be more than happy to babysit whenever he had to be out.

"You know I can't beef with you Jah. You're right. It's gonna bring crazy heat. On the same token, I can't abandon the lil' nigga. I'm not! If I get bagged or whatever I'll hold my own. You know I will. What I need for you to do for me, if you will, is to get me some legit paperwork for him. Work with me on this Jah, please!"

"Dammit Koran!" Jahad stood up catching the stubborn look in Koran's eyes. "It don't matter what I say, do it. You just gonna do what you wanna do, huh?"

"Nah, it ain't like that, but look at him Jah. Look at him!" Koran pleaded. "Where can he go? What can he do?"

Jahad glanced stone faced at Jamel as he slept with his thumb in his mouth and felt his defensives weaken. The child reminded him a lot of Koran when he was a baby.

"I couldn't leave him in there Jah. I couldn't. I know I'm a cold hearted muthafucka, but I ain't that cold. He's a lil' trooper too. He ain't cried all day."

Jahad blew out a breath. "A'ight Koran. We gonna keep this

between us, though. Don't think I'm a be doing no damn baby sitting, and don't be adopting no more damn kids. As much as you been busting your gun, before long we gonna have an orphanage in this muthafucka."

Koran laughed, relieved. "I gotcha, Jah. Now lets get down to business." He opened the briefcase. "I got $160,000.00. He only had seven ounces left so I ain't fuck with it. I'm hoping the Jakes won't investigate too much once they see it's drug related."

Jahad nodded. "Good thinking. We'll split the dough since you took the time to search the crib. I ain't giving the other Heads shit."

"Why? What's up?"

"They voted with Sha'. I didn't want you to do that shit," Jahad replied, screwing up his face.

"What you mean? Do what?"

"Nothing. Check this out. It's time you slow down. You doing too damn much. Since we brought you in you done bodied like fifteen muthafuckas. I..."

"Only ten," Koran broke in.

"Ten, fifteen, what's the damn difference," Jahad scowled. "You need to fall back. Your pride got you feeling like you got something to prove and you don't. You proved everything when you bodied Premo so all that extra shit ain't necessary. What you need to do is take a trip. Go visit mom's. New York ain't going nowhere nigga."

"I can't. I gotta keep my shorty's serviced. I'm a stay low for a while though. At least until that heat blows over."

"Yeah, do that. I just thought of something too. You don't even know how to change a damn diaper."

Koran grinned slyly. "That's what my shorty's are for."

For close to six months Koran had been juggling five girls. He had a five day schedule with a day for each girl. Lisa, his good girl from Webster Avenue, get's Monday. Monica, his Puerto Rican from Castle Hill, get's Tuesday. Kim, his conceited girl from Harlem, get's Wednesday. Tasha, his gangsta bitch from Brooklyn, get's Thursday. And Erica, his model chick from Queens, get's Friday. During the weekdays, his Range Rover stayed in traffic more than a dollar cab. Taking Jahad's advice he made it known that he wasn't looking for a steady girlfriend. His girls were free to date anyone they chose, just as he was. So far everything was working out fine. Well, Lisa and Monica were showing signs of falling in love, but that was their problem.

"You trickin' ass nigga." Jahad laughed. "Remember what I told you about bitches. Use them like niggas use fuck boys in jail. Once you get your nut, put them bitches back on the shelf. Don't fall in love man."

Koran snorted. "Me? Fall in love? C'mon. That'll be like seeing a skinhead in a 5% cipher. It'll never happen," he said, having no idea how wrong he was.

Chapter Eight

Jamel woke Koran bright and early the next morning bouncing up and down on the bed. Koran, who was used to sleeping by himself, sprung up and reached for the Ruger 9mm he kept in between his mattress.

"What the... Oh, it's you lil dude. What's up?"

"Wet. I wet," Jamel replied, still bouncing.

"Wet? Oh your diaper." Koran slid out of bed and walked to his dresser. "I don't got no diapers Jamel so I'ma have to find something for you." He grabbed a pair of his boxers, shook his head, then settled for a tee shirt. "This will have to do for now. I'll have to wrap it around your little ass."

Use to this routine, Jamel lay back on the bed and Started fumbling with the sticker on his pamper. Once it was off, Koran went to wrap the tee shirt around him and Jamel shot a stream of piss right at his chest.

"Oh shit!" Koran shouted backing into the dresser. He looked down at Jamel, who had a crooked grin on his face and burst out laughing. "Oh word. You pulled an R. Kelly on me. What if I pissed on you? One of those hard long pisses. I betcha' wouldn't find it funny then."

Jamel paid him no attention and kept grinning.

"I tell you what, Since you wanna piss on me, you're gonna stay butt ass naked until one of my shorty's get her to change you. And you better not shit on my bed either."

"I shit! I shit!" Jamel giggled.

"You better not. Now chill here and let me call Lisa."

"Mommy. Mommy. Where Mommy?"

Koran froze and felt a fresh wave of guilt. He had stayed up late last night terrified to fall asleep knowing the nightmares would come. He didn't want to believe, although it was true, that he was so ruthless to kill an innocent woman, then steal her child. But, Jamel was now his responsibility. He would feed, protect, and raise him as if he were his own flesh and blood. That's all that mattered. If he continued to dwell on what had been done, he would be no good to himself or Jamel.

"I know you won't understand this," he said, lifting Jamel to his lap. "But I'm your Mommy now lil' homey. I'm your Moms and your Pops. And from now on, your lil' Kay, a'ight?"

"Aw'ight."

"And I'm Koran."

"Ka-wan." Jamel dabbed his finger in Korans' chest.

"Yeah, that's close enough."

An hour later they were in bed watching cartoons when Lisa arrived with breakfast and pampers. Koran answered the door in his boxers and Jamel was still naked, both grinning.

"Hi sweety." Lisa kissed Koran on the cheek before kneeling down in front of Jamel. "And look at you sexy. All baby fat and smiles."

Standing at only five one and 115lbs, Lisa had the innocent face of an angel and the personality of a talk show host. Out of all his girls she was Koran's favorite. Their fling Started back in high school. Never once had she asked for anything other than what he was willing to offer, which was a quality he liked most about her.

"This is my nephew Jamel. He's cooling out with me for a while."

"Jah-mel," Jamel said, holding his arms out so she can pick him up.

"Well, let's get a pamper on you." Lisa dumped the diapers and food on the couch, then scooped Jamel up and buried a kiss on his chubby cheek.

Following them to the bedroom, Koran couldn't help resist palming her bubble butt. "You'll change my diaper too?"

Lisa giggled. "Sounds kinda kinky, but maybe."

While she tended to Jamel, Koran went to the closet where he kept his stash. Jahad constantly hounded him about keeping so much money in the apartment, but Koran liked having his money close for easy access. Eighty thousand, along with his weekly salary of five thousand dollars, would allow him to trick lovely for a minute. He spent money on his girls for the sheer fun of it. It had nothing to do with love. He had always been kind-hearted to women. A value instilled by his mother, sister and Emma.

"Lisa I need a favor," he called out. He took five individual thousand dollar stacks from a Nike shoe box, one of ten he kept stacked with money.

"If it has anything to do with putting a diaper on you I'm still thinking about it."

Koran laughed. "Nah, I need you to go shopping for Jamel. My sister and her husband are doing some traveling for their anniversary, and Since my mom's is going with them, I'm keeping Jamel until they get back. She dropped him off bare assed, though," he lied, casting a sad smile.

"Aren't you sweet."

"I know right. So you got me? You can take my truck and I'ma give you a 'G' for yourself."

"Say no more." Lisa smiled hosting Jamel up. "You hear that sexy? We're going shopping."

"Jamel can't go," Koran said quickly. "My brother is on the way to pick him up."

"I go!" Jamel cried, clinging to Lisa.

Koran shook his head. For a while he and Jamel wouldn't be going anywhere. "Nah, lil' homy. You want some ice cream?"

"Ice came!" Jamel pushed away from Lisa and reached for Koran.

"You sold me out for some ice cream." Lisa laughed while tickling his pot belly. "You want me to spend four thousand dollars on baby clothes?"

"Yeah. Hit up Fordham Road. Get clothes, sneakers, toys, and mad pampers. Cop him a chain and a bracelet too. Think you'll need some more dough?"

"Are you kidding!"

"Nah, this my lil nigga right here." Koran smiled, ruffling Jamel's curly black hair.

~~~~

For a straight week the story of the missing child played every night on the news. Koran cancelled all his dates with the exception of Lisa, whom he allowed to come over every few days just to see if she had an idea of who Jamel really was. As much as he would hate to do it, if she ever found out, he would be left with no choice but to kill her. Jamel was his now and he would kill anyone who posed a threat.

Time seemed to slow down the first three months they stayed cooped up inside the apartment. The only time they went out was after dark for quick runs to Baskin and Robbins. The time also proved to be a blessing. A bond was formed between Jamel and

Koran deeper than any father and son. To hear Jamel laugh, or see a smile on his chubby face, warmed Koran's cold heart.

They were on the couch watching a Disney movie the day Jahad came home with a brown manilla envelope under his arm. Unlike Koran, Jahad's relationship with Jamel was just the opposite. He wanted no dealings with Jamel period. He felt the child would somehow interfere with Koran's loyalty to the M.G.s. This would soon change.

"Here's your paperwork." He tossed the envelope on the coffee table, then grabbed the remote control and turned to ESPN missing the scowl Jamel gave him. "There's a birth certificate and social security card under the name Michael Copeland, born April 8th 2004, at Jacoby Hospital. "It's all legit."

Koran inspected the birth certificate finding his name typed beside the spaced labeled father. "Good looking, Jah. Word up."

"Good looking my ass. That'll cost you fifteen hundred. I want my dough too."

"Turn TV!" Jamel shouted, sliding off the couch with his little hand bunched into a fist. "Turn TV!"

Jahad smirked. "And if I don't? What?"

Jamel looked around, grabbed Korans' cell phone and hit Jahad on the leg. "Turn TV, now!"

They glanced at one another a second, then Jahad burst out laughing as he turned back to the movie. "You see this shit! The lil' nigga thinks he can beat my ass."

Koran smiled proudly. "C'mon Kay. You don't gotta fuck him up."

"Fuck up, Nugga," Jamel said, giving Jahad one last scowl before climbing in Koran's lap. Jahad laughed so hard tears ran from his eyes. From that moment on he accepted Jamel as a part of the family.

Chapter Nine

After seven months of being cooped up inside the apartment Koran Started to feel like they were in a well equipped prison. He was fed up with their daily routine of watching cartoons, playing video games, and nightly runs for ice cream. It had become downright boring. It was this same boredom that persuaded him to finally take Jamel out during daylight hours. Months of going without sunlight had lightened both their complexions. Jamel's chocolate skin to a light caramel brown and Koran's high yellow to a pale chalky beige.

Jamel's hair had grown out which Lisa kept cornrolled or either in Single plaits. Koran doubted if anyone would recognize him. They were only going to the ballpark anyway. He dressed Jamel in a Roc-A-Wear jean suit, a pair of brown suede timberlands, and a brown Phat Farm sweat shirt matching his own outfit. Jamel, excited to be going out, ran circles around Koran's legs as he took the battery Operator Hummer from the pantry.

"Outside Ka-wan. Outside?"

"Yeah, Kay. We going outside. Now chill before you make me bust my ass."

Jamel giggled while trying to climb in his truck. "Kay drive!"

He had one foot inside when Koran lifted him out. "Wait 'till we get to the park, then you can drive all you want, a'ight?"

"Aw-ight. Ice came Ka-wan?"

Koran shook his head, smiling, something he did often with Jamel around. "I'll think about it. Now c'mon big head."

"You big head," Jamel laughed, running to the front door while, Koran pushed the truck behind him. Exiting the building they bumped into Derrick, Jahad's head lieutenant and childhood friend who lived on the third floor in the building. Derrick was one of the original M.G.'s. His loyalty to Jahad dated back to grad school. Dressed in a black Sean John velour sweatsuit, a plain white tee shirt, and a pair of white Nike Air Force Ones, he could still pass for a teenager although he would turn twenty seven in August. His face was hairless except for a neatly trimmed mustache. He had thin eyebrows that curved over his small close set brown eyes. He stood six-one with a slim build and wore his hair in four thick cornrolls.

"What's up, Koran? Where you been nigga?" he asked, giving Koran a hug.

"Took a lil' vacation. What's up with you?"

"I'm chillin. Who you got with you?" Derrick looked down at Jamel, who was caught up in the sights.

The weather was nearly perfect. Temperatures hovered at a comfortable sixty degrees while a light breeze ruffled the last of the fall leaves. Huge clouds speckled the rich blue sky changing Sha"pes every few seconds. Although it was the beginning of March, people strolled through the project grounds in wife beaters and shorts as if it were Spring. Jamel took it all in through awestruck eyes. Seven months of being cramped inside made everything new to him.

"This is my son, lil Kay."

"Son! I ain't know you had kids."

"I didn't either until his mom sprung him on me."

Derrick studied Jamel for a second. "Yeah, lil' dude looks just like you. So what's up? Where you headed?"

"To the park for a lil' while. Why, what's up?"

"I got some haze nigga."

"Word!" Koran's eyes lit up. "Come to the park with us then. We can get toasted while Kay playing."

"Kay drive," Jamel said, while climbing into his truck.

When they made it to the park Koran and Derrick sat on a bench not too far from the swings and Started rolling blunts. Jamel rode around in his truck leaning to the side in an effort to mimic how Koran drove. In all directions kids were out playing. The basketball courts were packed with teams waiting to play next and old men sat the chessboard tables in deep thought over their next move.

"A yo, this shit crazy," said Koran before he took a pull from his blunt and looked around.

"What's that?" asked Derrick.

"I mean, look around. All these kids and shit, but soon as it gets dark this muthafucka be flooded with drug dealers, crackHeads, and stickup kids."

Derrick nodded, his eyes nearly closed. "I know right. It's been like this Since I was a kid. Probably long before that. When crack hit the streets back in the day it fucked a lot of shit up."

"Yeah. Them crackers some smart muthafuckas. I know the shit we do is ill," Koran said, referring to the M.G.'s, "but them crackers, they the illest! Look at Bush. He got niggas raping the Middle East frontin' like he's looking for terrorist. What he's doing is putting down a mean stick up game and its legal."

Derrick looked up at Koran with a straight face, then laughed. "Let me find out you on some political shit. Jesse Jackson ass nigga."

Koran laughed, although he was a news freak and stayed in tune with world affairs. "I'm saying, shit is real over there. Bush gonna fuck round and pop off World War Three. You think them Muslims gonna keep going for that shit? Hell no! Look at what Ben..."

His words trailed off when he noticed a couple walking with a lil' girl close by Jamel. The young woman screamed at her man who blatantly ignored her while the lil girl clung to her leg fearfully. Koran took a closer look and realized it was the same woman from the night before he killed Premo. The strong feeling that he knew her came across him again. His eyes traveled from her face to the tight Apple Bottom Jeans she wore which showed off her fat, heart shaped butt.

She wore her hair in thin corn rolls that hung well past her shoulders, stopping in the middle of her back. Bright red lipstick detailed her small thick lips giving them the look of a juicy plum. Her high yellow complexion was emphasized by high cheekbones, a small, slightly upturned nose, and deep green eyes the color of the sea. The whole package sent a tingle through Korans' genitals.

Jamel equally engrossed watched wide eyes as she yelled and dabbed her finger in her boyfriends face. Suddenly, the boyfriends patience broke and he slapped her so hard she dropped to one knee causing the little girl to fall with her. A muscle twitched in Koran's jaw seeing him hit her, but it wasn't his business, so like everyone else in the park he sat still. It wasn't until Jamel jumped from his truck and ran towards the commotion that Koran moved.

"Kay chill!" Koran shouted, but there was no stopping Jamel. When he reached the couple, after stumbling twice, he wrapped his arms around the man's leg and sunk his small teeth into his thigh before he could hit her again.

"What the hell!" The man looked down at Jamel, who was latched to his leg like a leech and roughly pushed him to the ground.

"I ought to stomp your lil' ass!" he snarled, grabbing his girlfriend by the collar.

Beside her the little girl tugged at her arm desperately trying to pull her away while Jamel pushed himself off the ground, a scowl on his baby face. Instead of crying like other two year olds, he turned to Koran as he ran up. "Ka-wan! Ka-wan get'im!"

Koran would have laughed if he hadn't been so pissed off. The only thing on his mind was murder as he drilled the boyfriend with an overhand right straight to the nose. The force shattered the bone and lifted him off his feet before he landed flat on his back.

"You fucked up nigga!" Koran yelled, reaching for the 45. Automatic he kept tucked at the small of his back.

"Bang bang, Ka-wan! Bang bang!" Jamel shouted.

Koran had to laugh. "Ain't no bang bang poppin' off Kay. Go get in the truck. We'll go get some ice cream later, okay?"

Jamel wasn't trying to hear it. "Me bang bang! Me bang bang, Ka-wan!" He jumped up on his stubby legs trying to reach the gun.

"A yo Dee, come get Kay, man before he body this nigga."

Derrick laughed and picked Jamel up as Koran turned his attention to the young woman and the little girl who sobbed uncontrollably. "You a'ight shorty?"

She gave Koran a sad smile. "Yes. Thank you, Koran." She stood up and hugged the little girl. "It's ok Dej'a. Don't cry baby."

"How you know…" Koran was about to ask how she knew his name but she walked to where Derrick stood holding Jamel. He followed her with his eyes, trying to figure out where he knew her from and came up with a blank.

Being a sucker for a woman's affection, Jamel held out his arms for her to take him. "Okay?" he asked, gently touching the bruise forming under her eyes.

"Yes, baby. I'm fine. You're my little hero."

"Okay?" Jamel asked again looking down at the little girl.

She smiled, showing three missing baby teeth, two on top, one on the bottom. Two long pigtails hung around her small oval shaped face and stopped at her shoulders. Her large hazel brown eyes were the same color as Jamel's and was a shade lighter than her smooth brown skin.

"Yes, I'm okay. Let me hold him, Sin," she said in a small voice reaching for Jamel, who was more than happy to share himself.

"Sin?" Koran glanced at her as her boyfriend stirred awake and realized that he knew her. He knew her well in fact. Her name was Serenity. Sin for short. She lived in building 1790 which was right across from his building. He also remembered having a huge crush on her when they were in Junior high school and that was the last time he laid eyes on her until recently.

The boyfriend, still dazed, looked up at Koran through watery eyes. "You broke my fucking nose man!" he cried, as blood and mucus ran freely from his nose.

"Shut the fuck up!" Koran kicked him in the side wishing he could kill him right there. "Stand your bitch ass up!"

The malicious look in Koran's eyes sent a shiver of fear through him. "A yo Money, I ain't mean no harm man."

Koran shook his head, his mind set on killing him. "What's your name?"

"Trouble. Derrick knows me. We went to school together."

"Oh word. Dee your man?" Koran glanced at Derrick, who rolled his eyes. "You lucky then. I was about to merk your ass. You need to apologize to my lil' man, though."

Trouble quickly nodded and walked to where Serenity stood holding Jamel. "My fault lil nigga. You gotta mean lil' bite on you. And Sin, I'm sorry…"

Serenity slapped him so hard his face jerked to the side. "Get the fuck out my face you sorry bastard!"

Jamel squirmed in her arms, trying to hit him. "Fuck face! Fuck face!"

"I think you better leave Duke," Koran said, standing in between them. "Ain't nobody feeling you right now."

"Fuck face! Fuck face!" Jamel yelled as Trouble walked off holding his sweatshirt over his bloody nose.

"A'ight Kay, chill."

Jamel covered his mouth grinning and looked at Dej'a. "Ice Came, Ka-Wan?"

"Yeah, we on for ice cream," Koran answered, unable to take his eyes off Serenity. With warmth all over his body, he still felt the same nervousness he felt around her in junior high school.

"You get ice came too?" Jamel asked Serenity and a smile broke out on Koran's face. "That's up to your father, handsome. Do I get ice came too Ka-wan?" Serenity mimicked grinning.

Koran laughed. "No doubt. You and this lil' cutie right here. What's your name pretty?"

"Dej'a." She blushed shyly.

"You definitely do that with your pretty self. And Sin, pardon what just happened, but your man was way outta line."

"You don't have to tell me," Serenity rubbed her cheek.

For a few seconds they were stuck staring at one another until Koran caught himself. "Give me a sec' and we'll be out." He turned towards Derrick and nodded towards their bench.

Jamel, playing the ladies man, squirmed out of Serenity's arms. He stood between her an Dej'a, and took hold of their hands. Missing his mother's touch made him seek a woman's attention. When alone with Lisa and Koran, all of their affection was his. At times Koran wasn't even allowed to touch her. Jamel would calmly remove his hand and proclaim the spot he touched "mine." If Koran got a kiss, Jamel got two. That was the law. Being the two were so closely bonded, Koran understood completely and went along with the program.

"A yo, you know that nigga Trouble?" Koran asked once they made it to the bench. "Yeah, I know scrams." Derrick reached in his pocket for a cigarette. "Why, what's up?"

"Oh, nothing. I'ma body his ass for putting his hands on Kay though. Do me a favor and bring him to the roof tonight at eleven. I'll meet you there."

"Body him! C'mon Koran, it ain't like he hurt the lil' nigga."

"That ain't the point. He fucked up when he put his hands on Kay," Koran snapped and turned to walk off. "I'm good though. I'll get his ass."

Derrick grabbed him by the shoulder. "Hold up nigga. I'll bring the nigga, but damn son. It ain't that serious."

"If it was your son or daughter what would you do?"

Derrick gave him a thoughtful look before answering. "I feel you. What's up with shorty. She trying to look out for you holding her down?"

"That's what I'm about to find. One!" Koran winked, then jogged back to where Serenity stood with Jamel and Dej'a'. "What up? Y'all ready?"

"We ready Ka-wan," Jamel tugged at Serenity and Dej'a's hand.

"If you don't mind, can you walk with us to my building so I can put his truck up."

"I need to go home too, so I can put something on my cheek. Sorry ass..." Serenity glanced at Jamel and cut her words off.

"Trouble your man or something?"

She rolled her eyes. "Was my man. If anything he was my dog. Every other week I hear he's with a different tramp. And that's the last time he'll ever put his hands on me. I'd rather be by myself."

"I'm saying, you don't gotta be by yourself. You need to find the right nigga."

"And where might the right nigga be?"

Koran hunched his shoulders. "You gotta know where to look."

"Think so?"

"Know so."

While Koran lay down his game, Jamel did the same thing with Dej'a' although his words couldn't be understood.

"I wonder if the right nigga is the same one who use to sweat me all the time at school but never said anything."

"Maybe." Koran grinned. "I'm saying though, if you peeped dude sweating you, why you ain't say nothing to him?"

Serenity shrugged. "I don't know. Shy I guess."

"You shy, please! As I remember you were the complete opposite."

In Junior High Serenity hung out with four other girls nicknamed the F.A.B. which stood for Fly Ass Bitches. They were just that. They wore the latest fashions, sported the hottest hair-doo's and wore tons of jewelry usually brought by their drug dealing boyfriends. When they entered a room all Heads turned. At fourteen Koran couldn't help but feel a little intimidated by her.

"Looks can be deceiving. I always thought you would get the nerve to ask me out."

"Now you're making me blush," said Koran smiling. "You were too fly to notice me back then. Where you disappear to after Junior High?"

"That's a long story, but I definitely noticed you. You use to be so serious. Always to yourself. I hardly ever saw you smile. As crazy as it may sound, that's what attracted me to you."

Thinking back Koran guessed his seriousness came from watching Jahad and his knowledge of the M.G.'s. Gangsta's didn't do a lot of smiling.

"On the low you had me kinda shook. That was then, though. So what's really good?"

Serenity looked at him through slanted eyes. "What you mean?"

"I ain't speaking French, Ma. You know what I mean."

She hesitated and looked towards the projects. "I won't front like you still don't spark my interest, but you saw what I went through. I can't jump into another relationship just like that." She snapped her fingers.

"Relationship! Whoa Ma. I don't get down like that. All I'm saying is we can hang out sometimes, you know? Ain't nothing wrong with that right?"

"No"

"Good, because I don't do relationships anyway. I do friendships."

"What you mean by friendships. You mean like we just cool or... you know."

"What difference does it make Since we only gonna be friends?"

"None I guess, but I hope you're strapping up if it's like that," she said wrinkling her nose.

"To satisfy your curiosity." He reached in his back pocket and pulled out a row of magnum condoms. "I stay wrapped up. That's my man right there." He glanced down at his crotch. "I gotta hold him down."

Serenity laughed. "You stay wrapped up, huh? Do your friends know each other. I mean are you all friends?"

Koran gave her a devilish grin. "Nah, I like the idea though."

"Dog." She rolled her eyes.

"Nah, I'm saying." His grinned stretched from ear to ear. "When I say friends I mean just that. We hang out, shop, or whatever. It ain't like I'll be in and out, pun intended. I'll put in some time. We're friends, you know?"

"Un huh. Let me ask you this and it's my last question."

"Go ahead. You gonna ask anyway."

"Why all the friends? You said it like you had at least two or three. What, you scared of commitment or does it take more than one woman to satisfy you?"

Koran's expression sobered. "It ain't too many things I'm scared of. And maybe if I found the right chick, then yeah, I could stay faithful. I don't do that though."

"Do what."

"You keeping it hot with the questions ain't you, Ma? I plead the fifth," he said, holding up his right hand.

Serenity giggled. "I sound like a reporter, huh?"

"Are you?"

"No, just curious."

"Uh huh."

~~~~

Back at the apartment feeling like he was twelve again, Koran ran some bath water, then went to the stereo and put on 50 cents 'Get rich or die trying just so he could hear 21 questions.

If I fell off tomorrow would you still love me?

If I didn't smell so good would you still hug me?

He rhymed along with 50 on his way to the bathroom while behind him Jamel bobbed his little fat head hard enough to snap his neck. When they finished bathing, after he cleaned up the water Jamel splashed all over the floor, they walked to the bedroom both wrapped in towels.

"You ready to go get fly Kay?"

"Get fry," he said, pointing towards the closet.

Koran laughed. "Yeah, you know what time it is. We gonna stunt today."

He dressed Jamel in a silver Roc-A-Wear velour sweatsuit, gray Timberlands, and a silver and white New York Yankee's hat. For himself a light brown Gucci velour sweatsuit, white Gucci sneakers and a white tee shirt. Since they were going to stunt, Koran pulled out the jewelry. He grabbed Jamel's baby platinum Cuban links with a Mickey Mouse piece crusted with diamonds and the matching bracelet he always broke. For himself, a rose gold Gucci link with a sun piece flooded with yellow diamonds.

"You ready to play lil' dude?" Koran asked, looking in the mirror. "You got a shorty and I got a shorty. What's up?"

"Ice came," said Jamel looking up at him grinning.

"Hopefully I'll get some cake with that," Kuran said while checking his clothes.

"I get cake too."

"I don't think you can handle the kinda cake I'm talking about."

On their way out Jahad walked in followed by Derrick. His face was screwed up into a frown until he saw Jamel running towards him. Since the two bumped Heads over the television Jahad had fallen under his spell. Jamel's innocence had a way of making Koran and Jahad forget what they really were, killers.

"What's good lil' nigga?" Jahad scooped him up and tossed him in the air. Jamel fell into a fit of giggles.

"Up Jah! Kay up!"

"Nah, it might wrinkle your gear. You all Gee'd up. Where you headed?"

"Ice came. You go Jah?" Jamel asked, trying to pull Jahad's platinum chain over his head.

"You wanna rock my chain or you trying to house my shit?"

"I wock chain."

Jahad sat him down, then laid the hundred thousand dollar chain glowing with huge blue diamonds around his little neck. Jamel being a clown folded his arms over his chest in a B-Boy stance imitating Jahad.

"Kay you something else lil' nigga." Jahad laughed and turned to Koran. "Dee told me what happened earlier. Want me to handle it?"

"Nah, I got Duke."

Jahad nodded and dropped to his knee in front of Jamel. "That nigga fucked up didn't he Kay?"

"Uh huh. Fuck up. Nigga fuck up."

Chapter Ten

Serenity and Dej'a' stood out in front of the building when Koran and Jamel walked out. They both were pimping hard. Well, Jamel tried his best. Catching sight of Serenity, Jamel took off at full speed and nearly tripped from the weight of Jahad's heavy chain. Luckily for him, Serenity ran to meet him before he could flip over.

"Well, look at you fly guy." She picked him up and planted a kiss on his forehead.

"I fry," Jamel said proudly, then looked over his shoulders at Dej'a'. "Give Kay a kiss."

Dej'a', looking cute as ever, was dressed in a light blue Baby Phat one piece skirt, white Reebok classics and a sky blue and white leather jacket to complete the ensemble. She made no attempt to move towards Jamel, so he slid from Serenity's arms and ran to her intent on getting his kiss.

"I see he's a ladies man like his father," Serenity said smiling. "Where we going?"

Koran was too consumed in admiring her outfit to answer. She wore a pink and white DKNY sweater, white Azzure's jeans, and a pair of pink and white Air Max sneakers. He noticed for the first time that her legs were slightly bowed and the picture of getting in between them flashed through his mind.

"Um, Um, Um," he grunted, looking her up and down.

"What?"

"You, Ma. I know you already know this, but you look good as hell. You just don't know the work I could put in."

"Stop it!" Serenity said blushing. "Now where are we going?"

"Ice came," Jamel called out, walking up holding Dej'a's hand.

Koran smiled and shook his head. "After he gets his ice cream we can hit *Fun World* or either the zoo, then catch a movie. We can top the night off at Chucky Cheese. He's a sucka for Chucky Cheese burgers. Ain't that right, Kay?"

"Chucky Cheese burger!"

"See," Koran said, leading them to his truck.

~~~~

"From the moment Koran pulled away from the curb there was nothing but good vibes. Jamel, talkative as ever, held a steady incoherent conversation with Dej'a that she seemed to understand. As the day progressed the attraction between Serenity and Koran grew stronger. So much so that it made Koran uncomfortable. A casual glance often turned into a Stare, causing him to swerve in traffic. An innocent touch tended to linger longer than necessary. By the end of the night the conversation of being friends was no more than wasted air. Still, Koran told himself not to push. What was happening between them was nature, it would take his course.

Just shy of ten thirty Koran parked in front of his building in his usual parking space. Eleven o'clock was showtime. Across the street the park was crowded, although the temperature had dropped to a chilly thirty five degree's. Street and park lights cast a dullish maroon tint over the monkey bars, swings, and basketball courts. This provided just enough light for the drug dealers to make their sales in private and the stick up kids to lurk in the shadows like preying lions.

In the back seat Jamel and Dej'a slept quietly. Dej'a was leaning against Jamel's car seat wearing a Chucky Cheese hat holding an IPod Koran bought for her. During the day he paid special attention to her Since Jamel refused to part from Serenity. For a seven year old, she was shy, and extremely pretty. She would definitely be a heartbreaker for sure someday.

"You get Dej'a and I'll get Kay," Serenity said once he turned off the engine.

Koran glanced at the purple bruise on her cheek as she stepped from the truck and felt anger bubble up in his chest. Never again would she have to worry about Trouble putting his hands on her.

"A yo Sin, I need you to do me a favor," he softly. He hoisted Dej'a up and she wrapped her arms around his neck and was fast back to sleep.

"What type of favor?"

"I need you to…." His cell phone went off interrupting him. He shifted Dej'a in his arms before answering. "Yeah, what up?"

"Hi baby," a sexy female voice purred. "You forgot the sound of my voice? It's Monica, Poppi."

"Oh, what's up, Ma. How you?"

Serenity cut her eyes at him, frowning.

"I'm missing you Poppi. I haven't seen you in ages and I need some attending to. I mean the works."

Koran pictured Monica's butter colored thick thighs and smiled. "Oh word. You know I'ma specialist so I can fix you up right. What you wanna...?"

"Don't you think that's rude?" Serenity cut him off as they walked up the walkway towards the building.

Koran forgot all about Monica. "What you mean, Sin?"

"Nothing," she said, picking up her pace.

"Who you talking to Koran?" Monica asked snappishly after hearing Serenitys' voice.

"A friend. I'ma get back at you later, a'ight?"

"Get back at me! Nigga I...."

Koran hung up and caught up with Serenity before she could make it inside the building. He couldn't explain it, but her mood affected him in ways he didn't understand. Usually he could care less about a woman's jealousy. It was nothing a new outfit couldn't fix. With Serenity it was different. The little time they spent together seemed to equal up to all his girls put together.

"What were you saying back there?" he asked, placing his key in the door.

"Nothing. But let me explain myself before you get the impression that I'm jealous."

He grinned. "So you saying you ain't?"

"That's exactly what I'm saying. What you did was disrespectful. What if I were the one talking to one of my boyfriends after....."

The grin left his face. "What boyfriends?"

"Jealous?" Serenity arched her eyebrow grinning. "This what I'm saying. If the shoe was on the other foot, I wouldn't hold a conversation with another man in front of you. Especially if I just finish entertaining you. It would be rude."

Koran gave her an apologetic smile. "You right. I still think you were jealous though."

"Would it give you the big head if I said maybe a little?"

He laughed. "Probably."

Upstairs Serenity looked around surprised by the lavishness of the apartment as Koran led her to his bedroom.

"You live here by yourself?"

"Nah, me and my brother." He laid Dej'a down on the bed beside

Jamel and then glanced down at his watch. "You still gonna do that favor for me?"

She placed her hands on her hips. "And what might that be?"

"Oh, it's like that?" He took a step around the bed towards her.

"Yes, it's like that." She smacked her lips, thinking he was about to ask for sex. "I want to kill that illusion before it goes too far."

"Don't kill it just yet, but that ain't the favor I wanted. Not at the moment anyway." He took another step toward her. "I need you to watch Jamel for like thirty minute. I'll be right back. I promise."

Serenity screwed up her face. "I know you don't think I'll sit here and babysit while you go see one of your girlfriends."

Koran laughed. "Nah, man. I mean no, Sin. Why would I wanna see one of them when I have you here in front of me?"

"Uh huh. Come back Koran like you said or I'll be pissed. I have to get Dej'a…."

He cut her off with a quick kiss that surprised them both. "I'll be right back."

~~~~

On his way to the roof a lopsided grin was plastered on Koran's face as thoughts of Serenity and what would happen when he made it back to the apartment played through his mind. For some reason she made him feel giddy and carefree. It was a warning sign he should have picked up on, but he was too absorbed in his feelings to realize what was happening.

Jahad and Derrick stood talking to Trouble near the ledge like they were old friends when Koran walked through the roof exit door. A spark of fear flashed through Trouble's eyes as soon as he laid eyes on Koran and he quickly turned his head towards Jahad.

"What's good?" Koran said, still grinning as he approached. Then, once he was in swinging distance he struck out with the speed of an animal and hit Trouble with a hard left jab followed by a vicious right hook that knocked him off the roof knowing sudden death was fourteen floors below. Turning, his expression casual, Koran met shocked eyes. "I gotta go, Jah. I left Jamel with one my shorty's."

"What the hell!" Jahad turned to Derrick, who kept glancing from the ledge where Trouble went over and back to Koran.

"I'm saying, that nigga wasn't worth talking shit to. I'm out."

"Hold on nigga. I got some shit to put you up on," Jahad said, grabbing him by the shoulder. "I'm feeling some ill ass vibes I can't put my finger on."

"What you mean?"

"Some shit ain't addin' up. I'm hearing two different stories about some shit that's supposed to be going down."

"What's supposed to be going down?"

"Nothing, that's just it. I'm hearing some shit is going on that don't suppose to be going on. Then again, I might be p-noid."

Koran blew out a frustrated breath. He hated when Jahad spoke like this. "I still don't know what the hell you talking bout, Jah."

"Tell him what you heard Dee."

"Some niggaz suppose to be eating in Bronxdale. Some Puerto Rican dudes."

"Okay, so what's the different story?"

"We just had a meeting a few weeks ago and Sha' said he heard some shit about nigga's moving weight around his way, but ain't shit coming from the watchers," Jahad answered.

"So what's the verdict?"

"On the low, Dee gonna send five nigga's out to Bronxdale. Just regular nigga's. I spoke to Sha' and he gonna do the same thing just to be sure it ain't no funny shit going on with the watchers. Until we find out what's going on, I want you to go down south with Kay for a few weeks."

Koran frowned sensing something serious was going on. "You sending me down south just because some nigga's might be hustlin' in Bronxdale? C'mon Jah. You know that shit don't even sound right. What's really going on?"

Jahad hesitated before answering. "It really don't concern you since you won't be here, but we about to expand. We been peepin' how these escort services are run and it's basically the same way drug organizations are ran."

"Escort services?" Koran said, confused. "You mean we bout to start pimpin' ho's?"

Jahad nodded. "Not us exactly, but yeah, something like that. The only difference in what we about to get into is the product. In this case the bitches are the product. The dude who runs the escort service pushes the work, but you always have a supplier. That's who we about to move on."

"Ok, I understand that, but what that has to do with me going down south?"

"Because behind every supplier, no matter what he's supplying, there's always a team. We about to go at it the same way we muscled in on the drug game, by force!" Jahad slammed his fist into his palm. "By this time next month shit gonna be crazy hot 'cause a lot of people gotta die. Some heavyweights who got long money and big guns. I don't want you around when the bodies Start poppin' up."

"I gotta be here when it pop off!" Koran said outraged. "You act like my gun don't go off or something!"

"It ain't about your gun going off. One of us gotta make sure Kay is a'ight. I think that's your responsibility."

Jamel had become a major part of Jahad's life in many ways Koran didn't see. Like at one point all things revolved around the M.G.'s, but now Jamel came first, and then the M.G.'s. Jahad would be sure he was somewhere safe before any moves were made.

"Won't nobody be safe when this shit goes down. Me, you or Kay. We dealing with some dangerous dudes this time around. One mistake could cost me more than I'm willing to give, so y'all gotta go."

"I'm saying, ain't no pimps built like that, not for the M.G.'s anyway. You talking like these dudes are monsters or something. We the monsters!"

"I told you, it ain't the pimps. It's the muscle behind the pimps."

"Who?"

"The Italians."

"You mean the mob?"

"If that's what you wanna call them. They ain't nothing but a bunch of spaghetti eating white boys to me."

"Oh shit!" Koran's mouth dropped open at the thought of the M.G.'s going up against the Mafia. "You for real?"

Jahad rolled his eyes. "When have you known me to bullshit? You looking awestruck, but the mob ain't really a power force no more. Not like they use to be back in the 80's. I mean, don't get me wrong, Gotti was a helluva white dude with an ill team. Back then, niggaz couldn't move them. They were too organized and bringing them wild ass dudes over from Sicily. They were bodying shit just to stay in the country. Sammy fucked that up when he ratted. The mob as a whole lost mad respect with the wrong people; the Columbians and the Chinese."

"At one time most of the drugs that came through New York

went through the mobs hands first, then they'd pass them down to the Dominicans and Puerto Ricans. After all that, they'd pass them down to the niggas. That all changed when Gotti got bagged. The Columbians fuck with whoever got enough paper. The gangs down in China town be pushing the heroin, as far as heavy weight. Now the mob be on some white collar shit. Prostitution is their only tie to the streets, but the whole prostitution game has changed. You got thousand dollar pussy out there, for real! They getting fat off that shit I mean sloppy fat. We about to get some of that money."

Marvelled, Koran shook his head. "How in the hell you know all this shit?"

"It's part of my job description." Jahad smiled as he reached in his pocket and took out a single key. "Take this. It's to a storage compartment at Port Authoughrity. The number is on the key."

"What's in it?"

"Some dough Pops left us. Give it to moms when you get down south. Don't lose it either."

Koran unable to comprehend what he was feeling felt a bad omen. "C'mon Jah. Let me stay and get down with what's about to pop off. That's why I'm on the Body Squad, right? Mrs. Harris can watch Kay while I do my thang. Just let me know what to get at."

"I said no," Jahad said forcefully, knowing how stubborn Koran was. "Your first obligation is to Kay. Why you think I took you through all that shit before making you an M.G.?"

"To get me right. I..."

"Yeah, to get you right," Jahad broke in. "But if something happens to me, you taking my spot. You can't do that if you're locked up or in a grave beside me. I know you get busy, but it's a time to get busy and it's a time to fall back. Now is the time to fall back, you understand?"

Koran nodded, but no, he didn't understand. There had to be a way to get around leaving and before that time came, he was determined to think of it.

~~~~

Serenity was asleep with Jamel on her chest and Dej'a cuddled up beside her when Koran walked into the bedroom. For a while he stood in the doorway hypnotized by the sight of her. Never in his life had a woman affected him so strongly. The urge to make love to her made his dick throb against his leg. But this was only the physical side of what he felt. Mentally, he felt the strong urge to protect her and make sure no one ever hurt her again. With that thought in mind, he crossed the room and gently shook her awake.

"What?..." She looked around confused until she realized where she was. "Shh." Koran put a finger to her lips and eased Jamel off her chest. "Come with me for a second."

Curious, Serenity missed the look of desire burning in his eyes as he helped her from the bed and led her to the hallway. Before she could ask what was going on he pressed her against the wall with his body and kissed her slightly on the lips.

"What are you doing?" she asked automatically wrapping her arms around his waist. He ran his hands down her sides slowly until they rested on her hips.

"Something I can't help, Ma."

"I...I gotta get Dej'a home."

"No you don't. Dej'a good where she at." He kissed her again with passion and felt her melt in his arms. Yearning to feel her heat he bent his knees and pressed his erection into her midsection. "Damn, Ma. You just don't know how bad I want you."

Serenity's knee's grew weak as his hardness pressed against her sex. She wanted so bad to give herself over to him. Had thought about doing it all day, but sex was a physical act that usually led to problems if the right feelings weren't involved. At the moment she didn't know what Koran's intentions were. Earlier, he made it clear that he wasn't interested in a relationship. She on the other hand had just ended a bad relationship and wasn't the type to be a part-time girl.

"Wait. Wait, Koran," she said flustered. She flattened her hands on his chest and pushed him away. "You know we can't do this."

"What you mean? Shit, we grown. We can do whatever we want."

Serenity shook her head. "What you said earlier about us being friends, did you mean it?"

"Yeah, I meant it, but..."

"But what? Now you wanna fuck me and expect me to be one of your other chicks. Am I right?"

Koran didn't answer. That's exactly what he expected.

"I might be a project chick, but I think more of myself than to be another one of your fuck friends. So if you wanna be my friend, then be my friend. If not, miss me with the bullshit!"

"What bullshit?" Koran shot back. "You saying me wanting you is bullshit? C'mon, Sin. I know you feeling the same thing I'm feeling."

"Yes, I feel it. I've been feeling it all day. What you think I don't wanna give you some? I do. If we're gonna be friends, though. I mean a real friend and not someone who thinks he's gonna fuck me whenever it's convenient for him. I want you to get to know me first. That way you'd know I'm not one of them bird head bitches you're used to dealing with."

For a second he was lost for words and surprised by her realness. His want for her also intensified a great deal more. "You know, you're absolutely right. I'm entitled to make a mistake, though." He looked at her from head to toe and smiled "Well, I can't really say it this would have been a mistake."

"Um huh," she mumbled, rolling her eyes. "I want you to know this too. Before, or if, we cross that line from being friends to whatever, these other girls have to go."

"Yeah, yeah, I pretty much know that, but that ain't the issue right now. Getting to know you is. So what's up for tomorrow?"

"You don't waste time do you?"

"My time is too valuable to waste."

Serenity cracked a sly smile. "Since you put it like that. What you're trying to get is valuable too. That's why I don't come off it easily."

"Is that right," he said, giving her hips another glance.

"Now about tomorrow," she said, smiling. "I'll be in school until four o'clock."

"School?"

"Yes, school. This project chick is going places. I'm taking paralegal classes at the local community college right now, but once I get my money together I plan on going to Columbia so I can become a lawyer."

Again Koran was lost for words and Jahad's warning about falling in love was no longer fresh in his mind. His mind was made up that he had to have her regardless of the outcome. "I'm feeling that. Word up. I'll pick you up from school tomorrow, then, a'ight."

Serenity gave him a curious look. "Let me ask you something. Since you have so much valuable free time on your hands what do you do?"

"Oh, I do a lil' bit of this, a lil' bit of that."

"I guess that means you won't tell me."

"I just told you. A lil'…."

"Forget it." She waved her hand dismissively. "It's none of my business anyway."

Koran smiled. "You right, it ain't none of your business, but if you think I sell drugs you wrong."

"Oh yeah? Then how you live like this and drive a range?"

He hunched his shoulders. "A lil' bit of this, a lil' bit of that."

"Well, I need to be doing a little of whatever it is you do. Maybe I could come up with law school money."

"Nah, all you gotta do is keep looking pretty. Law school money will come… Trust me."

Chapter Eleven

Falling in love affected Koran similar to the way it did Jahad years before. His first reaction was to back away from Serenity and stop spending so much time with her. The problem was, he couldn't. He began to think she had a spell on him. She was his last thought before going to bed and his first though when he woke up in the morning. What really bothered him and drew him deeper was that it felt so right being with her.

In Serenity he saw the female version of himself. She was smart, focused, and funny, with a dark side. Although he couldn't say exactly what it was, a hint of it could be seen in her green eyes. He still saw his other girls, however, the time was cut considerably short though. He stayed long enough for a quickie and then he was gone.

While getting to know one another, he and Serenity found so many things they had in common. They liked the same food, music, and movies. They both were well versed in the New York gossip line. Every day from Monday through Friday he and Jamel would pick her up from school and then swing by the projects so she could pick Dej'a up. From there they would explore the city together.

Koran treated every day as a special occasion. Knicks games and Yankee games which Serenity could follow play by play. She even talked him into going to a few Broadway plays. Weekends were set aside for the kids. The Bronx Zoo, Fun World, and of course Jamel's favorite, Chuky Cheese.

On their outings Jamel usually clung to Serenity leaving Dej'a and Koran to themselves most of the time. Soon she opened up to Koran and showed him a side of her that surprised him. There wasn't a subject she couldn't talk intelligently about. From science, music to politics, she always had a comment ready. Strange as it may sound, he Started seeking her opinion is his obsession with the Iraq War after learning that she stayed in tune with the news. By the end of the third week he found himself attached to Dej'a the same way he was with Jamel.

They were returning from Jamel's birthday party that was thrown at Chucky Cheese a few days before Koran had to leave for North

Carolina when he made it known that he was ready to be a one woman man. Jamel and Dej'a slept in the back seat, both full of cake and ice cream. Usually Koran would walk Serenity to her mother's apartment carrying Dej'a before going home. Tonight he had different plans.

"Sin, come upstairs with me. We need to talk," he said once he had Dej'a in his arms.

"About what?"

"Just come upstairs and you'll see."

Once they put Dej'a and Jamel in bed Koran led Serenity to the hallway. During most of the day he'd thought about the best way to break the news to her, but he still didn't know how to begin. The whole process of falling in love was new to him, so formulating his feelings into words boggled him. Fumbling nervously with his hands, he tried to force the words from his lips, but they refused to come.

"What is it Koran?" Serenity asked, taking hold of his hand.

He took a deep breath. "It's kinda hard for me to explain it, but I'm ready to get on some dolo shit with you. I mean, you know. I'm feeling you like that."

Serenity smiled. "I think I know what you're trying to say. The question is are you serious? Another question is why me when you had so many to choose from?"

"You can't be serious. Why not you? I mean, I'm ready to fall back with you and only you. Why is it so hard to believe?"

Tears swam in her eyes as she looked up at him, her expression casting him doubt. "Because I want to believe it so bad, but every time I put my faith into someone, I end up getting hurt."

Koran took out his cell phone. "Well actions speak louder than words," he said dialing Lisa's number.

"Hello?" Lisa answered on the second ring while Serenity Stared at him confused.

"Yeah, Lisa. Check this out. I know you probably won't be feeling this, but I can't see you no more. I have a shorty now. You take care a'ight." He rushed the words out, hung up, then called the rest of his girls and gave them the same line. "Believe me now?"

Serenity's mouth hung open for a second. "What... What did you need all those girls for?"

"I didn't. They gave me something to do at the time."

"I bet they did," Serenity smirked.

"Like I was saying before I was interrupted," he said trying not to smile. "That's the past. We have the present and the future. So how we gonna do this?"

"You don't have to ask. We can do this however you like."

"However I like?" Koran pulled her into his arms.

"Do I have to say it twice?"

"Hell nah!"

The hallway was dimly lit, but he could see the lust sparkling in her eyes. Teasingly, he sucked on her bottom lip, tasting the cherry lip gloss she wore. Serenity placed her mouth over his and buried her tongue inside. The kiss aroused him almost to the point of making him explode. Never in his life had he wanted someone as much as he wanted her.

"Hold up, Sin," he said, breaking the kiss. "You about to make me bust off."

"Uh uh. Come on." She pulled him back to her and found his lips once more. Unable to resist her, he slid his hand under the jean skirt she wore and felt damp heat through her panties. He continued to stroke her while she unzipped his jeans. A second later he felt her hands close around his dick and had to back away from her again.

"What's wrong?" she asked, reaching for him.

"Nothing, but let's make this more convenient." He dropped to his knees and pulled her red panties down to her ankles. Serenity looked down confused as he planted kisses along her thighs. "Prepare for the ride," he murmured before burying his face between her legs.

"Wait. What are you…" She took a sharp intake of breath and opened her legs wider when his tongue brushed across her clit. She then gripped his head and held him firmly against her sticky wetness while grinding her mound into his face. "Ohhhh Koran! That feels sooooo gooooood!"

The taste of her made his heart race. Using his middle finger, he eased it inside her, rotating it as he drew her wild flickering his tongue lightly over her clit. It was a trick he'd learned from his freaky chick Monica. Suddenly, Serenity's hips began to jerk sporadically.

"Ummmmm!" she cried out as hot cum flowed over his fingers like thick honey.

Koran stopped and stood up. His dick was standing straight out like a board as he took a condom from his back pocket. Once out, he rolled the wrapper over his long, thick tool preparing to do some serious work. Serenity was still leaning against the wall trembling from her orgasms. He raised one of her legs around his waist and pushed inside her. He groaned finding her hot and tight as he slowly began working his hips until she responded by arching out towards him.

"Come on, Koran. I'm ready. I'm so ready baby." Serenity moaned sweetly near his ear and began rotating her hips to the few inches he had inside her.

Needing no further encouragement, he lifted her off the floor, cupped her ass, and Started drilling into her with powerful strokes. "Is this what you want? Huh?" He began to drill her deeply while trying not to concentrate on how good she felt. "Answer me, Sin! Is this how you want it?"

Sweat dampened her braids to the side of her face as she worked her hips to his rhythm. "Yes! Oh God, yes! Give it to me baby! Give it to me!" With her arms latched around his neck, her hips moved seductively while using her muscles to contract around him. "Does it feel good baby? Tell me it feels good."

Koran Stared deep into her green eyes, connected physically and mentally in their love making. "It's the best, Ma. You the best!"

"Cum for me then, baby. Show me how good it feels."

Feeling the explosion building inside, he gripped her hips and Started slamming her off and on his dick in a frenzy. Her eyes rolled back into her head and spasms took over his body. To conceal his scream, he covered her mouth with a passionate kiss and held himself deep inside her. A few seconds later they slid to the floor out of breath, sweat pouring off their faces and their bodies still twitching.

"You a'ight?" Koran asked, nudging her.

"I hope I am. I can't feel my legs and I think I pulled something in my back. Damn, you don't be playing, do you? You almost killed me."

"You asked for it, so don't complain. C'mon, let's get you in the bed so we can pop off round two."

Serenity stood on wobbly legs while Koran pushed himself up against the wall. After gathering up their clothes, he noticed she still hadn't moved and he smiled.

"Think you can walk without falling?"

"I think so. I'll try."

"Tell you what, hold these." He placed the clothes in her hand

and then scooped her up in his arms and carried her towards the guestroom.

Serenity giggled. "Boy, put me down. I can walk."

"Don't want you to waste no energy. You gonna need all your strength to keep up with me."

"Oh really? Who you suppose to be Superman?"

"Shit, Superman don't got nothing on me. I can get through jeans in a single stroke and make you come faster than a speeding bullet."

She burst out laughing. "Boy, you crazy."

In the guestroom Koran discarded the rest of his clothes, lay back on the bed, and watched Serenity as she undressed. Just looking at her made him rock hard again, but his lust went far deeper than sex. He wanted everything she had to offer; mind, body, and soul. This feeling, although invigorating, also scared him because it was so sudden.

"Yours for mines," Serenity said, snuggling up beside him.

"What?"

"Your thoughts for mines."

"Oh, I was…" He paused, wondering if he should reveal how he truly felt. He had been taught to keep his emotions concealed and Jahad's lessons were embedded deep in his mind "I was thinking how stupid your ex was to lose you. He must be smoking dust or something."

Serenity turned on her side to face him. "I wonder if he was on something myself. I found out a few days ago that he was dead."

"Oh word!"

She gave him a look that told him that she knew the truth, but kept the masquerade. "Uh huh. From what I heard he jumped off the roof. So he was high or something or either crossed the wrong person." Her eyes held his as she spoke.

"He probably got a bad batch of dust. Let's change the subject. I don't wanna talk about that dude. That shit killing my vibe."

"What you wanna talk about then?" she asked, edging closer until his dick pressed into her lower stomach.

Koran forgot all about using a condom as she put a leg over his hip and guided him into her wetness with a jerk of her hips.

~~~~

Sleep took hold of them around four o'clock that morning. By then, they were both well acquainted with each others body. They knew exactly what to do, where to touch, and how to make one another beg for release. In between sessions they talked a little. Koran told her about the scholarship he turned down and Serenity confessed that her mother was an off and on drug addict. It was a confession that made him want to help her fulfill her goal of becoming a lawyer.

Jamel woke them up three hours later.

"Up ka-wan! Kay eat!" he yelled, tugging on Korans' arm. Koran raised his head sleepily and noticed dried tears on Jamel's cheeks. Since the day he brought Jamel home, they slept in the same bed together, so Koran figured he was pissed at waking and finding him gone. The scowl on his little face spoke for itself.

"My fault lil'dude." Koran picked him up and sat him on his chest. "Where's Dej'a?"

"DJ watch T.V. and Kay eat!"

"A'ight lil nigga. You putting pressure on me ain't you. Whatcha' want, cereal or pancakes?"

"Pancakes, eggs and juice juice," Jamel answered and then shook Serenity awake. "Sin, up. Eat pancakes."

She sat up and pulled the comforter over her breast. "Hi, cutie. What you say?"

While Serenity held Jamel's attention Koran slid out of bed and grabbed a terry cloth robe from the closet.

"Eat pancake. Ka-wan cook good pancakes, egg, juice-juice. You eat too."

"Yeah, she gonna eat too Kay. C'mon and help me cook," Koran said, noticing how Jamel's attention was drawn to how Serenity held the comforter to cover herself.

"Uh uh, let me see." He pulled away from Koran and tried to pull the comforter down. "Kay see titties."

Serenity burst out laughing as Koran snatched him up. "C'mon lil' nigga. And don't let me hear you say that again. I mean it."

Koran tried without much success to stop Jamel from cursing so much. It had gotten to the point where when he was mad every other word out of his mouth was a curse. Jahad didn't help. When the two hung out together Jamel always seemed to learn a new curse word. Jahad thought it was cute, but Koran knew that when Jamel started school it could become a problem.

"I sorry Ka-wan." Jamel poked out his bottom lip.

"It's a'ight Kay. You can't be talking like that though, feel me?"

"Feel you."

Dej'a was sitting Indian style on the couch, remote in hand, watching CNN when Koran walked by the living room carrying Jamel. He paused and studied the intense look on her face while she watched the coverage of the war. What's going through her mind, he wondered. She looked so serious, like the weight of the world was on her shoulders. No seven year old should have so much on their mind, but Dej'a wasn't the average seven year old.

"DJ eat pancake," Jamel said, drawing her attention. She looked up confused

"Huh?"

"I'm about to whip up breakfast. You wanna place an order?"

"Oh." She walked over and gave Koran a hug, which surprised him and made his heart melt. "I'll have whatever's on the menu."

"Kay hug." Jamel pushed away from Koran.

"So you aren't mad at me anymore?" Dej'a asked, giving him a hug. "He cursed me out this morning when he woke up and then made me get out of bed."

Koran shook his head. "That's Kay for you. Wanna help me cook?"

"I'll pass. Wanna finish watching the news. America is sending more troops to Iraq."

"Well, let me know how close Bush is to blowing up the world."

Dej'a laughed and gave him another hug before returning to the couch. A few minutes later Serenity entered into the kitchen fully dressed with her pocket book slung over her shoulder. Koran was in the process of breaking eggs into a bowl when he spotted her out the corner of his eye.

"What's up, you leaving? Thought you were staying for breakfast."

"Sin no leave. Eat pancake." Jamel pouted

"I'm sorry Kay but I need to get home. I wanna make sure my mother is there, plus I'd like to soak in the tub for a while." She winked at Koran driving home her meaning.

"You know where the phone is and the bathroom too. You can rock a pair of my boxers and use my toothbrush. After breakfast I want you and Dej'a to go home and change clothes, then come straight back so we can go shopping."

"I..."

"No I's or but's," Koran said firmly.

Serenity put a hand on her hip. "Are you always this demanding?"

"If Kay and Dej'a weren't woke I'd show you how demanding I really can be."

"Promises, Promises."

Chapter Twelve

Koran and Jamel took a bath not long after Serenity and Dej'a left and were in the living room watching video's on B.E.T. when Jahad, Derrick and Sha" stormed in. All of their faces were twisted with anger. Jahad went straight to the bar, poured a double shot of Henessey and downed it with one toss. Koran knew something had to be wrong. Jahad never drunk during the day.

"What's up?" Koran asked alarmed.

"That Puerto Rican bastard bodied the niggaz we sent to Bronxdale. Muthafucka!" Jahad hissed through clenched teeth.

"Who bodied who?"

"Hector," Derrick answered. "The dudes we sent over there to scope shit out were found this morning in the middle parking lot with head shots. Hector sent a message through a bitch saying every nigga we send to Bronxdale was getting merked."

"What! Who the fuck he think he is? That was our shit!" Koran was pissed now. "Who the bitch?"

"Nobody, she's dead. The faggot is good for sending messages through bitches. I should have bodied his ass years ago." Jahad paused as a sudden thought struck him. "How in the hell did Hector know we sent them niggas?" he asked under his breath looking off at the wall.

Koran looked over at Jahad. "So what's up?"

"You know what's up. We bout to go through Bronxdale and tear shit up. He calls himself sending me a message. I'm about to send his ass one."

Sha' shook his head. "C'mon, Jah. We talked about this already. I mean, I know you heated. We all are, but don't go thinking with your emotions."

"Emotions!" Jahad was about to explode, but took a deep breath and studied Sha' for a moment before speaking. "Check this out homey. And what I'm about to say stays in this room. When we first popped this shit off on the Island we planned and worked out every single problem that could come up. Am I right?"

"Yeah, that's why…"

Jahad held up his hand. "Hold up. Hear me out. Now ask yourself the same question I asked myself a few minutes ago. How in the hell did Hector know we sent them niggas? Think, Son! Don't nobody know who we are or what we do. If they did the Feds would probably have our asses by now? See what I'm saying?"

Sha', Derrick, and Koran Stared at Jahad stunned. Even Jamel, who had been looking back from Sha' to Jahad following their exchange, stared at Jahad like he knew what was going on. The implications were somewhat unbelievable, but the fact he presented was undeniable.

"So you saying we got a snake around us?" Sha' asked breaking the silence.

"What else can explain it? Why is it we ain't heard shit about niggas being in Bronxdale in the first place? I'm willing to bet money that the shit you said about niggas moving weight in your hood is true too. Only ten people, eleven counting Koran, knew what we were planning."

Jahad started pacing back and forth as his mind started putting shit together. "The head's, our top lieutenants, you, Derrick, and Koran I can cancel out, but I ain't taking no chances with the others. Not right now. So before we hold any kind of meeting we should blow Bronxdale up. Fuck holding a meeting, then risk having some niggas waiting on us. Ya feel me?"

Sha' nodded. "Yeah, no doubt, but what's up with the snake shit?"

"We sit back and watch. Sooner or later whoever it is will crawl from under his rock. For now though, we keep this shit to ourselves. That's our advantage."

Off to the side, Derrick reached into the backpack he carried, took out a brand new black M-P5 Heckled and Koch, and passed it to Koran. "Think you can get busy with this?"

Koran admired the gun as if it were a woman. Since Jamel became a part of the family he had taken advice about killing so much, but the desire was still there. "Hell yeah I can rock with this! Shit, let's go."

"You gotta take Kay over to Mrs. H crib." Jahad glanced at Jamel where he stood beside Koran looking up at the gun."

"Kay go. I bang bang too." Jamel began to pout poking out his lip.

Jahad laughed. "Nah lil' dude. When you get older I'll let you get your bang bang on."

A knock at the front door drew their attention.

"I'll get it," Koran said, passing the gun back to Derrick. "Put that up. It's probably my shorty, Sin."

When he opened the door Serenity stood in front of him wearing a red and white Roc-A-Wear sweatsuit. The pants hugged her hips causing Koran to stare. Her hair, which was usually kept braided, was parted down the middle in the two long plaits giving her the Pocohantas look. Beside her Dej'a wore a white Baby Gap jean suit, a yellow sweater, and a pair of yellow Timberlands on her small feet.

"Look at you." Koran smiled as he dropped to one knee and kissed Dej'a on the cheek. "Ain't you pretty."

Dej'a giggled. "Thank You."

"Dej'a's the only person you see?" Serenity asked with her hands on her hips.

"You know better than that." He stood and put his mouth close to her ear. "I had to catch myself before I ripped your clothes off."

"Um huh. You ready?"

Koran shook his head. "I can't go, something important came up. I still want y'all to go though." He put an arm around Serenity's shoulder, took Dej'a's hand and led them inside the apartment.

Serenity pulled away from him, frowning. "It better not be one of your friends and I don't need to go shopping," she said stubbornly.

Koran sighed and ran a hand over his face. "Here we go. First off, I didn't ask if you needed to go shopping, you are going. Second, and I hope I don't have to repeat this again either. I only have one shorty, that's you. I wouldn't have done what I did last night if I had plans of fuc...messing around on you. So I'd appreciate it if you never bought that up to me again. Are we clear on that?"

"Yes." Serenity smiled and kissed him lightly on the lips. "How long you gone be gone?"

"I can't say. Probably a couple of hours, though."

"Want me to wait?"

"Nah. I'm giving you Fifth Ave money, so you probably be gone all day."

Serenity bunched up her face. "Fifth Avenue money?"

"Yeah. Louie, Gucci, Chanel and Prada. I want you and Dej'a to look like movie stars when y'all get back."

"What you trying to say you don't like the way I dress?"

"Oh, don't get it twisted. I'm feeling the ghetto side of you." He looked down at her outfit. "But I wanna see the other side though. The classy Sin. Tell her Dej'a."

"Um huh," Dej'a nodded. "The classy Sin."

"See. Dej'a know," he said, smiling.

"Do that mean I can expect to see you in a dress suit wearing some Italian shoe's?"

"Nah, Ma. Timbs, Jeans, a fitted and a tee shirt for me. I said nothing about me looking like a movie star. I'd have to fight the women off me then."

Serenity punched him on the shoulder.

"I'm playing, Sin," he said laughing. "I'm saying though. You already look like Beyonce. Shit... better. Now you gonna dress better than her. Am I right Dej'a?"

"Yep!"

Serenity rolled her eyes, but couldn't help blushing. "I see Dej'a is your little *yes* woman," she said following him down the hall.

Jahad, Sha' and Derrick snapped their Heads around when they entered the living room. Jahads' eyes nearly bulged out of his head when saw Serenity. For a second he studied her through slitted eyes before looking over at Dej'a. Koran smiled, catching his look. Serenity's beauty had the same effect on him when he first saw her too.

"Sin! Sin!" Jamel shouted, running to her with his arms out.

"Hi cutie. Looks like it's me, you and Dej'a today. You wanna go to Fun World?" she asked, picking him up.

"Ice came!"

"Sin," Koran dropped an arm around her shoulders. "This is my big brother Jah I was telling you about. And these are my boys, Derrick and Sha'. Jah, this is my shorty, Sin," he said proudly and Jahad frowned.

Serenity smiled. "How y'all doing?"

All three nodded as Dej'a tapped Koran on his leg. "Oh, and this is Sin's daughter, Dej'a."

"Niece," Dej'a corrected.

"Pardon me. Sin's niece, Dej'a." Koran gave Serenity a questioning look, but Jamel held her attention.

"Ka-wan we go?"

"Yeah. Let me get my keys for you, Sin." Koran walked off without noticing that Jahad was right behind him.

No sooner than he stepped into his bedroom Jahad grabbed him by the shoulder. "A yo, who that chick?"

"I told you, my shorty. Why?"

"Where she from?" Jahad asked forcefully.

Koran screwed up his face. "What up with all the damn questions? I don't be asking crazy ass questions about the chicks you be fucking."

"I ain't trying to hear that shit!" Jahad barked and took a step toward Koran with his hands bunched up into a fist. "Where she from!?"

Koran automatically got into his fighting stance. He could hold his own with the best of them, but had no illusion who would win in a hand to hand confrontation with Jahad. On the same token, he knew he wouldn't be the only one to get knotted up either. Jahad would take some licks too.

"Ain't none of your damn business where she from. I don't know what the fuck you thinking, but I ain't no kid no more nigga!"

Jahad Stared deep into Koran's eyes. "You in love ain't you?"

Koran didn't answer.

"Did you say something to that bitch about what I told you on the roof?"

"What! What the fuck you trying to say, Jah?"

"You heard me nigga. Did you say something about us having these niggas in Bronxdale on some pillow talking shit?"

In an instant all Koran saw was red. Without thinking he swung a quick left hook that Jahad slipped effortlessly. Before he could throw another punch Jahad scooped him up by the legs and slammed him on the bed.

"A yo word up, if you weren't my brother, I'd beat you to death nigga. Now answer my damn question. Did you tell that bitch!?"

Tears welled up in Koran's eyes at the mere thought of thinking Jahad could believe he would betray his trust. "You gonna ask me some shit like that, Jah? You for real man?"

Jahad noticed Koran's expression and loosened his grip. A bad mistake. Koran swung a hard right hook that connected squarely to the side of Jahad's head. The blow knocked him into the headboard. Moving quickly, he pushed himself off the bed and advanced to where Jahad rolled to the left side of the bed.

"I don't give a fuck who you suppose to be! I'll fuck you up for asking me some stupid shit like that."

As Jahad pushed himself up, Sha' rushed through the door.

"What the hell y'all doing in here?"

"It's nothing." Jahad kept his eyes on Koran as he spoke. "We chopping up about something. Give us a minute, we'll be out there."

Hesitantly, Sha' walked out while Jahad made his way around the bed. Taking no chances Koran put his guard up.

"Chill nigga. I ain't gonna fuck you up. Don't hit me no damn more though or I'll hit yo ass back." He gave Koran a crooked grin then turned serious. "I owe you an apology lil' bruh. Your shorty puts me in the mind of someone and it fucked me up. Like I said, my fault. But what I tell you about that love shit though. Don't front and say shorty don't got you open either. That shit in your eyes."

Koran shook his head miserably. "She got me Jah, but I couldn't help it man. Word up, I couldn't help it!" He shook his head again. "I mean it's like...it's...I... See, I can't even explain this shit."

Jahad smiled sadly. "I know lil bruh. I been there before and that shit is dangerous. Make sure you find out where shorty priorities are before you put your trust in her. I'm telling you this because I know how bitches are. I got caught up in that love shit and it damn near got me killed. So be careful."

"I got you, Jah. You taught me too well for me to slip."

Jahad rubbed the side of his head. "I know one thing. I won't underestimate your ass no more."

When Jahad left, Koran went to his closet and took out ten thousand dollars from his stash. He then found Sin in the guest room changing Jamel's diaper.

"You better watch out. He be trying to piss on you."

"My baby won't pee on me, will you cutie?" Serenity ticked Jamel's side and he giggled kicking his legs.

"No pee- pee, Sin."

"See, I..." She froze when Koran threw the stack of money on the bed.

"That should be enough to get you and Dej'a right. Remember what I said too. Not one penny left. Dej'a make sure she spends it all."

"I will. I want a notebook computer."

"You heard that?" He kissed Sin on her bottom lip Since her mouth still hung wide open. "We gonna talk about your school situation later too, a'ight. See y'all later."

"Ice came Ka-Wan," Jamel said frowning.

"Sin is taking you to get ice cream. You be good, a'ight?"

"Kay good!"

Chapter Thirteen

Jahad was tightening up the last of his plan when Koran entered the living room after walking Serenity to the elevator. The guns, extra clips, three sets of gloves, three ski masks, and three hoodies, were laid out on the couch and coffee table.

"How's it going down?" Koran asked once Jahad finished talking, "All I heard was Sha' is gonna be waiting in White Castle's parking lot."

"Me, you, and Dee gonna walk through Rosedale, hit the Bruckner Expression and go through the underpass. That'll bring us directly to the middle section of Bronxdale. The parking lot is right there when we come from under the underpass. That's when we'll pull on our ski masks. After we wet it up, we'll run through the first section to White Castle. Sha' will be waiting for us there. Got it?"

Bronxdale projects were only a few blocks from Monroe projects and different as night and day. Six, seven story buildings made up three sections, each separated by a side street and parking lot.

"Yeah, I got it. Let me get my baby and I'll be ready." Koran dashed to his room, went to his closet and grabbed his 17 shot Beretta 9mm. By the time he returned Sha' had left and Jahad and Derrick were ready to go.

"C'mon Koran damn!" Jahad glanced over his shoulder impatiently as Koran removed the Beretta from the small of his back and replaced it with the Heckler and Koch. The Beretta he tucked in his hoody pocket after checking to make sure it was cocked and ready.

"A'ight, I'm ready. Let's go send these bastards to hell." He grinned, feeling the old adrenaline rush he missed so much.

On their way through Rosedale apartment grounds Koran took in how peaceful it was compared to his projects. The lawns were neatly cut without a speck of trash in sight. The buildings were graffiti free. Rosedale's two, fourteen story buildings were exact replica's of Monroe projects. The difference was the armed guards and trained dogs that patrolled the grounds at night to keep stragglers away. For as long as he could remember everybody in Monroe projects looked at Rosedale as being the uppity projects.

Traffic was light when they made it to the Bruckner Expressway underpass, but overhead the roar of passing cars drowned out all other noises. The few cars that stopped at the light inside the underpass gave off thick exhaust fumes which caused them to cover their mouths and noses with their shirts to keep from choking. Exiting the underpass, the parking lot lay just ahead crowded with groups of people who stood out in front of the buildings. A few guys had their pit bulls on leashes with muzzles over the dog's deadly mouths.

"Get ready," Jahad said under his breath just before they crossed the street. Trying to be inconspicuous as possible they tucked their Heads in unison and pulled the mask over their faces, then pulled the hoods over their Heads. Koran took a quick glance up and estimated close to thirty people total. In a few minutes, thirty dead if he could pull it off.

"Spread out, left, right! I'll take the middle," Jahad snapped out once they made it to the parking lot about forty yards away from the building.

Derrick and Koran branched off from Jahad, Derrick to the left, Koran to the right, while Jahad continued straight towards the crowd. About twenty yards away Koran walked in between two parked cars. Derrick followed his lead on the other side of the parking lot. The crowds now were looking at them slightly confused as if to determine whether they were friend or foe, but a few weren't taking any chances and were reaching for their guns.

Suddenly, without warning bullets tore into the car Koran walked between and shattered its windows. He ducked, moved to the rear end of the car, calmly pulled the Heckler and Kock. After hitting the safety button he leaned over the trunk and sprayed three round burst into the crowds. Jahad, laying flat on his stomach directly in the middle of the parking lot, swung his gun from left to right, his face underneath the mask twisted in a snarl. Wanting to get closer to the action Derrick crawled to the front of the parking lot until only one car separated him from the shooters. Return fire came heavy from the left side of the building, but though in front were pinned in from three sides.

"I'm going around! I'm going around!" Koran shouted motioning to Jahad as he moved from the cover of the car. His intentions were to go around the right side so he could come behind the shooters on the left. Too much firepower came from their direction. From the number of shots he guessed it to be at least seven shooters. If Jahad and Derrick could keep them occupied long enough, he could sneak up from behind and end the gunfight.

"Chill nigga! Chill, we can't get them!" Jahad yelled over the shots, but Koran was already on the move.

The scene looked more like CNN live footage from the Iraqi war as Koran edged closer to the right side. Gun shots, agonizing screams, and howling dogs echoed loudly while everything else seemed to move in slow motion. The wounded tried to crawl to safety. The bullets that ripped into those who stood in front of the building tried to hold their ground. Bullets tore into anyone too slow to move and the bodies of though already dead.

Out the corner of his eye Koran spotted a black guy running towards him with a 40 caliber trained at his head just as he made it to the sidewalk boarding the parking lot. Luckily he tripped over a dead pit bull before the bullets reached its mark. Instinctively, he dropped to the ground and rolled to his right. A second later bullets chipped the concrete beside him and stung the side of his face. He rolled to his back, held his gun out preparing to fire when a hail of bullets stitched his assailants chest and face and sent him curling backwards. Stunned, Koran glanced over his shoulder to see Derrick running up at full speed. An excited grin was on his face as he pushed himself up from the ground, but then froze horror struck when Derrick's head exploded.

"Nooooo!" he roared, whipping his head around and screwing up his face at the two Puerto Ricans who ran toward him shooting. At that moment death meant nothing to Koran. Rage had taken over his thinking process and he only had one thought in his mind... Kill!"

"C'mon muthafucka's!" he screamed, running straight at them.

God or some other supernatural force had to be with him. He stood further than twenty feet away, exchanging shots with both men. In the midst of action he heard Jahad scream his name, but he was too far gone to respond. The man on his left fell first as bullets ripped the top half of his head off and sent blood and brain's flying through the air.

Hearing his gun click, Koran dropped the Heckler and Koch and reached for his Beretta. At that same moment Jahad shot the other Puerto Rican in the stomach dropping him to his knees. Still in his zone Koran walked up to the man while he clutched his stomach and shot him twice in the head. Before the body could fall, two more men ran from the left side of the building, their guns blazing. To their surprise, Koran ran to meet them and was cloSing the distance until Jahad tackled him to the ground.

"What the fucks wrong with you nigga!" Jahad barked pulling Koran away.

"C'mon, let's kill these muthafucka's!" Koran yelled out in fury.

Jahad jerked his arm so hard he nearly pulled it out of place. "Bring your stupid ass on before I fuck you up. We can't do shit for Dee now. We're outnumbered ten to fucking one. What, you wanna die here too?"

Koran nodded, accepting Jahad's logic. He glanced over at Derrick's lifeless body just as three men rushed from the left side of the building. From the right about twenty yards away, two more men came running, guns in hand. Moving with the speed of a cheetah Jahad grabbed Korans' hand and sprinted off, ducking and weaving while bullets whistled dangerously close by their ears.

A taunting thought filled Koran's head and echoed repeatedly when they made it to the first side street. Why am I running? I don't run. I kill…I kill…I kill. Without a moments hesitation, he snatched away from Jahad, spun around, dropped to one knee. He lifted his gun and lazered in on each target all in one fluid motion.

Boom! Boom! Boom!

Three precise shots slammed through the first three purser's head in rapid sessions. Zooming in on the other two, he was in the process of squeezing the trigger when Jahad snatched him around by his shoulder.

"If you don't bring your ass on I'ma knock you out right fucking now!"

"I got them. They right…"

Before Koran could finish the sentence Jahad swung a hard blind right hook that connected flush with his chin and put him to sleep instantly. Just as his knee's buckled Jahad slung him over his shoulder and took off again. As he drew closer to the car, exhausted from the extra weight, Sha' opened the back door.

"He hit?" Sha' asked as Jahad tossed Koran into the back seat.

"Nah, I knocked his ass out," Jahad answered hopping into the passenger seat. "C'mon, let's get the fuck outta here before the Jakes show up."

"Where's Derrick?"

A shimmer of grief flashed in Jahad's eyes. "He ain't coming. Now c'mon, pull the fuck off." In the backseat Koran grunted but stayed down.

"What you mean he ain't coming?" Sha' asked once he pulled out into traffic.

"He's dead Sha' and right now I really don't wanna talk about it. We'll build later a'ight?" Jahad turned to the window indicating the subject closed.

Ten minutes later, they passed numerous police cars heading towards Bronxdale. Sha' pulled in front of Jahad's building. Jahad helped Koran, who was still slightly dazed, from the car. Sha' left to dispose of the guns and the stolen car.

"What you swing on me for?" Koran asked as Jahad opened the door to their building. Jahad didn't bother to answer. Didn't even bother to acknowledge Koran until they stepped inside the apartment.

"Don't ever do no stupid shit like that again!" he roared slamming Koran into the wall. "Who the fuck you think you are, super fucking man?! Bullets don't bounce off your black ass!"

"I ain't trying to hear that shit!" Koran shoved Jahad back and put up his guard. What you swing on me for man!"

"To save your stupid ass life. And if you don't calm the fuck down I'ma knock your ass out again. Now try me."

This was the second time today Jahad tried to chump me, Koran thought. He took a deep breath, then released a flurry of wicked combination's: left jab, right cross, left cross, overhand right, left hook, right hook, left hook, straight left, right jab, left hook, right cross.

In front of him Jahad weaved and ducked with mechanical movement from each blow until a right hook slammed into his jaw and knocked him into the wall.

"A'ight, let's get busy then." He gave Koran a crooked grin and started bouncing on his toes, his attention focused on Koran's shoulders. "You think you can beat my ass, huh? I taught you nigga, so you should know I can put you to sleep at will."

Koran kept his eyes on Jahad's face as they squared off. Koran was in a firm stance, his eyes slit. Jahad was bouncing lightly on his toes, his grin wide, both waiting for an opening.

"You won't be mad at me if I break your jaw will you?" Jahad taunted. "Yeah, I'm gonna put some steel in your mouth. Or do you want me to break your nose so your shit will be crooked like mine?"

Koran ignored him knowing that Jahad was trying to piss him off, in the process cloud his thinking. The first thing old man Jimmy taught him when he started his boxing lessons was to never take a fight personal. It was a sport that required thinking, like a chess match. A physical chess match.

"You think your shorty would like that?" Jahad continued to taunt him while slipping into a 52 hand block. "If I crack that jaw, she won't be able to kiss you then. But don't worry. I'll kiss her for you."

The mention of Serenity set Koran off. He snapped three rapid left jabs, a left hook, followed by a right cross. Jahad weaved the blows with ease, then dropped to his knee and drilled a powerful right into Koran's solar plexus.

"Oof!" Koran exhaled loudly doubling over, his breath gone.

"When you get your shit together come to the living room 'cause I ain't finished chewing your ass out." Jahad smiled as he walked off.

A few minutes later Koran stepped into the living room still holding his stomach. Jahad sat on the couch, a shot of Patron in hand, a blunt hanging from his mouth, staring at the wall. He took a deep pull from the blunt, coughed, then looked up at Koran slowly.

"What in the hell got into you out there man?" he asked quietly.

Koran glanced at him before answering. "They bodied Dee, Jah. What the fuck was I suppose to do?"

Jahad sprung to his feet. "Think, dammit! Fucking think! That's what you were suppose to do! Them niggas could have bodied your ass and you the only damn brother I got." His voice was thick with emotions as he yelled angrily. Then suddenly he burst out laughing as he wrapped Koran in a fierce hug. "Crazy ass dude. I almost shit on myself when you pulled that Rambo shit. You gotta always think, Koran. Always."

Koran nodded. "I feel you, Jah, I feel you. I mean, I wasn't trying to do no heroic shit, but when I saw Dee go down something inside me snapped. All I could think about was killing those niggas. What we gonna do about Dee?"

Jahad released Koran, his face masked with sorrow. Derrick and Jahad had been friends Since grade school. Closer than friends, so his pain went far deeper than Koran's although he wouldn't express it out in the open. Later tonight when no one was around tears would stain his cheeks.

"I'll see his moms after the police get at her so she'll know she won't have to sweat funeral expenses. As far as his kids, they'll be straight for life. That's about all I know to do besides bodying the muthafucka's responsible."

After taking showers and changing clothes they sat in the living room reminiscing over Derrick while playing video games. At exactly one o'clock the Heads, along with their top lieutenants, showed up escorted by Sha'. Once everybody was seated Jahad explained what had happened, down to the last detail, except for what was discussed prior to going to Bronxdale. All eyes were focused on Koran when he finished.

"What y'all looking at me for?" he asked looking around. "Shit, I spazzed out when Dee got lit. Ain't like I was trying to be a fireman."

"What in the hell y'all go out there for anyway?" Star directed the question to Jahad. "We could of planned it out first and came up with a better way."

"Yeah, you probably right, but we didn't, so it's not no need to talk about what if."

"No need!" Star raised his voice. "What you do falls back on all of us, so there is a need to talk about what if."

The tension in the room grew thick as Jahad and Star glared at each other hostilely.

"Star made a good point, Jah," Prince said breaking the silence. "You need to get at us before you make a wild ass move. What's done is done though, so instead of beefin' lets move forward."

"No doubt," Jahad nodded. "And pardon me if I offended anyone," he said, looking around wondering which one was the snake.

"Now that we've kissed and made up, I got some information to put y'all up on." Lord stood up grinning. "I put some Watchers on this Lenny Leopardi dude and he's like thirty strong from what we can tell so far. We don't know who though."

"I'll get at Valentino tomorrow and see what's up. He should be able to break down who's who, but it ain't necessary. If we kill the head the body dies."

Sha' shook his head. "With these Italian niggas there's always someone to step up and fill a position just like with us. I say we kill all them muthafucka's."

Everybody nodded and Jahad shrugged his shoulders. "So be it."

"What up with Corsello's?" Star asked. "Valentino still ain't told you nothing?"

"Nah, not yet. I'll see what's up tomorrow. About that situation with Hector, I'm bout to go on his ass hard...no homo. It's obvious he's been getting money in Bronxdale right under my nose. How that happened I don't know." Jahad made eye contact with each M.G. before continuing. "Today we bodied about twenty of his people so most likely he'll crawl his stinking ass in a hole somewhere until he regroups. Whenever he pops back on the scene, it'll be his last!"

"Word!" Koran nodded.

"Word my ass," Jahad smirked, his eyes boring into Koran. "I want you outta New York after Dee's funeral."

"C'mon, Jah!" Koran stood outraged. "I'm going, but it's gone be a few weeks. I wanna be here when we get at Hector...for Dee."

"No nigga, you going after the funeral like I said. That shit you pulled today was the last straw. You bout to take a long vacation."

"I don't need no vacation. I'm good."

Jahad shook his head. "Nah, I see it in your eyes Koran. You like killing too damn much. At first I thought you were trying to get your rep up, but you took that shit to another level today. As long as there was somebody else to kill you ain't give a fuck if you lived or died. You frontin' like killing don't effect you, but what you did today was one of the effects. You stopped thinking."

"I'm saying..."

"He's right Koran," Sha' cut in. "You'll fuck around and get bodied with that gun ho shit you on."

All types of emotions coursed through Koran, mostly anger. *How in the hell do they figure I'm doing too much, he thought. Nobody said shit when I was doing the hits. I make one mistake, now I'm killing too much.*

"So what y'all trying to say is I'm out the picture." He snapped his fingers. "Just like that."

"Nobody said you were out," Star answered. You need to chill for a while, that's all. It's for your own good."

"My own good!" Koran looked at each head as anger bubbled

over. "A yo word up, y'all on some real live bullshit. Fuck y'all!" he yelled, then walked out wanting to punch something or someone.

Jahad's face came to mind, but he rubbed his stomach and thought against it. In his room, he rolled a blunt of Purple Haze then lay back across the bed and Stared up at the ceiling as the blunt started to ease his tension. Closing his eyes the scene flashed through his mind when Derrick got hit and he realized that Jahad was right.

At that moment it didn't matter if he lived or died. Jahad was also right about his desire to kill, although it wasn't because he liked it. Killing was his job. So what if he became a little excited. The thought sent chills up his spine as reality struck him in the face. He did like killing, regardless of the effect it had on his conscience. It gave him a buzz. It made him higher than the potent weed he now smoked.

"What the fuck have I become?" he asked himself out loud, feeling a deep sense of shame.

The truth hurts and the truth was he no longer held any regrets for human life. Much worst, he was no longer Koran Copeland, the bright kind hearted young man his mother raised. His short time being an M.G. had turned him into a monster. A monster posing in a human body. All at once depression engulfed him filling his head with suicidal thoughts. He wondered how long he could continue living the life he led while yearning for a simpler life if possible. The M.G.'s were a permanent fixture in his life and there was no turning back. Then he thought of Serenity, Jamel, and Dej'a and nearly burst into tears.

"You a'ight now or you wanna fight again?" Jahad asked entering the room.

Jarred from his thoughts Koran snapped his head up. "Nah, I'm good. I mean, you right. I need a break." He paused and looked up at Jahad through misery filled eyes. "I'm...I'm... This shit is fucking with me, Jah."

"You don't have to tell me, I know. I told you when you first came to me about becoming a M.G. how this shit was. The killing becomes addictive. That rush is better than busting a nut. Am I right?"

Stunned Koran nodded. Jahad knew exactly how it felt. "Word up, Jah. That shit is crazy! Knowing I'm bout to stop a muthafucka from breathing and that I have that power, makes my dick hard. Afterwards, I feel like shit though. But I can't help wanting to kill again. I mean, lil' Kay slowed me down some, but the urge is still there."

Jahad sat on the bed beside Koran and reached for the blunt. He took a few pulls, coughed, then spoke in a knowing voice. "Let me explain something to you lil' bruh. It ain't the killing you addicted to, it's the power. That's where the rush comes from. As far as you feeling like shit, that's natural. It proves you're still human. No normal nigga can keep killing over and over without it fucking with them. Shit, unless you a serial killa and them muthafucka's are crazy," Jahad smiled. "That's the whole reason for the system we got up with the Body Squad. So niggas won't have to keep killing over and over. You'll be a'ight though. The time you spend down south will help you get your shit together."

"I really don't have a choice but to go, do I?"

"Oh, you have a choice. You can go down there, cool-out and enjoy yourself or stay here and have me beat your ass. Choose one," Jahad replied with a crooked grin.

Chapter Fourteen

Jahad left a few minutes after their talk and Koran decided to troop it to Kana's Friend Chicken once the munchies get the best of him. On his way to the elevator, he bumped into Emma coming out her apartment dressed like she was on her way to church.

"Hey baby! Come give me some sugar," she smiled, showing all her dentures.

Koran kissed her on her wrinkled cheek. "I'm headed to the chicken spot, you want something?"

"No. No thank you. Where's that bad butt Jamel? I haven't seen him all week."

"He's out with my Shorty. You sure you don't want nothing?"

"No baby, I'm on my way to Pastor's house. He invited me to dinner this afternoon."

"If I had my truck I would give you a lift. You got money for a cab right?"

Emma nodded. "I already called a cab."

Koran looped his arm around hers. "Well, let's roll out then."

Exiting the building Emma's cab waited parked beside the curb. Koran walked her to the cab promising to bring Jamel to see her tomorrow, then strutted off up Story Avenue towards Kana's Fried Chicken. He glanced over at the park as he walked and memories from his childhood flashed through his mind. Jahad wasn't around much back then so Tony, Derrick, and the rest of Jahad's friends filled the role of big brothers often chasing him home when he was up to some mischief. The thought made him smile, then he thought of Derrick's death. The smile evaporated.

Instantly he was filled with an untamable rage while in the back of his mind a voice whispered seductively, Go back to Bronxdale and kill them all! Kill them all Koran! You know you want to and you can do it all by yourself. Kill them all! Kill them all! Kill them all!

Repeatedly the voice taunted him until he couldn't fight it anymore. Tensed as a coiled spring, his teeth clenched, he started back toward his building to get his guns as if in a trance.

"Koran!" A female voice called out behind him before he could reach the end of the block.

The trance broke and he turned to see Lisa crossing the street. Three reactions hit him at once. He was thankful for the distraction, felt a tug of arousal by the brown tight Prada dress she wore, and was annoyed feeling she had come to put pressure on him about their relationship after he clearly made it known that it was over.

"I was on my way to your apartment. We need to talk for real."

Koran frowned. "I know damn well you ain't about to tell me you're pregnant. If so, you can save that shit for the next nigga."

"No, I'm not pregnant. Happy now." She rolled her eyes. "But how can you just cut me off like that."

He rubbed a hand over his face. "I can't beef with you, but I got a shorty now Lisa. What, you expect me to cheat on her?"

"No, but I thought we were cool like that. You changed your number, you don't call. Maybe I want to check up on you sometimes to see if you're a'ight. It has nothing to do with sex. We didn't start our friendship based on sex. We were friend's remember?"

"No doubt. We were friends, still are friends. It's just that my shorty...."

Before could finish the sentence a dollar cab pulled up beside them and Monica jumped out scowling. She wore a skintight Chanel body suit that emphasized her heavy breast and Buffy the Body ass. On a scale from one to ten, as far as looks, she was pushing a six, but her body added the extra four points.

"So this the bitch you dumped me for!?" She glared at Lisa. "I guess her pussy is better than mine."

Koran shook his head, sighing. "You on some other shit Monica, word up. I don't...."

"Bitch?" Lisa smirked while taking off her earrings. "The only bitch I see is you, Bitch!" Koran placed himself between them before they could start clawing at each other.

"A yo, you two need to chill with the bullshit. Monica you way outta line and furthermore, I don't belong to you. I never did. I..."

Lisa stepped around him while his head was turned and slapped the shit out of Monica. It was on then, a live girl fight! Monica retaliated by kicking Lisa on the chin, then ripped the front of her dress open exposing her apple size breast. Without caring that most of the park, passing cars, and bystanders were getting a good view of her titties, Lisa started swinging wild with her eyes closed. Monica ducked her head, unable to block the blows and grabbed a fist full of Lisa's hair.

"Stop yo! Stop this shit!" Koran shouted forcing himself in between them again. "How the fuck y'all think y'all look out here doing this stupid shit!"

"Fuck that! And fuck you too!" Monica screamed, then hauled off and slapped him so hard his head jerked to the side.

During the commotion, no one noticed when Serenity had pulled up beside the curb until she jumped out the Range Rover and ran towards them with an orange box cutter in her hand.

"Sin, No!" Koran yelled, but she was already in motion. With one precise swing she cut Monica from her temple ripping a straight line down to the bottom of her jaw. Shocked, Lisa quickly backed away clutching her arm over her breast, while Serenity raised the box cutter for another swing. Luckily for Monica, who foolishly hadn't moved, Koran grabbed Serenity's arm.

"You buggin' Sin!" he said, pulling her towards his truck. "Let's get the fuck outta here before you get locked up."

"I'll kill that bitch if she ever puts her hands on you again!" She snatched away from him, her eyes wild with fury, and lifted the razor as if she were about to cut him. "What the hell are they doing here anyway!"

Koran grew still. "Don't do some shit you'll end up regretting, Sin. And you will regret it," he said coldly.

"You better not, Sin!" Dej'a' screamed, running up to them. She stood in front of Koran protectively scowling at Serenity. "Put that thing away!"

Koran smiled while Serenity looked at her niece confused. "It's cool Dej'a. Go back to the truck so me and Sin can talk."

Dej'a shot Serenity another warning glance before walking off.

Koran shook his head, grinning. "That's my baby right there. Now to answer your question, they popped up while I was on my way to the chicken spot."

He looked around at the crowds still staring, Lisa among them with tears running down her pretty cheek. For a moment he felt a pang of sympathy for her. To show he still considered her a friend, he decided to do something special for her without Serenity knowing. "C'mon, let's go before somebody call the Jakes."

He led Serenity to the Range Rover, got behind the wheel, then turned in his seat and gave Dej'a a wink. She blushed holding her notebook computer up. Beside her Jamel slept in his car seat with a large Super Soaker water gun lying in his lap. A few minutes later he parked in front of his building and looked over at Serenity who still held the box cutter.

"Why you still got that? Still thinking about cutting me or something?"

Serenity blinked, then shook her head. "You know I couldn't cut you."

"Um huh. That's what your mouth say."

"I'm serious. I kinda lost it when I saw that bitch hit you."

"Kinda?" Koran snorted. "I know not to leave my ratchet around you. Where you learn how to use a razor like that anyway?"

Serenity smiled. "Oh, you think I'm just another pretty face huh? All the drama me and my girls went through in junior high, we had to learn how to use razors or anything else we could get our hands on. That was the price for being down with the F.A.B Five, and how this face stayed pretty."

"That's what y'all get for stuntin' so much. Where you disappear to after junior high anyway? The last time I asked you said it was a long story. I'm all ears."

The smile left Serenity's face as quick as it came. She stole a glance at Dej'a who was busy tapping keys on her computer before speaking. "We were having some personal problems in my family. Actually, it was my sister, Dej'a's mother. She was caught up in some mess that I still don't understand. Whatever the case she got us the hell out of the Bronx in a hurry."

"Oh word? You never said nothing about having a sister. She prettier than you?" he asked with a sly grin in an effort to brighten her mood.

"Yes, but she's..." Serenity stole another glance at Dej'a. "I don't know what happened, but she's...she's like a zombie Koran. She hasn't left our apartment in years. Dej'a sits and talks to her for hours, but all she does is stare at the wall." Tears glistened in her eyes. "It's so sad."

Koran cut his eye at Dej'a wondering if her quiet demeanor came from her mother's condition. "Damn Sin, pardon me for asking."

"It's ok, boo. C'mon, let's go upstairs so I can show you what I bought. I got some stuff for you too."

Koran grinned devilishly. "You only got one type of stuff I want."

"Oh really?" She arched her eyebrow returning his grin. "Then stop talking about it and come get it."

~~~~

Upstairs, once Koran and Serenity made two trips to bring all their shopping bags up, Jamel woke up being his usual animated self. Water gun in hand, he ran through the apartment yelling Bang! Bang! for hours until Koran put on a Disney movie. Afterwards, Dej'a and Serenity put on a fashion show while Jamel played hostess and escorted them both through the living room to show off their outfits. Around nine o'clock the night finally wound down. Dej'a slept in Koran's lap, Jamel drooled on Serenity's shoulder.

"Let's put these two to bed so you can get your stuff," Serenity said, smiling while cradling Jamel in her arms as she stood.

Jahad walked in coming from work just as Koran scooped Dej'a up. Briefcase in hand, reading glasses on, he looked exactly like a legit business man. He called it his Clark Kent outfit. He gave Koran a sly grin without bothering to acknowledge Serenity, whom he made no attempt to hide his dislike from.

"Family man, huh? Looks good on you. You sucka for love ass nigga," he muttered grinning on his way to the bar.

Serenity rolled her eyes as she brushed past Jahad bumping him intentionally. From day one it was established that they did not like each other. Why? Serenity had no idea.

"Chill with the jokes, Jah."

"Oh, you sensitive now lover boy?" Jahad's grin stayed in place while he poured a shot of Crown Royal. "Let me find out you getting soft."

"I'd show you how soft I am if I didn't have Dej'a," Koran hissed, feeling blood rush to his brain. "Why you keep fucking with me about shorty anyway?"

Jahad downed his drink and let out a slow breath. "Because I know it pisses you off. Smart as you are, I thought you figured it out."

"Nah, I thought you were past all that. I love her Jah, and can't shit change it. You fucking with me all the damn time definitely won't change it."

"I know something that will," Jahad said under his breath as

Koran walked out.

~~~~

Koran was awakened the next morning to breakfast in bed. Strawberry pancakes dripping with maple syrup, two sonny side fried eggs, a slab of turkey bacon, and his favorite drink, cherry cool-aid.

"Eat Ka-wan. Get up!"

Serenity sat on the edge of the bed, holding the tray across her lap. Dej'a was beside her while Jamel pulled his arm. "C'mon sleepy head, get up. I cooked for you this time."

Koran sat up on his elbows yawning. "What time is it?"

"A little after ten and I'm missing the news," Dej'a answered, leaning over to kiss him on the cheek. She then bounced out the room casting a warm smile before turning the corner.

Koran grinned. "She gonna be something special."

"I know." Serenity smiled after her. "Did you have somewhere to be?"

Koran lifted Jamel, who was scrambling trying to climb on the bed. "Nah, but I gotta get some stuff together so we can bungee this weekend. We going down south."

"Down south!" Serenity looked stricken. "I can't go down south and leave my mother with my sister."

"Damn! I forgot about that. Find somebody to chill with her until we come back."

"Who? And I can't miss any classes either. What's in the south anyway?"

"My Mom's. Plus Jah' is putting pressure on me to take a vacation. We gotta figure out what to do with your sister. Don't sweat your classes. You ain't going to be a paralegal no more."

Serenity screwed up her face, holding the tray like she was about to launch it. "You or no other nigga will decide…"

Koran patiently held up his hands. "You wanna be a paralegal or go to N.Y.U. and study law first hand?"

The tray lowered a fraction. "What are you talking about Koran?"

"I'm talking bout putting you through law school. If you can make the grades I'll put up the dough. What up?"

"Are…are you serious?"

"Yep." Koran smiled, taking the tray from her hands. "Might need you to represent me one day. Now, about your sister. Mrs. Harris can…"

Too overwhelmed to speak Serenity covered his face with kisses.

"Chill Sin." He laughed, pulling away. "I'ma speak to Mrs. Harris. She's like my Nana. She won't mind holding your sister down. You cool with that?"

"I'm cool with anything you do baby."

Chapter Fifteen

The assault on Bronxdale played heavy on Hector's mind as he drove his black 745 I BMW through the thick traffic on Beach Avenue. Close to twenty of his people were dead. Dead all because he chose to take advice from an unknown stranger, a faceless voice. It was that voice who convinced him to move his people into Bronxdale against his better judgement. His thirst to kill Jahad had blinded him to the fact that this stranger could be playing him, paving the road to his death. The thought was fresh in Hector's mind when his cell phone rung.

"Hola?"

"Listen good, 'cause I'll only say this once. Opportunity only knocks once in a lifetime, so consider it at your door. I'm sure you know where the Shell gas station is on Story Ave, right across the street from Kana's Fried Chicken. There's a car wash that sit's right beside it. This Friday between one and five I suggest you have some of your people posted there. Jah will be driving a black 600 with mirror tinted windows. If you do it right, you might be able to have your cake and eat it too."

Familiar with the Operator's voice, Hector quickly pulled over and double parked in front of a McDonald's. "What the hell are you talking about?"

"You ain't stupid man. You know what I'm talking about. Jah and his brother, they'll be sitting ducks if you handle your business right."

Hector snorted angrily. "I took your advice recently and look what happened. I killed those five Moreno bastards and it costs me most of my new recruits. You told me you were in control, what happened?"

"That shit couldn't be avoided. It was a spur of the moment thing. What I'm telling you now is good money, so I strongly advise you to use it to your advantage," the Operator said, then hung up.

Hector sat Staring at traffic while a million thoughts ran through his mind. Was it a set up? Could he trust the Operator again? As hard as it was to believe Jahad would be delivered into his hands. The bait was too enticing. He wouldn't be there personally anyway. The way

Hector saw it, if it was a trap the chance to murder Jahad was worth risking a few more of his people. No, this was one opportunity he wouldn't miss out on.

Chapter Sixteen

Friday at one o'clock Derrick's funeral was held at A.M. Zion Church in Harlem where his mother relocated after the drug war in 2000. A hint of summer hung in the air with sunny skies and a light breeze blowing off the East River. Koran's reluctance to leave New York changed a little after seeing Derrick dressed in an all white Armani suit, arms folded across his chest, looking like a bronze statue. It made him realize his own mortality. The roles could have easily been reversed. He could see himself lying lifeless in his coffin while Derrick along with the rest of his loved ones walked by to get one last look before he was planted into the earth.

After the funeral the Heads and their lieutenants met up at Prine's brownstone to put together assault teams to hit Corsello and Leopardi. A special team of ten was being put together for the sole purpose of finding and killing Hector. A team Jahad personally volunteered for. Derrick was the first M.G. ever to die in battle. His death was taken personally by every last M.G.

From their plans they calculated Corsello and Leopardi would be the easiest to hit Since they had no idea what was about to come at them. Hector didn't fit into that equation. No one could pinpoint his movements, so random assaults would be aimed at Bronxdale and his other known drug spots. For this, the big guns would be bought out; M-16's, AR 15's, AK 47's, and altered fully automatic mini 14 assault rifles. The cause was to kill everything moving, but it would open two doors. One: weaken Hector's team. Two: eventually someone would betray Hector once they realize the killing wouldn't stop until Hector was dead. At least that's what they hoped for.

After the meeting, Jahad and Koran left. Jahad drove to the diamond district to buy gifts for Michelle and Latrice, then hit Bransan for an ounce of Cush before heading home. All the while he stayed unusually quiet. Koran figured his brother's thoughts were on Derrick. Finally, once they reached the Major Deegan, Jahad spoke in a low raspy voice.

"You know lil' Bruh. I've been wondering how my life would have turned out if I would have never started this shit."

Koran snapped his head away from the Hudson River choppy water. "What you talking about about, Jah? Started what?"

"I mean, I can't front, it has its rewards." Jahad went on as if he hadn't heard Koran. "The money, the bitches, the power. I can go on and on, but now I see the downside. The death, stress, fear of a muthafucka bodying somebody close to me on some revenge shit. Not to mention always having to look over my shoulder. I can go on and on about that too. I mean, it is fucking worth it?" He looked at Koran eyes burning intensely. "A yo, word up. Between me and you, after this last move, I'ma give it four or five more months and then I'm leaving this shit alone."

Koran's mouth flew open. "Get the fuck outta here!"

"I'm dead ass. I got money to last me six or seven lifetimes. I'm thinking about coppin' a crib out in Jersey, invest some dough in the rap game, then sit my ass down somewhere and live. Make a few babies and whatnot. I'm twenty seven and don't have no damn kids. Yeah, I feel like it's time I fall back."

"So who's gonna handle business in the Bronx, Prince?" Jahad smiled. "Nah nigga, you are."

"Me!"

"Yeah, you. Now it's time to see if all that shit I taught you stuck in your head or went out the other ear. When you come from down south I'll show you where the stash house is. In fact, you already know. B-10 on our floor."

"Mrs. Harris! Stop fucking playing!"

"Shit, Mrs. Harris likes money too." Jahad laughed. "Nobody will suspect that shit either. You already know how to run Joe's. I gotta teach you how to freak the books though. I could have been showed you that shit if you didn't spend all your damn time with that chick."

Koran looked away. Since he began dating Serenity he had been neglecting a lot of his duties.

"Hit a nerve, huh?" Jahad smirked. "That's what the truth does."

"You act like you ain't never been in love, Jah!" Koran said sounding pissed off.

"I have and know what, that shit almost got me bodied. You gonna have to learn that for yourself though 'cause you ain't trying to hear a damn word I'm saying," Jahad replied bitterly, then changed the subject. "Now pay attention to what I'm about to put you up on. This is how I distribute the drugs. First, I would hit Derrick with everything that would be out for the week. The coke, heroin, and tree's. He would pass it down to the three lieutenants. They pass it down to their individual soldiers who turn around and pass it down to the middle men. Now the middle men don't have shit to do with the M.G.'s, but they deal with the hustlers who push weight. Tell me why it's done like that?"

Koran was lost. "Shit, I don't know."

Jahad chuckled. "A'ight, say one of the weight pushers gets knocked and starts snitching. The soldiers body's his ass and whoever the middle man was. That way it'll never reach the top. Understand now?"

Koran nodded marveled by the set up. He knew that no M.G. was directly involved with drugs, but had no idea how complex the operation really was. "So you saying the only person who could say they got something from you was Derrick. The other M.G.'s under him didn't know shit pertaining to you," he said fully grasping the concept.

"Exactly. That's how we been going at it so strong for so long. Can't nobody tie us to shit. Plus everything we own is accounted for on paper from our businesses. Our paper is crazy long though, you know that. That's where the stash houses come in at. You and the other four Heads should be the only ones to know where they are. Since this snake shit happened, I moved out most of the money from the stash on my end. Mrs. Harris crib is my personal stash spot. That's where most of the dough is now and a few bricks. I got a couple mill' stashed at an apartment in Rosedale, but I'm leaving it there. Until we find out who's behind the bullshit we keeping this between us, a'ight?"

"Whoa! A couple mill'? What? You mean like two million dollars?" Koran asked stunned.

"Nah. That's nothing' but sneaker money."

Koran shook his head. "Hold up Jah. You fucked me up with that. If two mill' is sneaker money, how much dough is stashed at Mrs. Harris Crib?"

"Sixty million. I'm slowly washing it through Joe's, but it's gonna take a minute. I been meaning to spread it out to some new stashes, but I been so busy with this other shit. But check it, you should collect at least five mill' a week. The money comes up the same way the drugs are passed down, so when it reaches you everybody should have their cut. It's a lot more shit I got to put you up on, but I'll wait until you get back."

"Them B.M.F. niggas ain't got shit on us!"

"They had a good operation poppin' off. You see what took them down, right?"

"Yeah. They were too damn flashy."

"Yep, so keep that in mind and don't let this shit go to your head. This move with the prostitution will blow us all the way out the water. I'm talking billions in the next few years, so you gotta keep your head on straight."

Koran nodded slightly overwhelmed. Fear crept up his spine wondering if he could fill Jahad's position with all its responsibilities. He was only nineteen on the verge of being one of five people controlling a billion dollar operation. The thought was staggering.

His mind still reeled as Jahad stopped for a light on Story Avenue right across the street from Kana's Fried Chicken. He glanced out his window at a group of young kids being chased by the old Puerto Rican who ran the bodega when a red and white 1100 Kawaski pulled up beside his window. The rider was dressed in a black and red Averex motorcycle jacket, black leather pants, black Gore-Tex hiking boots, and wearing a black and red helmet. He cut his head towards Koran's then looked straight ahead. Koran admired the bike wishing he knew how to ride just as an identical motorcycle pulled up beside Jahad's window. The sight made goose bumps break out on his arms.

"Jah, go!" he screamed, his eyes wide with shock.

At the same time bullets shattered the passenger side window and tore into the door. A split second later his whole right side felt as if it was on fire.

"Koran, get the fuck down!" Jahad yelled, reaching for the Tarus 9mm he kept under his seat.

Outside the two gunmen emptied their clips and reloaded while pedestrians scrambled for cover, some stunned frozen by the sight. Traffic had come to a stop. Hitting the seat lever Koran threw himself back and reached for the 45. Automatic stashed in the middle console panel. Gun in hand, he pointed out the window shooting blindly praying his bullets reached their mark. Jahad, full of rage, sat straight up in his seat exchanging shots with his attacker paying no attention to the slugs that pierced his upper body. He was too outraged at being attacked.

"Jah, go man! Press the fucking gas!" Koran shouted over the roar of gunshots once his gun clicked empty.

Hearing Koran's plea, Jahad pressed the gas pedal down to the floor. The Mercedes shot forward with a burst of speed as bullets shattered the rear window. The car traveled about 100 feet, then came to a jolting halt when it crashed into a car double parked in front of the Chinese restaurant. Koran slammed into the dashboard air bag the same time Jahad barrelled into the steering wheel air bag before they both fell back into their seats.

"Somebody sat our asses up!" Jahad barked. Blood soaked the front of his white shirt, but he was more angry than hurt. "Koran! Koran! You a'ight?"

Dazed, Koran weakly lifted his head. "Yeah, I think so. I'm hit, though." He turned his head to Jahad's direction and his pain immediately went away seeing Jahad's bloody chest. "Oh shit, Jah! I gotta get you to a hospital!" He quickly grabbed his cell phone and dialed 911 unaware the police and ambulances were already on the way. Leaning over, he tried his best to cover Jahad's wounds as blood poured through his fingers. "Hold on Jah, everything's gonna be a'ight."

"I...don't know Koran." Jahad's voice grew weak as he spoke. "Those...those bastards got me good. Listen, don't ...don't trust no...nobody we...we fuck with except...except Sha'. Somebody close to...to us did this shit. Let...Let Sha'..."

"Shhh! Save your strength," Koran hissed, his vision blurry. In the distance he could hear sirens approaching and prayed they would get there before it was too late. "I know exactly what you trying to say and believe me, I'ma use everything you taught me to get this shit straight. That's my word! Just hold on 'cause if you die I swear to Allah, I'ma die right here with you. You see this?" Koran held up his gun so Jahad could see it. "I'll put this muthafucka in my mouth and chew on as many bullets as I can if you leave me nigga. I swear I will!"

Tears gleamed in Jahad's eyes as he held Koran's stare.

"You hear me nigga!?" Koran cried, putting the barrel in his mouth.

"I...I won't... die Koran so...so stop talking...fucking crazy."

Koran removed the gun, then let out a sigh of relief. Jahad had never let him down before, so he knew he wouldn't now. As the sirens drew closer he looked in the rearview mirror and saw two ambulances followed by three police cars racing up Story Avenue. His thoughts automatically went to their guns. He had to get rid of them or they both would be hit with weapon charges.

"A yo Jah, I gotta get rid of these guns before the Jakes get here. You gonna be a'ight. The ambulance is only two blocks away. I love you nigga!" he said, grabbing Jahad's gun from the floor board.

Jahad nodded, giving him his signature crooked grin.

As Koran exited the car clutching his right side a large crowd had gathered on both sides of the street, but no one made a move to help him. Typical New Yorkers. Half stumbling, half jogging, the crowds parted for him like the Red Sea while he made his way up the avenue glancing over his shoulder every few seconds to see if the police were behind him. Luckily Monow projects were only a half block or he may not have made it being he was losing blood at a rapid pace. By the time he made it to his building he was out of breath on the brink of passing out. Too tired to go any further, he leaned against the iron rail leading up to his building gasping lungs full of air.

"Koran! Koran, they hit you?" Tom-Tom a crackhead who lived in his building asked as he approached with a bottle of Wild Iris Rose wine in his hand. He wore a pair of dirty Pelle Pelle Jeans, a dingy brown sweatshirt and a pair of old construction Timberlands. On his head was a crinkled New York Knicks hat two sizes too big for his small head.

Koran raised his head weakly. "Tom-Tom?"

"Damn man! What the hell happened to you?"

"Get me upstairs, Tom-Tom. I'ma look out for you."

Tom-Tom took a swig of his wine and sat his bottle down. "I gotcha' man, but you bleeding like a muthafucka. You need to get to a hospital."

"Just get me upstairs man." Koran rested his head on Tom-Tom's smelly sweater while he led him towards the glass door. Once they made it upstairs, Tom-Tom helped him off the elevator. Koran reached in his pocket and pulled out a wad of money placing it in Tom-Tom's hand. "Good looking Tom-Tom. Go cop…a bag or something and smoke 'till you can't smoke no more," he said, stumbling off leaving Tom-Tom staring down hungrily at the money.

When he opened his apartment door, he would have fallen over if the wall hadn't of caught him. Blood ran freely from his right sleeve creating a puddle at his feet. A few seconds later Jamel came dashing down the hallway. "Ka-wan, we go see Gan Ma..." Suddenly, Jamel paused catching sight of the blood. "Sin! Sin! Ka-wan bleed! Ka-wan bleed. Sin!" he yelled, racing back to towards the living room. He returned seconds later pulling Serenity and Dej'a by the hand.

"OH MY GOD!" Serenity screamed, rushing toward him. "What happened!"

Koran looked up breathing hard. "Get...get these guns off me, and...and find out where...where they took...Jah," he managed to say before everything went black.

Chapter Seventeen

A few hours after the assault, the Operator sat in the living room of his two story five bedroom brick house, naked on the couch. His head was thrown back into the cushion and his hands were gripping the armrest as a young, beautiful mixed black and Asian woman gave C.P.R. to his dick using a technique he figured she learned from her Asian ancestors. To take his mind off the tingling feeling that crept from his toes up towards his groin, he forced his thoughts on what lay ahead while she slurped and sucked him like a vacuum.

On the way from Derrick's funeral the Operator had called Hector to make sure his people were in place. Now Jahad and Koran were out the way, or so he thought. This cleared the slate as far as his revenge went. Now it was time to start phase two of his plan. The other Heads. One by one they had to die, but in a way not to draw attention to his purpose which was total control of the M.G.'s. It would have to wait until the prostitution move was secure.

Next came the Sicilian lawyer. The Operator was well aware that Valentino played a major role within the organization. Still, he didn't feel comfortable with everything he knew about them. It would be a challenge, but one he was determined to accomplish. He was in the process of working out the beginning details when his phone rung.

"Yeah, who this?" he answered as the young woman gently took his balls in her mouth causing his toes to curl.

"It's Lord. A yo, Jah and Koran got hit up, Son!" his voice was strained with anger. "I just got the call from Joey."

"Word! They dead!?" The Operator feigned concern as a slow smile came over his face.

"Nah, but from what Joey told me they got hit pretty bad. I'm on my way to Einstein General now. The other Heads are already on the way, so get your ass in gear!"

The smile vanished from the Operator's face. "I'll be there. Who did it?"

"Damn if I know, but when I find out, I'm gonna torture the muthafucka real fucking slow. One!"

As soon as Lord hung up, the Operator slung his phone at the wall. "Goddammit! That Puerto Rican bastard can't do shit right!" he fumed, pushing the woman away from him. "Get your shit and get the fuck out!"

"I don't…"

The Operator jumped up, snatched up her clothes, then grabbed her arm and dragged her to the front door. "I don't like repeating myself," he said, pushing her out the door, tossing her clothes behind her.

He returned to the living room with the intent of calling Hector just so he could curse him out. How in the hell could he fuck up something so simple. He thought Hector would be the perfect pawn to kill Jahad without drawing attention to the game he set forth. Now it was evident that Hector didn't have what it took to accomplish the mission. A brilliant idea interrupted the Operator's thoughts. An idea that made him smile from ear to ear and would add a little more spice to his game. Instead of going against the grain, why not flow with it and use Hector's mistake to his advantage. It would definitely be interesting.

Chapter Eighteen

The sound of incoherent voices seeming miles away pulled Koran from his coma induced sleep. For a while he faded in and out of consciousness until the voices became clearer. A voice from his earliest memory as a child caught his attention. His eyes fluttered open to a bright light.

For a moment he thought he was dead, but he wasn't. Once his eye adjusted to the light, he took in his surroundings. He lay in a small bed, a white sheet pulled around his chest. To his left a hospital monitor set with small clear tubes attached running to his right forearm and one going up his nose. Turning his head slowly towards the sound of voices, he saw his mother sitting beside his bed talking quietly to his sister who sat at the small round table near the bathroom.

"Ma," he called out in a hoarse voice. His mouth felt drier than autumn leaves.

Startled, Michelle shot from her chair. "My baby! Thank you, God!" she cried out bending to kiss him forehead Tears of joy ran from her eyes dropping onto his face as she rambled on and on.

"Where's…where's Jah, Ma?"

Michelle was too emotional to speak so Latrice answered. "He's upstairs in intensive care. The doctor said he has a 50/50 chance, but you know Jah. He always fought against the odds," she said, giving him a weak smile.

"He gonna make it," Koran replied confidently. "Where am I?"

"Einstein General. You been in a coma close to three weeks."

"Three weeks!" He tried to sit up and a sharp pain ran through his side. That's when he noticed the condition he was in. His right arm was in a cask, his ribs heavily taped. "I gotta get out of here. C'mon, help me up."

"Take it easy, Koran!" Michelle said sternly easing him back down. "You aren't going anywhere. Have you lost your mind? You been in a coma boy!"

Being in a coma was the last thing on Korans mind. Someone had tried to kill them and now he was laid up in the hospital, a sitting duck without a gun. Jahad was in an even worse predicament and the hospital was the last place he needed to be. There was no way he could explain this to his mother though.

"Sin? Where's Sin?"

"She's in the waiting room with Jamel, Dej'a, and John-John. Tony is upstairs with Jah. Why you ain't tell us you had a son?"

Michelle gave him a sharp look. "Yes explain that."

Koran blew out a breath which hurt more than trying to move. "Jamel ain't my son, Ma. His parents died so I took him in."

"Nonsense!" Michelle rolled her eyes. "I know my grand babies when I see them. That boy and John can pass for twins."

John was Koran's four year old nephew. Tony and Latrice's son named after Korans father. "I'm telling you Ma, Jamel ain't..."

Serenity walked in carrying Jamel with Dej'a and John at her side at that moment. A smile lit up Koran's face as she and Dej'a rushed him while Jamel squealed his name.

"You... You're okay!" Dej'a cried, taking hold of his hand.

"Yeah, I'm good Dej'a so stop crying."

"I...I thought.." She began to sob pitifully burying her face into the side of the bed. Koran wrapped his good arm around her. "It's okay Dej'a, it's okay."

"Ka-wan home!" Jamel yelled squirming in Serenity's arms. "What up lil' dude. You been good?"

Jamel nodded. "Kay good boy. Sin cry so Kay be good. Ka-Wan you come home?"

Koran held back tears seeing the sad look on Jamel's face. "Yeah, Kay. I'm coming home real soon so we can go get some ice cream, a'ight?"

"A'wight Kawan. I wuv you."

"I love you too, Kay. Word up! I love all of you." Koran looked up into Serenity's ocean green eyes and felt an intense wave of love.

"Thank you, Sin. For everything."

Serenity shook her head. "You don't have to thank me. I would gladly switch places with you right now. All I ask is that you hurry and get well." She leaned over and kissed his dry lips, then whispered... "So we can kill whoever did this to you!"

The intensity in her voice sent chills up his spine and at that moment he had no doubts that she was his soulmate. Now he understood completely Jahad's warning of falling in love. If he had to choose between Serenity and the M.G.'s, she would be his choice without any hesitation.

"I wanna thank you anyway." He motioned for her to come closer. "Get me outta here, Sin," he said in a low voice so Michelle couldn't hear him.

"I can't baby. You need to heal first."

"You can't what?" Michelle asked, frowning. "I know you not trying to get her to sneak you out of here Koran! She will do no such thing!"

"Ma, you don't understand."

"Why don't you explain it to me then? Better yet, explain to me why we should take you outta here when you have cracked ribs and a broken arm. If Serenity had of been one minute late getting you here we wouldn't be having this conversation because you would have bled to death. Do you understand that!?"

"Calm down, Ma. I'm a'ight now."

"You are not alright! You almost died!" she shouted with tears streaming over her cheeks as the doctor entered.

To Koran's surprise, he was black, literally. His skin was the color of charcoal. He wore a white doctor's coat over a pair of brown slacks and a pair of brown wingtip shoes on his huge feet. His features were blunt. Thick purple lips, a broad nose and large brown eyes behind a pair of specs. When he smiled his large horse teeth looked like polish ivory.

"Mr. Copeland, I see you're awake. That's a very good sign. I'm Doctor Johnson and I'll be tending to you during your stay here at Einstein." His voice was deep and jolly.

"How long will I have to be here, Doc? I mean, I feel like I'm good to go now." Koran tried to sit up again and cried out when the same sharp pain ripped through his side like electric heat.

"Hurt's doesn't?" Doctor Johnson said, placing his hand on Koran's side. "You'll be here at least another two months. You have two big holes in your right side. Two big holes that although are sewn up, still need to heal none the less. Also, you have two broken ribs where the bullets passed through and damaged your right lung. We were lucky to save it, so until you're completely healed this room will be your home. He turned away from Koran to Michelle. "I'll have to ask you to leave now. There's one test I have to run, and after he takes his medication, he'll go out like a light."

"Hold up Doc. I just woke up. Let me…"

"Ka-Wan home!" Jamel pouted.

Koran smiled. "You heard lil' man. Tell him again, Kay."

"I'm sorry, Kay," Doctor Johnson said, then chuckled. "Your father can't come home now. He has to stay here until he heals up. Understand?"

Jamel screwed up his little face. "Fuck heal! Ka-wan home!"

"Jamel!" Michelle shouted, taking him from Serenity. "Watch your mouth boy before I beat your butt."

"Ka-Wan come home! Ka-Wan! Ka-Wan!" Jamel cried, reaching out for Koran as Michelle marched him out the room.

The scene made tears well up in Korans eyes. Regardless of how long it took, whoever was responsible for causing his family to suffer, would pay. Pay dearly!

Chapter Nineteen

That next morning Koran sat propped up in bed reading The Village Voice when Valentino burst into his room out of breath. Sweat beads were on his forehead, looking as if he was on the run from the police. A few seconds later, three nurses and security guard ran in after him.

"Sir, you will have to vacate the premises," the white bullet head security guard said while the three nurses glared at Valentino. "You were told at the front desk that only immediate family was allowed. Or would you rather have me call the cops?"

"I don't give a damn who you call!" Valentino spat placing his briefcase on the small table. "You have no idea who I am. I'll file so many lawsuits against this... this..." He looked around Korans' room with disgust. "This poor excuse for a hospital that you'll be out of your rent-a-cop job!" He pointed a finger at the old white nurse who stood in the middle with bluish dyed hair. "I told you that I was the Copeland's family lawyer and I had to see him!"

Koran watched from his bed amused. He didn't really know Valentino except for what he heard from Jahad. Actually, this was the second time he had ever laid eyes on him. The first being years ago when Valentino represented Jahad for two homicides. One thing he knew for sure though, Valentino had been a valuable asset to Jahad and could possibly be a valuable asset to him in his helpless state.

"A yo, let him stay. He's cool," he said and all eyes turned in his direction.

Valentino gave Koran a satisfying nod, then turned back to the security guard and nurses. "You heard my client. Now if you'll excuse us, we need some privacy."

He walked off towards the bed without looking back. The nurses and security guard stood staring harshly at him until Koran shooed them away. Valentino pulled a chair beside the bed, sat, then shook Korans' hand.

"Koran we haven't formally met, but I'm Vincent Valentino. Your brother..."

"I know who you are. I'm in the family business too."

Valentino nodded in understanding. "Can you tell me what happened? Do you remember?"

Koran studied Valentino debating on how much he should reveal. From what Jahad told him Valentino had no knowledge of what went on within the organization. His involvement dealt strictly with money laundering except for the new move with the prostitution. So Koran's main concern was could Valentino be trusted. Playing his cards close to his chest, he decided to tell him little as possible.

"A muthafucka set us up is all I can tell you right now."

"But you know more. Am I correct?"

"Maybe."

Valentino nodded. "Well, how about we begin like this. I'll tell you what I already know and you fill in the blanks"

Koran arched his eyebrow. "What blanks?"

"These. A few days ago your brother and I met at his moving company to discuss some business ventures."

"Yeah...and?" Koran said, knowing exactly what meeting he was talking about.

Valentino looked surprised for a second. "Yes. Apparently you're well informed."

"Let me make this simple for both of us. It ain't nothing that goes on that I don't know about. Now I have a question for you. How in the hell did you know I was in the hospital and who the hell are you for me to tell you anything? For all I know you could be the one who set us up," Koran said matter factly with a slight frown.

"Though are good questions." Valentino smiled. "Now here are your answers. I'm not in a position to betray you or Jahad. What he does has never been any of my concern. I don't ask and don't wish to know. Another thing, being as you're well informed, you should know I need Jahad to make our new business venture work. So why would I want to kill him? As far as me learning of you and Jahad being in the hospital, I received a phone call from Mrs. Harris the day you two were shot. She's who informed me that you were out of your coma."

"Mrs. Harris?"

"Yes. Sweet old Mrs. Harris. Does that answer your questions?"

Koran nodded, lost for words.

"Good. There's one more thing I would like to add. Your brother is a dear friend to me as well as a business associate. I would like to help put an end to this threat on his life if I'm allowed."

"Oh word. How can you help? You gonna bust your gun or something?" koran asked grinning.

"I'm a lawyer. I'm far from being a gangster," he said, holding up his hands. "However, being a lawyer does have its advantages. I've made lots of friends and I may be able to get certain information you don't have access to. All I need to know is what to look for."

Koran studied Valentino again, then made his decision. "Has Jah ever mentioned a dude name Hector to you?"

"Hector!" Valentino wrinkled his face like he smelled a bad odor. "So it's him again. Yes, Jahad mentioned him a time or two. This was a few years ago."

"Well, that muthafucka is back and he has help. Somebody close to us is rolling with him, but we don't know who."

"So that's what Jahad was hinting at."

"What you mean?"

"After our meeting he mentioned that some things were not as they should be, but failed to go into details." Valentino paused giving Koran an intense look. "You, nor Jahad, are safe here without protection Since it's obvious that you can't trust anyone close to you. How long will you be here?"

"The doctor said two months, but as soon as I can, I'm getting the fuck outta here. Valentino shook his head. "No, stay until you're healed. With your wounds an infection could be the death of you. I'll provide protection while you're here."

"Just bring me a rachet and I'm good. Make sure Jah…"

"A rachet?"

"A gun. Bring me a gun. Make sure Jah has someone holding him down though."

Valentino laughed. "You and your brother with that street slang. That's the first time I heard that one. I'll bring you a rachet and for extra precaution, I'll have two bodyguards assigned to each of you."

"I'm feeling that, but do it on the low. Like I said, whoever is behind this shit is close to us. I don't wanna put him on point."

"Don't worry, I'll speak to the hospital's administrator and arrange things. Your bodyguards will be dressed as nurses. The only difference is they'll be carrying rachets."

Koran smiled. "I'm with that. How soon can you make it happen?"

"This afternoon, hopefully. When I leave, I'll try to contact the administrator. All it should take is a little money in the right hands."

"No doubt. Good looking too. So what up with the prostitution situation? Is it still on?"

"Definitely not! Until Jahad is in control of things again, it's off. If he can't trust his own comrades, I'm not about to trust them. I've only dealt with Jahad and that's how I'm keeping it."

"How bout you deal with me," Koran said, holding Valentinos' eyes.

"Deal with you? Elaborate."

"I'm saying the information you gave Jah has already been passed around so you may as well go head with it. Our people might move on both families anyway."

"They can't do it without Jahad!" Valentino snapped angrily.

"Who's to stop them? Jah is only one of five, including me since Jah is out."

"You?"

"Yeah, me. I'm taking Jah's spot Since he's out. Between me and you, he was planning on retiring after this move. So I'll ask again, will you deal with me? I mean, you're the missing link in all this. Well, you and Jah, since he was the link between you and the other Heads. Without you, they can't see no dough. So let me be the go between, at least until Jah gets better. It might buy us some time to find out who's on the bullshit."

Valentino shook his head. "None of this makes sense. I understand your logic, but why would one of the four want to kill Jahad when he's needed for what we're about to do? It doesn't add up."

"Who's to say its one of the Heads? Not that I'm excluding them, but it could be one of their top lieutenants. Then you gotta think about this. This new move will bring in crazy paper, but we don't really need it. You have no idea how much dough we see. All you know about is what's in the bank. Then it could be that whoever the snake is may feel like he can deal straight with you once both families are out the way. What I'm getting at is whoever it is evidently feels like he don't need Jah, feel me?"

Valentino nodded. "Yes, you've made some good points."

"So what's up? You gonna deal with me or what? At least you'll know what's poppin'. And if you wanna help like you said, if that muthafucka contacts you after we do what we do, let me know so I can handle it."

Valentino was silent for a moment, thinking. After a minute or so he nodded. "Alright, I'll do it. Tell your friends, if you can call them friends, that the date has been pushed back until you get out of here. It's your show now."

Koran was about to speak when Tony walked in dressed in a pair of Red Monkey jeans, a plain white tee-shirt, and all white Air Force One's. He walked up to Valentino and gave him a hug. "Valentino, what up man! Damn, it's been a minute."

Tony and Valentino's relationship dated back to Jahad's time spent on Rikers Island. "How are you Tony? Jahad tells me you're a disk jockey now."

"Yeah, something like that. What you doing here?"

"Just came to pay my respect. I'm on my way upstairs to see Jahad. I know he's still out, but maybe my presence will be felt." Valentino turned to Koran, reached in his pocket and pulled out a business card. "Use this number whenever you need to reach me, day or night. When your bodyguards arrive, I'll make sure they make themselves known, alright?"

"Yeah, no doubt. I'ma get at you soon and let you know what's up."

"Make sure you do. You take care Tony."

Once Valentino left Tony took a seat beside the bed. "What was that about? And what is it you gotta get at Valentino about?"

Koran held Tony's Stare. "I'm saying Tone, do you really wanna know?"

"What kinda question is that? Hell yeah I wanna…"

Tony's words froze on his lips as it dawned on him what Koran was really saying. He had played a major role in Starting the M.G's but had no idea that Koran was now part of the organization until now.

"Nah man, not you." He shook his head sadly. "What the fuck was Jah thinking bringing you into that shit! You had a future Koran. The only thing this shit gonna do is get your ass bodied or 25 to life!" he spat angrily.

"It's what I wanted Tone. It ain't Jah fault" Koran replied, feeling like a kid again.

"What you wanted? Well look at you now. You got exactly what you asked for. I told Jah what this shit was gonna lead to but he didn't listen. Now look, both of y'all asses are fucked up. Who did this shit anyway?"

Tony stood flush with anger and began pacing. He was mad at Jahad for making Koran a M.G, mad at Koran for getting involved in the first place, and mad at whoever put them in the hospital. Beneath his anger there was a deep sadness he felt for Koran. In Tony's eyes Koran was just as much his brother as he was Jahad's and like any brother, he held high expectations for him. Koran's intelligence at a young age proved that he could have become anything he chose to be. Now he's just a murderer.

On a much deeper level, he knew that what had happened could possibly change the life he set out to live. Until whoever was responsible for the attempt on Jahad and Koran's life was dead, he couldn't return to North Carolina. His loyalty to Jahad wouldn't let him leave, therefore he was drawn back into the life he tried so hard to escape. With that thought he cursed Jahad under his breath, then focused back on Koran who stared up at the ceiling.

"Who did it Koran? I know you know."

"Yeah, I got a pretty good idea, but it's complicated."

"Complicated how? Either you know or you don't."

Koran exhaled a painful breath. "Check it Tone, this ain't got nothing to do with you, so it ain't no reason to tell you. When I get outta here, I'ma handle it, a'ight."

Tony's face twisted up into a scowl. "A yo Koran if you weren't already fucked up I'd beat the shit outta you for saying that dumb shit! This has everything to do with me. Derrick gets killed, which nobody bothered to tell me. Now the two niggers I care about the most are laid up in the goddamn hospital and I wanna know who the fuck did it!"

A few seconds passed before Koran answered. "I can't say for sure, but I think it was this Puerto Rican dude name Hector."

"Hector!" Tony shouted. "You talking about the same dude we were beefin with from back in the day?"

"Yeah, the same dude. I think he's the one who had us ambushed, but we were set up by somebody close to us."

Tony's mouth dropped open as he digested the information. "Whoa! Whoa! What you mean somebody close to you? You can't be talking about another M.G."

"Yeah, I can. Somebody is on some bullshit and right now we can't say who. That's the reason for the bodyguards. I can't trust nobody in our circle."

Tony sat down and placed his head in his hands. He couldn't believe another M.G. would want to kill Jahad or Koran. Their structure was too tight, or so he thought. "You have no clue who it can be?"

"I know it can only be one of the Heads or one of their top lieutenants." Koran went on to tell Tony how Jahad first picked up the deception.

Tony stood and shoved his hands in his pockets. "I ain't leaving till this shit is over, but we need to get your moms and Trice back down south. If I were you, I'd send your shorty too. Who is she anyway? She looks mad familiar."

Koran ignored his question. "Nah Tone, don't get involved in this shit. I told you I got it."

"Don't get involved? You buggin, Son. I'm about to..."

"No, listen!" Koran snapped. "The only advantage we have is whoever is behind this shit don't know that we know. If you start hanging around it could put him on point and that's the last thing we need. Out of the Heads there is only one I can trust, and that's Sha'. Some funny shits been going on out in Brownsville around his spots too. He's the only M.G. who knows what's poppin. Together we gonna get to the bottom of this shit."

"I feel you Koran, but in a situation like this you can't afford to trust nobody. Especially a Brooklyn nigga. And I'm staying whether you like it or not. At least until Jah gets out the hospital. I'll play in the cut so niggas won't know I'm around though. I'll let your Moms and Trice know what's up. And like I said, get your shorty and lil man outta New York."

"Why?"

"Nigga you already know why. You dealing with some heartless muthafucka's. And with this nigga Hector involved, he'll kill anybody close to Jah or you on some revenge shit for what Jah did to his brother."

Koran's interest sparked. "You talking about what happened before you moved down south. What was that about anyway? Jah would never tell me."

Tony sat back down and collected his thoughts before speaking.

"It all started when Jah came home from Spofford."

He relayed the story from the beginning to the end, telling of their lost music career. He explained how Hector and Jose initiated the beef with them because of Jahad's relationship with the Coco Twins half sister Janet. Then he told him how the M.G's were formed on Rikers Island. Then there was Cream's betrayals leading up to the night the assaults were made on the Coco Twins drug spots when Jahad kidnapped Hector's twin brother Jose.

Koran stared at Tony when he finished with all types of thoughts running through his head. He finally understood the reasoning behind a lot of what Jahad had taught him. His respect level for Jahad deepened. If it wasn't for his brother there would never be no M.G's.

"Whatever happened to the chick Janet?" he finally asked.

"I think she got bodied the night Jah killed Jose."

"Word! Jah bodied her?"

Tony shook his head. "Nah. From my understanding she got hit by a stray bullet from one of Hector's men. Jah was fucked up over shorty too. Did Jah ever tell you about your pops?"

Koran shook his head.

"The Coco Twins bodied him. They bodied their own pops too, and took shit over in the South Bronx. That's how they came into power."

"Get the fuck outta here! That shit ain't true!" Koran said heatedly.

He wasn't about to let anyone disrespect the memory of his father. He was only four years old when John Copeland was murdered, but from what he vaguely remembered, his father had no time to be in the streets. His job with the transit system took up most of his time.

"My pops wasn't no fuckin drug dealer!"

Tony held up his hand. "Don't think I'm trying to throw dirt on your pops name, but it's true. Ask Jah. Your pops was like the Nicky Barnes of the South Bronx. The only difference is he stayed crazy low and he wasn't a rat. But the Coco Twins pops... Damn, I forgot his name. He and your pops used to get money together. Your pops provided the work and the Coco Twins pops handled shit on the street."

Koran closed his eyes and shook his head. "This shit is crazy. Why would they body their own pops?" he said, speaking more to himself.

"I don't know, but it gives you an idea of what type of person Hector is. If he could body his own pops, you know he don't give a fuck about nobody else."

Koran nodded. "Yeah, you right. I'll..."

He cut his words short when the door opened and Serenity walked in with Jamel and Dej'a at her sides. She wore a pair of tight apple bottom jeans, a white blouse with a pair of white Timberland boots on her feet. To her left Jamel was clad in a Phat Farm jean suit, a red tee-shirt with the superman emblem on the front, and a pair of red and white Air Jordands. To her right, Dej'a wore a pink Roc-A-Wear velour sweatsuit, and pink and white Air Force One's. Her hair was cornrolled with pink and white beads at the end of the plaits.

"Where y'all headed, the club?"

"Ka-wan I fry?" Jamel asked, crossing his arms across his chest.

"Yeah, lil dude, you fly."

Dej'a walked over to the bed and kissed him on the cheek while Serenity watched from the door with love swimming in her eyes. She wasn't superstitious, but it seemed like an invisible force had drawn them together knowing everything would coincide. Never had she imagined she would love someone as much as she loved Koran. The relationship he shared with Dej'a only intensified her love.

"What you standing over there looking all goofy eyed for? Come give me a kiss," Koran said making her blush.

Tony stood as Serenity approached the bed, his eyes on Dej'a. For some reason he couldn't get the image of Latrice out of his mind every time he looked at her. "A yo Koran, Ima go check on Jah. I'll swing back through before I leave."

"Trice is up there now with Michelle and Mrs. Harris," Serenity said, sitting in Tony's spot. "Their next stop is here. Mrs. Harris brought you some cookies too, Koran. I told her they probably wouldn't let you have them, but she wasn't trying to hear it."

"They gonna catch hell tryin to stop her. A yo Tone, make sure you come back so we can finish talking, and bring me something to smoke up in here tomorrow."

"No!" Serenity frowned shaking her head. "You heard what the doctor said about your lung."

Koran grinned sheepishly. "I'm saying, some haze might help ease my pain a little."

"You smoke some haze right now you might not make it out the hospital. Crazy ass dude." Tony laughed as he walked out.

"How you feeling, boo?" Serenity asked, taking hold of his hand.

On the other side of the bed Jamel tried his best to climb up until his foot slip off the rail and he crashed into one of the machines behind him. At once a loud piercing round filled the room. Jamel got up, his eyes wide, looked left, then right before he took off running around the bed to Serenity. "Po-lice Sin! Po-lice!" he yelled climbing into her lap.

Koran laughed so hard tears ran from his eyes as held his right side. A second later a nurse ran into his room looking around frantically.

Jamel glanced at her then buried his face in Serenity's chest. "They get me Sin!"

"What happened in here?" the nurse asked over the noise as she walked around the bed to unplug the machine.

Jamel kept his face hidden.

"It's nothing, Miss. My lil man made a mistake and bumped one of the machines."

The nurse shot Jamel a frown, then left. Once she was gone Jamel watched the door for a second before he looked up at Koran grinning. "They not get me Ka-wan?"

"Nah, you a'ight with your bad ass. You better be good though or she gonna come back."

Jamel looked back at the door. "I be good."

"Back to what I asked, how are you feeling?" Serenity asked again while Jamel played with her earrings.

"I'm a'ight. Could use some loving, but I'm a'ight." Koran smiled then turned serious. "Listen sexy, you ain't gonna be feeling this, but I want you and Dej'a to go down south with my Moms for a while."

"Why? And what about my sister?"

"Mrs. Harris will hold your sister down, so don't sweat that."

"Does it have anything to do with why you're here?"

"You gonna make a good lawyer," Koran said smiling. "And that's exactly what I'm saying."

"Why?"

"Cause it's not safe and that's all I'ma tell you. Now when you get back to the crib look in my closet and get some dough outta one of my shoe boxes. I'll ..."

"I ain't going nowhere until you tell me what's going on," Serenity said stubbornly.

"Dammit, Sin! I wouldn't be telling you to bounce if it wasn't important. Right now I'm not in no shape to protect you. I can't even protect my damn self. So stop being hard headed and bounce. When things…"

The door flew open and Michelle and Latrice stormed in followed by Tony, who wore a pained expression. Emma was right on their heels, carrying a platter of cookies.

"Koran what's going on!" Michelle asked, marching up to the side of his bed. "What's this about we have to leave?"

Koran looked at Tony, who shrugged his shoulders. Emma walked up behind Michelle and gave him a little shake of her head, which made him wonder how much she really knew.

"I don't know what's going on myself. I don't wanna take any chances though."

Michelle shook her head. "Jahad pulled this same mess years ago keeping me in the dark. You're mixed up in that mess he's in aren't you?"

Fear gripped him. She couldn't possibly know about the M.G's. "What you talking about, Ma?"

"I'm not stupid!" she yelled as tears spilled from her large brown eyes. "I know what he's into. He promised me he would keep you out of the streets. He promised!"

"Ma, I don't know what you talking about" he lied, unable to meet her eyes.

Chapter Twenty

The first week after Karen came out of the coma the Heads and their lieutenants paid him a visit. It took all the self control he could muster not to expose what he knew to be a fact. That whoever wanted him and Jahad dead was in his room smiling, laughing, and pretending not to be angry along with him. Somebody he and Jahad has risked their lives for and made a pact of brotherhood with was now trying to kill them.

But why? The question nagged him ever since he'd woke up in his hospital bed. Everyone got their fair share of money and no toes were being stepped on. So why would one of his own people want him dead? Lost on him was the motive, but he would have to dig deep to figure it out. His life, as well as Jahad's, depended on it.

A month and a half later, against the doctor's orders, he checked himself out of Einstein General. He was fed up with lying around, the bland hospital food, and the constant hounding from the N.Y.P.D once the detectives found out that he and Jahad were bother's. From eyewitness statements and his wound, there was no way that he could deny that he wasn't at the same crime scene. He made up a story of a botched carjacking, but the detectives weren't buying it.

If it were an attempted carjacking why would two men pull up on motorcycles and just start shooting? It was a question they asked each visit. So he simply left after sicking Valentino on the detectives even though his wounds hadn't completely healed. His right arm was still in a cast and staples were still in his side. None of this mattered. Since the cast wouldn't be coming off anytime soon, the first week after Valentino brought the gun he asked for, he'd started practicing every day in the bathroom using his left hand until he could, cock and aim with the same speed and precision he used with his right hand.

Before leaving the hospital Koran stopped by Jahad's room. After his operation in the removal of five bullets from his chest and abdomen, he was now listed in stable condition. Dr. Johnson claimed it was a medical miracle how his body took so much damage without dying. Koran thought otherwise. Jahad was a warhorse and five measly bullets wouldn't stop him.

Entering his room, Koran felt a load of sadness like he did every time he visited. Tubes ran from Jahad's nose and arms while a steady beep, beep echoed through the room coming from the vital signs monitor. He pulled a chair next to the bed and began talking as if Jahad were wide awake.

"I'm about to blow this joint big, Homie. I'm tired of these Jake's coming around all crazy, plus I need to get on the job. Me and Valentino been kicking it and it's still on with the prostitution thing. The Heads been coming through too asking mad questions, but I'm keeping them in the dark."

"A yo check it, Jah. I know you groomed me so I can take your spot, but honestly bro, I don't want this shit. If I got to worry about a motherfucka I done put my life on the line for trying to mark me…" He shook his head. "Nah, I don't want no parts of that. You think you gonna leave me to put up with this shit? Picture that! I'm coming with you nigga. We can both cop cribs in Jersey and invest dough in the rap game. Tone told me how you used to flow. On the low I can spit too. We can live your dream again and own our own label. Black Market Productions. Yeah, that shit sound tight. B.M.P., we all we got!" he said, holding back tears. Seeing Jahad in this hopeless state hurt worse than the pain in his side.

"I'm sorry, but visiting hours are over," a pretty red headed white nurse said as she entered carrying a clipboard in her hand. "We want to be careful that you don't tire him out."

Koran raised his head, scowling. "Come on lady. How the hell can I tire him out when he's not even woke?"

"That's what you think. Look," she said with a bright smile.

Koran snapped his head around stunned when he saw Jahad looking at him through cloudy eyes with a weak crooked smile on his face.

"You been woke the whole time?" he asked, then turned back to the nurse. "How long has he been woke?"

She blushed glancing at Jahad. "This morning when I came to check on him, he grabbed my butt. I thought it was a mistake until I came back to check on him an hour later he did it again. When I looked at him, he had that same grin on his face."

Jahad gave Koran an innocent look.

"Oh word!" Koran laughed. "So you heard everything I said?"

"Yeah. I heard you nigga." His voice was barely a whisper, but his eyes were alert.

"Well hear this. Hurry up and get your ass out of here. I need you, Jah. Word up, I need you bruh!"

"And Mr. Copeland," the nurse said, addressing Jahad with a wicked smile. "My butt is off limits... for now. You may get too excited."

Jahad winked as she turned to leave.

Later, on his way home in a cab, Koran called each Head and set up a short notice meeting at his apartment. A lot of things are about to happen and they probably wouldn't like what he was about to tell them, but so be it. Jah was the only one who knew of his intention and supported him all the way. Tony wanted in also, but Koran refused to pull him in though. Too much danger was involved and Latrice would never forgive him if something happened to Tony. So for the time being he would stay on the outside.

When he walked into his apartment and closed the door, he heard water running in the bathroom. He automatically pulled his gun and placed his back against the wall. Who in the hell would be in his apartment he thought. Tony was staying on long island with his aunt, Serenity was down south, so it could be one or two things. Either someone had broken in looking for something to steal or someone had come to kill him. Whoever it was, was as good as dead.

As he inched closer to the bathroom, the door opened suddenly and Serenity stepped out wearing a towel. His finger froze on the trigger as she screamed, her eyes crossed focus on the gun pointed at her face.

"What in the hell you doing here?" he asked angrily tucking the gun back into his waistline.

Secretly she was there to see him. "I...I," she stuttered.

"You what?"

"I came to check on my sister. I've been calling home, but no one answered our phone."

"She a'ight?"

"Yeah. I called Mrs. Harris when I got here. She brought her to her apartment. She said she didn't feel comfortable leaving her alone with my mother," she answered him, then turned the tables. "What are you doing out of the hospital? I thought the doctor said you'd be there for at least two months?"

Karan ignored her question. "How long you been here?"

"I flew in about two hours ago. Now answer my question, Koran. What are you doing out the hospital?"

Koran let his eyes roam over her body from head to toe. Her black hair hung loose and wet plastered to the side of her face, stopping right at the swell of her breasts. Unconsciously, he reached out to remove the blue terry cloth towel until Serenity slapped his hand away.

"Answer my question Koran," she said, backing away.

He grinned, stepping towards her. "If I answer will you give me some?" Serenity glanced down at the bulge in his jeans and felt herself growing moist.

"Maybe."

"Maybe ain't good enough." He held her eyes as he reached out and removed the towel letting it fall to the floor. Stepping closer he kissed her softly, then moved his lips over her jaw line with light kisses. Serenity let out a low moan while working at his jeans until she held his erection in her hand.

"Turn around," he whispered, licking on her earlobe.

Serenity complied placing her hands on the wall and spreading her legs wide. Koran started at the back of her neck with wet kisses that he trailed along her spine until he reached her round yellow buttocks. Dropping to his knees, he palmed and squeezed her plump cheeks. Turning her around slowly he ran his hands up her waist and across her flat stomach until he held her full breast in his hands.

Sin sighed loudly and Koran's dick hardened even more. His eyes roamed back down and smiled at the cute little heart shaped design of her pubes. Reaching between her legs, he parted her folds and covered her with his mouth. He used his tongue to dark in and out between her slick lips while she winded her hips. Her juices flowed heavily rolling down the inside of her thigh.

"Koran you're driving me crazy," Serenity moaned, clawing at his shoulders as he took her clit in his mouth.

He sucked gently like a newborn on a nipple until her body tensed, then shook uncontrollably. While she was still caught up in her orgasm, he stood up and lined his swollen dick head up with her glistening pussy lips. Teasingly, he moved up and down between her slit before pushing in. Her sex gripped him so tightly that he had to hold his breath to keep from cumming.

"Damn, Sin. You crazy tight," he said, holding himself still, scared that if he moved he would explode.

"C'mon Koran. I need you to fuck me, baby!" Serenity demanded.

With his good arm gripping her right side, he started pumping in and out of her with long steady strokes. Every time he pulled out he felt a sharp pain in his side, but he couldn't stop. The sight of his dick disappearing inside her made the pain worth it.

"You don't know how much I missed this baby," Serenity said, looking over her shoulder, her green eyes pouring it into his. "Is it good? Did you miss your pussy, baby?"

"You know I did. This shit about to kill me though," he winced pushing into her again. Serenity abruptly pulled back, leaving his dick sticking straight out glistening with her juices.

"Oh my God! Why didn't you say something!?"

"What you doing, Sin? I was almost there," he said, frowning reaching for her hand.

"Uh, uh. Its hurting you. We'll wait until..."

"Wait hell! I need to cum before I go crazy." He turned and placed his back against the wall. "C'mon, you can do all the work. Word up, if you let me get this nut, I won't bother you no more until my side heals. Please, Sin! I need to be in you, for real," he begged, stroking himself.

Serenity looked from his face to his dick, biting her bottom lip.

"Alright. But if it starts hurting you let me know, okay?"

Koran nodded eagerly as she backed her fat ass up on him halfway, then eased up off him. After a while she got into a steady motion sinking down and rotating her hips. Her pussy was making suction sounds that was driving him wild. Despite the pain, Koran pumped into her round cheeks met his short fast thrusts.

"Oh shit, Sin! Keep it just like that! Just like that!" He was just about ready to bust when he heard someone banging at the front door. Too far gone to stop, he reached around and fondled Serenity's clit until they both went over the edge together.

"Hold... Hold the fuck on! I'm cumming!" he bellowed as he continued to release his seed deep inside Serenity. When he pulled out he only gave himself a few seconds to catch his breath before he yanked up his jeans. Serenity trembled as picked up her towel and rushed into the bedroom. Koran smiled as he watched her disappear before he rushed off to answer the door with his gun in hand.

"Who is it?"

"It's us nigga!" Star barked. "Open the damn door."

After tucking his gun in his waist, he opened the door and faced all four Heads. Star stood in front, his dreadlocks covered with a gray Tam matching the gray wife beater he wore. To his left stood Sha' and on his right Prince, while Lord brought up the rear.

"What the hell took you so damn long?" Star asked, stepping inside. "We been out here knocking for like 10 minutes."

"My fault. I was in the middle of doing something," Koran replied just as Serenity walked up behind him wrapped in a white robe. Star glanced at Serenity then back to Koran with a sly grin. "Oh, I see. You were in the middle of something, huh?"

Serenity turned red in the face and Koran laughed. "Y'all niggas c'mon."

Once they were assembled in the living room, Serenity played hostess and brought everybody Heinekens. Afterwards, she returned to the bedroom to get dressed. She knew Koran needed to talk shop with his boys, so she left to go see her sister.

Once everyone made small talk, Koran stood up from where he sat in the recliner and addressed the Heads. "A yo, as you all know, Jah gonna be outta it for a minute. So until he gets back, I'll be holding shit down in the Bronx. I already…"

"Hold the fuck up!" Star interrupted. "You suppose to be going down south nigga. That's already been agreed on before any of this crazy shit popped off."

"And who gonna handle shit out here?"

"Prince. He can hold it down since he'll be here."

"That was then, because I ain't going no fucking where," Koran said with ice in his voice. "My brother is laid up in the fucking hospital and you think I'm leaving? You must be smoking some crack. Now like I was saying, Jah put me up on everything. The stash houses, the connects, the whole run down. He wouldn't have did it if he ain't think I could handle it and that's exactly what I'ma do. Handle it!" He glanced at Star and for the first time felt a vibe of dislike.

"You know what, I know how you feeling Koran. You're pissed

because of what happened, but use your head man!" said Prince. "This shit ain't no joke, Son. How you expect to do something with your arm in a cast? You'll fuck around and get bodied. Take your ass down south, at least until you heal up."

Korans' eyes narrowed. "First of all Prince, I ain't no damn kid, so don't speak to me like I'm one. Secondly, I can get busy with my left hand just as good as I could with my right. If I ain't mistaken I got more bodies than all you niggas put together which don't mean shit, but it should speak for me being able to protect myself."

Sha' nodded. "He made a good point. To be honest, since Dee is gone, I feel he's the best person to hold Jah's spot down. Jah said it himself a few months back."

Silence filled the room for a few seconds until Lord voiced his opinion addressing Koran. "I've been watching you ever since Jah started you out on that Karate Kid shit. The way you came up leaves me with no doubts that you can hold it down out here. This is the thing though, you can't be thinking with your emotions or making any immature decisions. Your actions fall back on us, remember that."

"No doubt, Lord. Before I make any important moves, I'll run it by y'all first, just like Jah did. As for emotions, the mistake I made in Bronxdale won't be repeated. I'm repping Jah by holding down his spot. I won't do nothing to let him down, believe that!" Koran said, giving the impression that he would work within the boundaries when he had plans to do just the opposite. He didn't know for sure that one of them in this room was trying to kill him and he wasn't about to take any chances trusting them. "Since we past that, I got some shit to put y'all up on," he continued, knowing when they were in for another shock. "Me and Valentino had a discussion and…"

"Valentino! When you talk to Valentino?" Star asked, screwing up his face. "We been trying to get in touch with that cracker since that shit popped off with you and Jah."

"Who's us?" Koran asked, wondering if all the Heads were in on the plot.

"Us nigga!" Star looked at the other Heads. "We ready to move, but we gotta know what's up with the dough."

Koran grinned. "I'll be handling that now."

"You!?" all four men said at the same time.

"Yeah, yours truly. Know how Valentino would only deal with

Jah? Well now he'll only deal with me. At least until Jah gets out the hospital. Now with the dough, everything is still set up the same. The numbered accounts are already set up in the Cayman Islands. One for each of us."

"A yo, this shit is crazy!" Star exploded looking at the other Heads. "This cracker acts like he can't trust us after he been eating off all our shit. And now he'll only deal with you?" he spat sarcastically glancing at Koran. "What type of shit is that?"

"You've got a problem with him dealing with me? Did you have a problem when he only dealt with Jah?"

"Nah, but…"

"But what, Nigga?"

Star squinted his eyes as he stood and took a step towards Koran. "You better calm the fuck down and watch how you talk to me!"

"And if I don't, what?" Koran threw up his good arm waiting for Star to get within swinging distance.

"Whoa! Whoa!" Lord quickly jumped in between them, his massive body making it impossible for them to reach each other. "Both of you niggas need to sit the fuck down! What the hell is wrong with y'all?"

Tension was thick as Koran and Star took their seats, never breaking eye contact.

"Check this out," Sha' said, walking over to where Koran sat facing the Heads. "If we stripped this shit all the way down it basically boils down to one thing. Do we accept Koran as being one of the Heads? If it comes down to a vote, Jah already made his wishes known. I'm for it and so is Lord. Am I right Lord?"

Lord nodded.

"So that's three against two if you feel the same way Prince. It's obvious how you feel Star."

Star held up his hand. "Hold up, Son. I never said I had a problem with him holding down shit for Jah. If y'all comfortable with it, shit, I'm cool with it too. All I'm saying is why can't this cracker deal with us?"

"A'ight, now think about what you just said. When Valentino was dealing with Jah you ain't have no beef with it. So why is it a problem now? I mean, back in the day when Jah first brought it to the table about Valentino washing our dough, it was agreed then that he would only deal with Jah. Just like we agreed that Prince would be the only one to deal with the coke and heroin connect. Just like we agreed that you and the Lord will deal with the weed connects. We all know who the connects are just like we all know who Valentino is. So what's the problem?"

Star looked at Sha' and then to Koran with a stern expression. "You right, Homie. I owe you an apology Koran." He stood and gave Koran a hug. "All this crazy shit going on got me stressed, Son. It ain't nothing personal."

"Everything good, Star," Koran returned the hug. "I ain't really want to knock your short ass out anyway."

Star laughed. "You one armed muthafucka. I woulda beat your ass then felt bad about it."

"What were you saying before you niggas got on that crazy shit?" Prince asked, directing his question to Koran.

"Oh, I got information that Hector is still getting money in Bronxdale. Since me and Jah been gone, he got his teeth in Castle Hill and Sound View too. He got three lieutenants. Money, he's a black dude from Castle Hill. Timbo, another black dude who's rocking the sound view area. And Carlos, this big Puerto Rican dude who's supposed to be holding down BronxDale. From…"

"Hold up, Son," Star butted in. "I don't mean to cut you off, but where you getting this information from?"

Koran didn't want to say, but saw no way around it. "Valentino. He said he had mad contacts so I had him use them. From what I got, Hector got Bronxdale and Castle Hill on lock. Prince you been holding shit down, right?"

"Yeah. Some dough is missing from the stash spots too."

"No, it's not. Jah was in the process of spreading it out when this other shit happened."

"Where's it at then?" Star asked.

"Chill, let me get back to what I was saying." Koran tried to keep the impatience out of his voice.

"Prince have you noticed a drop in what we usually pull in? Jah said we saw at least five mill' a week." Prince looked around uncomfortably. "Yeah, the money intake dropped. The most I've taken in is 3.5."

"See." Koran looked at each Head. "My information is correct."

Lord, who usually was the humblest, stood and started pacing. "What the fuck is going on? How the hell is this Puerto Rican doing all this shit without us knowing. A yo, we slippin' for real!"

"You gotta keep in mind that Hector ain't no slouch," Sha' said quickly. "How you think he stayed alive all these years?"

"I don't give a fuck how smart he is!" Lord snapped. "How can one muthafucka outsmart all of us? That shit ain't possible!"

"You right," Koran agreed. "It's about to be a rap for his ass though."

"What you mean?" Sha' asked.

"Valentino ain't got a bead on Hector yet, but his lieutenants be up at the Wedge on Hunts Point every weekend. I'm trying to put together how we should go at it. I mean, the whole set up as far as the assaults."

"Same plan," Prince answered. "Ten M.G's for Leopardi, ten for Corsello, and a ten man team to hit Bronxdale randomly. I guess we'll have to do the same for Castle Hill in Soundview. It's going to be crazy heat though trying to hit them all at intervals."

Koran nodded as his plan slowly started taking shape. "When we plan on doing it?"

"Two weeks from today," said Prince.

"A'ight, two Fridays from now. That's good because Hector's lieutenants should be in the Wedbush and it'll give me time to scope shit out. One of my old chicks used to step there and I already know the area. Next, the Friday after that, I'll send their asses to hell."

"You can't be serious," Star chuckled. "You one step away from being crippled and you talking about bodies against three muthafuckas. You bugging, Son."

Koran shook his head. "Here we go again."

In one swift movement he grabbed the Browning from the small of his back, ejected of the clip, and caught it in his cast hand. Still moving at a blinding speed, he caught the gun against his leg, ejected the bullet lodged in the chamber. In one smooth movement he inserted the clip and caught the gun again, chambering another round. The move took no longer than five seconds using his left hand only.

"I can aim and shoot, you fucking bastard. Still think I'ma cripple, Star?"

Star burst out laughing. "My fault, Son. With all that Clint Eastwood shit you just pulled, I know Hector's peeps are some dead muthafuckas. And yo, I know you be thinking I be coming down on you, but I just don't wanna see nothing happen to ya, you know?"

"I feel you Star, but I got me," Koran said with a slight grin to hide the pain he felt on his side. "Now back to business. I just thought of something. Prince is right about shit being crazy hot after we pop off, so we might not get the chance to hit Hector's spots back to back. I think it'll work to our advantage if we stick to the plan, but when we hit'em, we hit'em crazy hard then fallback for a good minute."

"Let me hear some more." Star said intrigued.

"I'm saying, the way Jah explained how the drugs were distributed, it makes it crazy simple. I mean, we're killa's and thinkers. We ain't the nigga on the street moving the weight. So we do what we do best, kill and think. Let the niggas on the street do them. We'll send like thirty niggas to Bronxdale, thirty niggas to Castle Hill, thirty niggas to Sound View and blow that shit up. Ain't no reason to bullshit. Get on some terrorist shit and body like a hundred muthafuckas at one time and be done with it. A move like that will put the fear of God in the coldest nigga heart."

For a few seconds the Heads were stuck staring at Koran awestruck. His words had the effect to put the fear of God in them also.

"You hear this nigga!" Star stood up, his eyes gleaming with excitement. "He's a fucking maniac. But I like it. We hit everybody, Leopardi and Corsello too at the same hour. The Jakes gone be fucked up! I'm feeling this!"

Prince stared at Koran as if trying to read him. "You dangerous for real," he said with a straight face.

"So it's settled then," Star said, getting back to business. "Two weeks from today. Same time."

"Hold up on setting a time. Let me watch Hector's lieutenants first. That way everybody can get busy at the same time. Oh yeah, I suggest we all bounce for a month or so after this shit over. I mean, every M.G. involved. You know the Jakes gonna be looking under every rock trynna figure out what happened. Even though it shouldn't tie back to us, why chance it?"

Again, they were stuck looking at him.

"Yeah, Jah taught you good," Lord said laughing. "Killa's and thinkers. Killa's and muthafuckin thinkers. Ain't that some shit."

U. E. Wynn

Chapter Twenty One

Koran sat in the living room contemplating the meeting after the Heads left. So much was riding on his shoulders, so many lives, and he wondered if he could handle it. Now college and the square life he once hated, didn't seem so bad. He was snatched from his thoughts when Serenity burst into the room excitedly.

"She's up! She's talking!" she shouted, her eyes brightly lit.

Koran stood up confused. "Who's talking? What you talking about, Sin?"

"Janet! Mrs. Harris said she was talking." Serenity engulfed Koran with a hug.

"That's what's up. Wow, she's been out for a minute too."

"Years! She would have never been messed up if it wasn't for my evil ass twin brother's."

Koran stiffened suddenly.

"What's wrong?" Serenity asked, taking in his expression.

"Twin brother's?" he repeated, stepping back. "What twin brother's?"

Serenity looked at him looking at her strangely. "Hector and Jose."

"You can't be talking about the Coco Twins?"

Serenity nodded. "How do you know my brother's?"

"Oh shit!" Koran staggered back, holding Serenity's eyes. The same eyes he recalled staring into as a child when he first met Janet. All of a sudden, all of Jahad's workings came rushing back. *Don't fall in love. Don't trust a bitch.*

"You're the Coco Twin's sister?" he asked, a sickening feeling began tightening his gut.

"Yes. Koran, what's wrong with you?"

He pulled his gun from his waist and slowly started walking towards her. "Say it's not you Sin. Say it's not you," he said, barely getting the words out. Thoughts of betrayal, the death Derrick, and his brother laid up in the hospital flashed through his mind.

Serenity's eyes widened. "Koran what are you doing?" she asked, eyeing the gun. "Please listen to me. Whatever you're thinking is wrong."

"Don't!" he yelled, placing the gun on the table in front of her. "I pray I'm wrong, but if not, kill me now." He turned his back expecting her face to be the last thing he'd ever see.

Instead of shooting him in the head, Serenity hugged him from behind and started sobbing on his back.

"How…How could you ever think I would do anything to hurt you?" she cried. "I would never do…"

Koran turned in her arms. "Shhh! I had to know, Sin."

"Know what?!" Serenity snapped. "You really think I'm that type of bitch? I mean, really Koran?! You think I would betray you?!"

Koran shook his head. "Baby, look at all this shit going on around me. I can't put nothing past anyone, especially with what Jahad is going through." Koran paused and his eyes grew wide. "Wait, if Deja' is your niece and Janet's her mother, who's the father?"

'Boy, I know my grandbabies when I see them.' His mother's words rung loudly in his head.

"Jahad," he said in a low voice.

"Jahad," Serenity stated at the same time.

Koran stumbled back into the couch and sat down. "This is too much." He looked up at Serenity. "This some TV shit, Sin. Jah, Janet…me, you. I mean…" He shook his head, trying to cope with all the new information he was getting.

"Yeah, it's a lot, but you have other things to worry about at this moment." Serenity sat beside him and grabbed his hand. "You have to find out who's trying to kill you."

Koran cut his eye at her. "Well, we know one person is your brother. But none of this is for you to stress over. You need to be getting ready to get you and your sister out of here. Wow Janet," he said, shaking his head again in awe.

"No Koran. Just hear me out. I think I can help. I can…"

"Stop right there."

"No, you stop! You're good at what you do, but not only are you injured, you have no one to trust except me. Yes, Hector is my brother, but I hate him just as much, or maybe more than you. He destroyed my mother and sister. Deja' grew up thinking her mother was a life size baby doll because of him. So even if you don't like it, you're gonna listen," Serenity said fiercely.

Koran hunched his shoulders. "Aight, I'm listening."

Serenity nodded. "You're gonna have to use me," she held up her hand when Koran was about to speak. "The only way to truly end this is to find out which Head is trying to kill you. Whoever this Head is, he's using Hector. Hector has no idea that you and I are together. If so, he would have been contacted me."

"How do you know?" Koran asked sitting up.

"That's how he works. He did Janet like that. He uses whatever is around him to get what he wants."

Koran shook his head. "If you went to him and told him you were with me he would know it's a trap."

Serenity nodded her head in agreement. "He definitely would because he knows how I feel about him. That's not my plan. In order to find out who the Head is, you need to tell them that you found out that I'm Hector's sister and that…"

"No!" Koran snapped. "It's too dangerous. They're gonna expect me to kill you or one of them will, just because of who you are."

"Just hear me out." Serenity continued unfazed. "Once you tell the Heads about me and that you plan on killing me, whoever the snake is will tell Hector and then Hector will contact me. When he does, I'll do whatever you need me to do." She stared directly into Koran's eyes so he would see that she meant what she said.

"There is a lot of *if's* though," Koran said, not liking the plan of putting her in danger.

Serenity shook her head. "No, it makes sense. Hector likes to manipulate people. This is a mirror situation of what happened between Janet and Jahad. He screwed that up and got Jose killed. He will jump at the opportunity to feel he's in control again. The difference this time is you and I are in control. Use me Koran," she said pleading.

"What about the Heads?"

"Only one wants you dead from what we know. Once he's gone, you can handle the rest."

Koran held her stare, letting her words sink in.

U. E. Wynn

Chapter Twenty Two

Serenity spent nearly thirty minutes running down her plan which Koran had to admit was worth trying. If it worked, his suspects would provide him with a name. If it didn't work, at least Hector would be dead. The problem what he wasn't willing to risk was having Serenity caught up in the middle. If he put it in motion, she would be targeted by both sides. When he tried to voice this, Serenity shut him up with a kiss, then changed the subject, determined to have her way. For the time being he decided to go along with her just so he could avoid the argument. In the mean time, his goal was to come up with another plan. One that didn't involve her.

Afterwards, on their way to Emma's apartment, butterflies fluttered in Korans' stomach. The thought of meeting Janet, the woman who had played a part in molding Jahad into the man he was today, made him feel a little apprehensive. He wondered how Jahad would react once he found out. From what Tony told him, Jahad believed Janet to be dead. Did he still love her? Did she still love him? The questions along with a million others ran through his mind as Serenity knocked on Emma's door.

"Who is it?" Emma's voice came from the other side a few seconds later.

"It's me Mrs. Harris, Koran."

It took a few more seconds for her to take all the locks off the door. It sounded like she had about ten dead bolts on that shit. The door opened and Emma stood with a wide lip splitting smile. "Hey baby." She kissed Koran on the cheek before turning to Serenity. "Did you tell him?"

"Yes, Ma'am. He wants to speak to her. We both do. How long has she been talking Mrs. Harris?"

"Y'all come in first and we'll talk. Janet is taking a nap right now, poor thing. I don't think she slept in two days."

The sweet aroma of cookies and cakes lingered in the air as Koran and Serenity followed Emma through the brightly lit hallway. Pictures of Black Jesus, crosses, The Last Supper and old photo's dating back to the seventies decorated the walls. Some showed Emma in her prime posing in front of Lincoln Town Cars and Cadillac Sevilles with an afro the size of a punch bowl.

"What you cooking Mrs. Harris?" Koran asked, his mouth watering.

"I'm in here doing a little baking for my church. How bout y'all try something out for me. I need to see if I still got my touch?"

Koran wrapped his arms around her shoulder. "You know I wouldn't turn down your cooking for nothing in the world." Emma giggled.

Entering the kitchen Koran felt like a kid again when he saw all the goodies. Seven cakes sat on the large round table. Two chocolates, two vanillas, two red velvets, and a pineapple pound cake. On the kitchen counter an assortment of chocolate chip, oatmeal, lemon, and peanut butter cookies were lined in plastic trays.

"You need to open a bakery Mrs. Harris and call it Emma's Sweet Treats. I betcha you'd get paid," Koran said, pulling out a chair. "All this stuff for your church?"

Emma chuckled as she walked over to the knife rack. "Yes, we're having a family day tomorrow. You two need to come. What will you have Serenity? I already know you want red velvet Koran."

"I'll take red velvet too, Mrs. Harris. Thank you."

Emma cut two healthy slices of cake, then turned to the refrigerator and took out a gallon of milk. "You know, this reminds me of the time I had Jahad and Janet together right here in this same kitchen. They'd had a spat over something, but I fixed it right up. Yes, I did."

Koran and Serenity exchanged a questioning look while Emma poured two glasses of milk. She sat the two slices of cake on small plates, added a couple of cookies and placed it and the milk on the table in front of them.

"For a while they had a good thing going. Jahad had a good paying job, although he worked his butt off. But hard work is good for a young man. He had his dream of doing his Be-Bop thing and Janet was right there supporting him."

"Hip Hop," Koran corrected.

"Be-Bop, Hip-Hop, it's the same thing," she said, waving her hand. "Anyway, they were off to a good start. Then them no good Puerto Rican boys came along and messed everything up." Her face hardened. "They should be a shamed of themselves for what they did to that girl. The devil has no shame though. For two straight nights I've held her while she cried her poor little heart out."

Serenity sat up in her chair. "That's how long she's been talking? Two days?"

"Yes. The first day was when I went to your apartment. I knew who she was right away, but she didn't recognize me. That is, not until the day I brought her here. I'd sit and talk to her for hours, but she just stared at me like I was a fixture on the wall. I've seen people like that before. It's the pain. It becomes so unbearable it shuts you down and that's exactly what happened to her. She told me when she came out of it how those boys threatened to kill her baby. Jahad's baby. And his stubborn butt had the nerve to accuse her of turning on him. When she shot that man, that did it. It pushed her over the edge. It's a wonder she didn't lose her mind."

"What brought her around?"

Emma smiled. "Sometimes when you're burdened with some bad memories all it takes is one goofy one to lift you up. I told you Serenity, your mother was doing something I didn't approve of, so I gathered up Janet's things and brought her here. And you know what? As soon as she stepped foot in my kitchen she smiled. That was the first time I saw her respond to anything so I started talking about the day she and Jahad were here."

"At the mention of that boy's name she broke down crying, a pitiful sight too." Tears threatened to fall from the corners of Emma eyes. "It look a while for her to get herself together, but when she did, she asked where she was. Her next question was where was her baby. When I told her Dej'a was down south with Michelle, I couldn't get her to shut up." Emma laughed.

"Before I could finish answering one question she was asking another. There's a gap in her memory too, Serenity. She doesn't remember anything after the time she shut herself down, so you'll have to bring her up to speed. She wants to see Jahad too. She's a little scared thinking he might try to hurt her. I told her he would do no such thing."

"He's awake now too. I spoke to him this morning before I left the hospital," Koran said, feeling like he was caught up in a soap opera. "Why you ain't tell me you knew Janet all those times you came to see me in the hospital?"

Emma smacked her lips. "Because there's a time for everything Koran. If I would have told you your mind would have been all mixed up when it needs to be on how you're gonna get you and Jahad out of the mess y'all in."

Koran eye's widened. "What you talking bout Mrs. Harris?"

Emma ignored him and turned to Serenity. "Will you please excuse us baby? I have a bone to pick with this boy."

Serenity shot Koran an 'ooh you're in trouble look' and he stuck his tongue out at her. Once she left Emma looked at him pointedly. "Are you mixed up in these streets Koran, and don't lie to me?"

He started to do just that, wanted to lie so bad so he wouldn't disappoint her, but he couldn't. Since he was filling in for Jahad he had to tell her since everything was stashed in her apartment.

"Yeah, Mrs. Harris. I'm taking care of things until Jah gets out the hospital," he said looking down at his hands.

Emma shook her head sadly. "For some reason I thought this life would escape you. Jahad I understand, but you. It wasn't forced on you like it was your brother. You're a bright young man Koran, with a short future if you continue to mess around in them streets. Just look what happened to you. That was a sign from God baby. Get out before it's too late. You're probably wondering why I keep Jahad's poison in my house. Well, believe me, it's not the money he gives me. I donate every dime to my church. You see, old Mrs. Harris use to be a young Mrs. Harris, and just like you and Jahad, I was a slave to them streets. I had a pimp I loved more than life itself, but…"

"A pimp!" Koran dropped the cookie he was about to bite into.

"Yes, baby. I use to sell my body and do all types of despicable things. You know why? I put my trust in someone who didn't care two red cent about me. When my body was all used up and my pretty face wasn't as pretty, I was no longer any use to him. By that time, I'd had so many abortions, I lost the ability to do one of the things a woman was put on this earth to do, have children. Now you, Jahad, Jamel and Dej'a are the closet thing I'll ever have to grand babies. And like any grandmother, I'll do all in my power to protect y'all. So, I'd rather keep the poison here knowing I won't betray him, then have him keep it somewhere else."

Koran nodded, feeling a deep, sympathetic love for Emma.

"Remember this baby," she continued. "With the life you're living trust ain't nothing more than an illusion. When it comes to money and power, if genuine love ain't involved, then be very careful. That's one thing them streets taught me. Now, while Serenity out, go look in the middle bedroom. Jahad keeps his mess in that chest beside the bed and the closet."

Koran stood with Emma's words bouncing around in his head. She definitely was right about one thing. Trust is an illusion. Something else echoed in his mind as well. Power! He couldn't picture any of the Heads, nor their lieutenants, trying to kill them for money. Power was another story. If one person controlled the M.G's, he would be one of the most dominate forces New York had ever held. Then another thought struck him. He and Jahad weren't the only ones in danger if the control of the M.G's was what the snake wanted.

With that thought in mind, he turned to walk out the kitchen just as Serenity and Janet turned the corner in the middle of a conversation. Immediately, the conversation came to a halt and Koran froze in his tracks. His eyes were fixed on Janet's almond shaped green eyes, which seemed to hypnotize him. The resemblance between the sisters were distinct. The green eyes, high cheekbones, pointed chins, and heart shaped faces.

But unlike Serentity, Janet stood at five eight with honey blond hair that hung almost to her waist, a long, sharp, delicate nose, wide sensuous lips, and a thin barely visible sexy mole near her eye. Her complexion was the color of champagne, pale from the lack of sunlight. She wore a pair of tight Azure Capri jeans that gripped her round voluminous hips, a white short sleeve button-up unbuttoned over a white wife beater that clung to her melon size breast, and nothing on her small narrow feet.

Koran held her gaze with all types of taboo thoughts running through his mind. She looked absolutely stunning, breathtaking. He saw how easy it was for Jahad to fall head over heels in love just as he did with Serenity. Both sisters carried an aura of untamed passion. A strong, magnetic, attracting power.

Janet studied Koran in a similar fashion, but in her eyes, she saw Jahad. The seven year gap in her memory puts Koran around the same age as Jahad when the two first met. He was close to the same build and height, and looked so much like Jahad she couldn't differentiate between the two.

"Hi Janet." Koran spoke with a little smile once he found his voice. The trance broken, Janet ran into his arms and kissed him, holding him firmly against her. Koran, without thinking, held her with his good arm and felt himself growing hard until Serenity broke them apart.

"What the hell you think you doing Janet! That ain't Jahad. That's Koran, my man!" she hissed. She then turned on Koran, her nose flaring. "And why in the hell did you kiss her back!"

Koran's face flushed red. "I ain't kiss her back."

"Koran?" Janet looked him up and down surprised. "Little Koran?"

"I ain't little no more," he said with a wide grin.

"Oh my god!" Janet laughed, embarrassed, then arched her eyebrow. "I can see you aren't little no more."

"Alright, that's enough!" Serenity grabbed Korans' hand possessively. "And you stop flirting with her before I knock that silly grin off your face."

"Leave him alone, Sin. I thought he was Jahad." Janet took hold of Serenity's hand and gave it a little squeeze. "I ain't trying to steal your man. He is a cutie though."

Koran blushed turning his head away from Serenity who looked at him with a scowl. "Janet, honey, what are you doing up?" Emma asked as she walked over drying her hands on a towel. "You need to get some rest baby."

"I'm fine Mrs. Harris. I've been resting for seven years. What I need is to get caught up," Janet replied and turned to Koran. "How is Jahad?"

"He's good. I spoke to him this morning. He's still kinda weak, but he gonna be a'ight."

Janet nodded. "You think… I mean, I want to see him. There's so much I have to explain. So much he doesn't understand. He thinks I set him up. I tried to tell him what Hector did, but he wouldn't listen. He just wouldn't listen Koran!" she cried, burying her face in her hands.

Instinctively, Koran wrapped an arm around her shoulder. "It's a'ight, Janet. We gonna straighten it all out tomorrow, I promise. Once you explain what happened and tell him Dej'a is his daughter, I betcha he'll apologize. I'll talk to him first so he won't spazz out. He thinks your dead, so all this gonna fuc…" He cut his eyes at Emma. "Mess him up."

"He doesn't know Dej'a is his?" she asked wiping her eyes. "But I thought she was down south with Michelle?"

"She is, but Jah still don't know. I sent her and Sin down there when I was in the hospital."

Confusion was written all over her face as she looked at Serenity then back to Koran. "I don't understand. What happened?"

Serenity coughed under her breath to draw Koran's attention, then gave him a little shake of her head. Koran picked up on it immediately. With all the stress Janet had been under, the less she knew the better. If she found out Hector was involved, fear could possibly make her slip back into her trance.

"I'll explain what I can later. For now, why don't you and Sin go out so she can show you how much New York has changed in seven years. You probably wanna do some shopping too. You should get all fly so when you see Jah tomorrow his tongue will fall out his mouth."

Janet smiled. "I like that idea, but I don't have any money for…." She paused and whipped her head towards Serenity. "I have some money put up in your closet that I took from Hector."

Serenity looked down at the floor. "I um…. kinda borrowed it. Well, some of it. When mommy got on that stuff I had to take care of me and Dej'a. I used some for school too. There's still a couple thousand left, though. I budgeted it as best I could."

Janet's face dropped. "I understand."

"What you looking all sad for?" Koran titled her head up. "Money is something you never have to worry about."

"What you mean?"

"Just trust me, you rich on the low. Sin, look in my closet and take out ten stacks so you can fix her up."

"Fifth Ave money?" Serenity grinned.

Janet shrugged her shoulders not knowing what they were talking about. "I wanna speak to Dej'a before we leave."

"You can call from my apartment. Now vamoose!"

U. E. Wynn

Chapter Twenty Three

Koran stayed at Emma's after Serenity and Janet left so he could check on Jahad's stash and figure out what to do with it. He managed to avoid telling the Heads where the money was stashed. But he didn't know how he could keep them in the blind without someone getting suspicious. Especially the snake if it happened to be one of the Heads. Eventually he would have to tell them something, so he figured his best bet was to move it. Well, at least some of it. Out of sixty million they wouldn't miss a few million. A little something he planned to set aside for Serenity and Janet in case something happened to him and Jahad.

As he stepped into the bedroom, he noted that it was decorated exactly the same from his childhood. Gold and white striped wallpaper layered the walls with pictures of himself, Jahad and Latrice through various stages of their childhood. A queen size bed sat directly in the middle of the room made up with one of Emma's handmade quilts. Flanked on both sides were two oak nightstand that held twin white and gold antique lamps. The chest Emma spoke of set next to the oak nightstand on the right. Beside the closet on the left side of the bed sat a highly polished oak dresser with a large wall mirror attached.

Koran knelt in front of the chest and unleashed the shiny brass latches. On top was another one of Emma's handmade quilts, one he remembered snuggling under as a child. His eyes grew wide when he removed the quilt. Neatly stacked compressed bricks of cocaine lined the top. Giving into his curiosity, he began taking the bricks out one by one. By the time he made it three quarters through the large chest, he tallied up a total of thirty bricks. That's when he came across the Herion. Packaged the same as the cocaine, it was set apart by its dusty dark brown dirt color. Five minutes later he came up with another thirty bricks.

Done with his inventory, he walked to the closet where the real shocker came. Inside were five large Louis Vutton suitcases and ten green army duffle bags, all stuffed with money.

"Sixty fucking million dollars," he whispered to himself in awe. He wondered if Emma knew exactly what she had in her apartment. Probably not. From the way she explained it Jahad could be hiding nuclear weapons in her apartment and she wouldn't care.

It took close to ten minutes to wrestle one of the suitcases from under the heavy duffle bags with his good arm. He had no idea how much money it was but figured it was over a million dollars by how much it weighed. If it wasn't, he could always come back for more.

Before walking out he made a mental note to come back tomorrow with two duffle bags for the drugs which brought about his first decision as being one of the five Heads. Who would be his lieutenant?

Since whoever he chose would deal directly with him, it had to be someone he could trust with his life, which left only two people: Jay or Kwan. Jahad's childhood friends and his surrogate brother as a kid. At the time they were in charge of passing down the drugs to their own personal lieutenants. It didn't matter which he chose, both were trustworthy, so he decided to leave the decision up to a flip of a coin.

He wrinkled his nose when he stepped into the hallway, catching a strong whiff of marijuana. He sniffed at his clothes, wondering where the smell came from. The mystery was made known when he entered the kitchen and saw Emma sitting at the dining room table smoking a joint the size of a cigarette.

"Mrs. Harris! What you doing?!"

Emma looked up with a grin. "What's it look like? I'm getting my smoke on as young people say."

Koran laughed so hard tears ran from his eyes. "Ah man! You something else Mrs. Harris. Now I see why you always keep a smile on your face. You be toasted."

"Ain't nothing wrong with smoking a little marijuana. I told Jahad the same thing. Besides, it's good for my eyes. Helps me see better."

"I bet it does. I'll be back tomorrow around one o clock." He walked around the table and kissed her on the cheek. "I'll bring you something for your eyes too. You'll have Superman vision."

"Hold on baby, take this key. I'll probably be at church," she said and handed Koran a silver key on a heart shaped key ring. "And listen, baby. If you're gonna be in them streets, then you have to play by the same rules the street play by. You can't chance nothing or put nothing past nobody. Remember that, baby."

He nodded, lodging the information in his mind. Don't chance nothing or put nothing past nobody. In his situation he couldn't afford to do neither or it could cost him his life.

After leaving Emma's, he dropped the suitcase off at his apartment, then called a cab since Serenity had his truck. He needed to scout for some stash houses and cruising in a cab was a low key way of doing it. Unlike Jahad who always used apartment buildings, he would use brownstones. From experience, he knew with apartments, there was always a chance the super would come snooping around when no one was home. Something he and Jahad had to stop their own super from doing when their apartment had been remodeled.

For nearly three hours, the cab driver chauffeured him around the South Bronx until he located four vacant brownstones. Still in the cab, he called Valentino to handle the paperwork giving him four of his ex-girlfriends names as host to rent the brownstone. The only thing left to do was have them furnished which would be done over the next couple of days.

By the time he made it home it was going on eight o clock. A sharp, tangy aroma smelling of steak and beans smacked him in the face when he entered his apartment. His nose led him to the kitchen where Janet stood over the stove dropping diced shrimp into a pot of what looked like gumbo. Serenity sat at the dining table, cradling the phone with her shoulder while chopping up a green pepper. Both women sported mirco cornrolls. Serenity's idea, Koran thought. The style suited them perfectly, showing off their heart shaped faces.

"What you whipping up Janet?" he asked, giving Serenity a wet kiss on the lips.

Janet turned from the stove with a smile bright enough to blind him. "Hi Koran!" She wiped her hands on a towel, then gave him a quick peck on the lips under Serenity watchful eyes. "I'm making Shrimp Asopao just for you. It's a Puerto Rican dish my father taught me how to cook. I think you'll like it." She winked turning back to the stove.

Koran blushed and Serenity shot him a warning scowl before she spoke into the phone. "Koran just walked in cutie… alright alright. Here he is." She looked up at Koran, the scowl still on her face. "Jamel wants to talk to you. And we need to talk when you get off the phone," she said briskly.

He gave her an innocent grin and grabbed the phone. "What up, Kay? You being good?"

"Ka-wan Kawan!" Jamel shouted happily.

"Yeah, Kay, it's Koran. How you feeling the country?"

"I come home, Ka-wan. Bug bite me. I come home."

The sadness in Jamels' voice broke Koran's heart. "You don't like Nana, Kay?"

"Nana like. Bug no like and bad doggie. Kay home!"

A second later, Michelle picked up the phone. "Koran this boy is a mess. He gets bit by one little mosquito now he won't go outside. Every time we try to take him out he curses us out like he's grown. Who taught him how to curse like that? You know that ain't right. I washed his mouth out about ten times already. Then there's my poor poodle. Either he's chasing her with that plastic bat of his or she's chasing him. I tell you, it's a job putting up with him. Dej'a is the only one he'll halfway listen to."

Koran laughed. "I'll send Sin to come pick him up this weekend. He said he don't like it down there anyway." Until the beef was over Jamel could stay with Emma. She'd like nothing better.

"You'll do no such thing!" Michelle snapped. "My grandbaby won't be going nowhere until he gets use to it down here. I don't care how many times he tells you he doesn't like it. He's gonna learn to like it!"

"I'm saying, Ma. You already got Dej'a, you gon…"

"What are you saying! Yes, I have Dej'a and she's staying for the summer. Janet and I had a long talk about it. She's coming to stay with me too. So I have Dej'a and Jamel and they're both staying for the summer. Now, what were you saying?"

"Nothing, Ma."

"That's what I thought. Now you listen to me. Tomorrow when you take Janet to see Jahad, you make sure that boy acts like he has some sense, you hear me? That girl's been through enough already. Don't let him hurt her again. Tell him if he does I'm coming up there to knock some sense into him."

"I'll tell him Ma. This whole thing is crazy though, right?"

"It's not crazy. Everything happens for a reason, Koran. Maybe all that's happened will make Jahad change his life, at least I hope so. And you, you know better. What got into you? You turned down a scholarship to one of the best…"

"C'mon Ma, not now." Koran cut her off and closed his eyes. With all that was going on with the M.G's he knew he had made a mistake by ever getting involved. A mistake that was too late to change. And he wasn't in the mood to have it rubbed in his face.

"Koran Copeland! You better watch how you talk to me! I'll still beat your ass," said Michelle, furious. She ranted for a full two minutes loud enough so that Serenity and Janet could hear her while Koran held the phone away from his ear.

"You hear me!"

Koran rolled his eyes as he placed the phone back to his ear. "Yeah, Ma. I hear you. I'm sorry."

"Um huh, you better be sorry. Now, here's that bad butt boy of yours. He's standing here with his arms folded over his chest, looking like he's ready to jump on me. I love you."

"Love you too, Ma," he smiled, shaking his head. His mother was a trip.

"Ka-wan Gan Ma mean. I come home," Jamel said as soon as Michelle passed him the phone.

Koran knew his little face was probably balled up. "Give her a chance Kay. Tell her to take you out for ice cream."

"No ice cream! Fuck ice cream! Kay home!" Jamel cried.

"Kay, what I tell you..." Koran paused when he heard a scuffle with the phone.

"Well, that ends that conversation," Michelle cut in after she snatched the phone out of Jamel's hand. "By the time he gets back to New York he's gonna like the taste of soap."

"Don't be too hard on him, Ma. He's homesick."

"He'll be soap sick before too long," she said chuckling.

"Ma, don't..."

"Don't what? This boy is too fresh and needs to be taught some manners. Now here's Dej'a."

"Hi Uncle Koran," Dej'a said with a smile in her voice.

Koran laughed. "Go head with that uncle stuff, Dej'a. Makes me feel old. So you spoke to your Moms, huh?"

"Yes, I spoke to Mommy. She's coming to stay with Nana for the summer. Nana said she's gonna try to talk Mommy into moving in with her for good. I think I'll be able to persuade her. I wanna talk to my Daddy too."

"Don't worry. I guarantee he'll call you tomorrow," Koran said, wondering how Serenity would feel about Janet and Dej'a moving down south. For seven years she had been Dej'a's mother, now Dej'a was about to be snatched from her life. "So how you feeling the south?"

"I love it down here. It's not so crowded and everybody is so nice. Nana's the best too. She's teaching me how to cook soul food. I can make cornbread from scratch."

"So next time I see you, you gonna cook for me right?"

"You bet. Nana said when Mommy gets here I can cook the whole meal. I'm thinking fried chicken, cabbage, mash potato's, string beans, fresh baked rolls and a chocolate cake for dessert. Then, when my Daddy gets out the hospital, I'm going to cook for him too," she said, bubbling with happiness.

"Go head with your bad self. Dej'a do me a favor. Try to keep Kay outta trouble. Mom is putting mad pressure on him."

"I know, but he keeps cussing everybody out. I keep telling him to watch his mouth. He's so stubborn though. I can hear him in the bathroom now cursing Nana out. He just won't listen Koran."

"Yeah, I know," he said, feeling sorry for Jamel. It wasn't his fault. The little guy was homesick. "You wanna speak to you Moms before I hang up?"

"Yes. I wanna wish her luck. She's going to see my Daddy tomorrow. You think they'll get back together?" she asked hopefully. "When I asked her, she said they had some problems that needed to be worked out."

"I can't say Dej'a, but Uncle Koran will try to work his magic, a'ight?"

Dej'a giggled. "Alright Uncle Koran. Love you."

"Love you too pretty lady." Koran smiled as he passed the phone to Janet. "Your baby girl wants to speak to you."

Serenity grabbed his hand, no sooner than Janet took the phone and led him to the living room. The sofa and loveseat were covered from one end to the other with large shopping bags from Macy's, Saks, and Apollo. Serenity cleared the bags off the sofa then motioned for him to sit down.

"What up, Sin?" he asked as she sat beside him. "And why you giving me the screw face all crazy for?"

"Because you're acting too friendly with my sister and I'm telling you to stop!" She kept her voice low, but it was laced with anger.

"Every time you get around her you get that stupid, silly grin on your face like a lovesick puppy."

"What the hell you trying say?"

"Stop playing my sister so close. She's stuck on Jahad and you look so much like him that it's messing with her mind. It's not helping that you're being so friendly either. I see how she looks at you. It's not an innocent look either."

Koran's temper flared. "You think I wanna fuck your sister? You gotta be joking. Are you comparing me to that nigga Trouble or some other bum ass niggas you use to fuck with?"

"No, but…"

"But what!?" he barked inches from her face. "Janet is my fucking brother's baby mother, so I look at her like family, and you coming at me with this bullshit! You got me fucked up for real!" he said angrily as he jumped up.

Serenity reached for his hand as he stood. "Koran I…"

"I ain't trying to hear shit you gotta say!" he spat storming off to his bedroom murmuring curses under his breath. He couldn't believe she would question his loyalty about something as crazy as trying to sleep with her sister. If she could think that, then she really didn't know him at all. It also made him question how well he knew her. Serenity came in a few minutes later, while he sat on the edge of the bed rolling a blunt. He glanced up, rolled his eyes, then went back to twisting up his blunt. Well, at least the best he could with one hand.

"A yo, Sin, whatever you gotta say, save it. I ain't tryin to…"

"Boo, I'm sorry," she interrupted crossing the room to him. Before he could speak, she kissed him softly, her hands circling his waist. "I got kind of jealous seeing how you two flirted. Janet is so pretty and the thought of you being with any woman besides me drives me mad. I mean, I've never felt these type of feelings before. No one has brought them out of me the way you do."

Koran bit the inside of his cheek to keep from smiling. "Stop trying to gas me up yo."

"I'm serious Koran." She looked deep into his eyes. "But I should have enough trust in you to know you wouldn't do something like that, so I apologize."

"Yeah, you should trust me. And yeah, Janet is pretty, but to me you're prettier. Now about your apology. The only way I'll accept it is you gotta show me just how sorry you are," he said with a sly grin.

"You want me to show you?" She ran a hand over his crotch. "How about I kiss it and make it better?"

"That'll work as long as you don't bite it."

She slipped her hand inside his jeans just as Janet opened the bedroom door. "There you are, Dej'a wanted... oh sorry." Janet giggled, closing the door. "Dej'a wanted to speak to you, Sin. I'll tell her you have your hands full at the moment, " she called out laughing.

Serenity was flushed with embarrassment. "Damn! She messed up the mood."

"Yeah, she did. It's cool though. You can apologize later on tonight. You know Dej'a is…"

"Staying with your mother," she finished for him, her eyes welling up with tears. "She told me she doesn't want to come back Koran. She's gone!" she said, sobbing on his shoulder.

"Whoa, Sin. C'mon, you know that ain't true."

"But she'll be way down there in North Carolina and I'll be here. I'll never get to see her."

"How bout we move there?" The words came out before he realized what he had said.

Serenity looked up at him wiping her eyes. "You for real?"

"Yeah, I guess I am. I'll probably keep this apartment so I'll have somewhere to come when I get homesick. But yeah, we can do that."

"Thank you! Thank you! Thank you!" she squealed, covering his face with kisses.

"You can do all that tonight. Now c'mon before I change my mind and stretch you out right now."

She grabbed his arm before he could stand. "Wait a minute. Did you do what we spoke about yet?"

"What's that?"

"You know, about Hector."

"Nah, not yet. I ain't feeling getting you mixed in this. We dealing with some dangerous ass dudes on both sides. I don't wanna chance it back firing in our faces."

Serenity blew out a frustrated breath. "We talked about this already Koran. I know exactly what I'm getting into. This…"

"Do you really?"

"Yes, I do. Stop cutting me off too, and listen. This…"

"If I don't, what?" Koran smiled as she covered his mouth with her hand.

"Stop it! You wanna play when there's someone trying to kill you. Now shut up and listen!"

Koran held up his hands, grinning. "A'ight, Sin. Damn."

She glared at him a moment before continuing. "This is the best way period and you know it. I can't approach Hector directly. He'll probably know it's a set up. I have to make him come to me."

"I never said it wasn't a good plan. I'm saying I don't like putting you in danger."

"Putting me in danger? I've been in danger ever since I started messing with you. I'm not about to leave you though, so we have to do something to eliminate the danger."

Koran nodded, hating to admit that she was right. Her plan was for him to inform the Heads that he found out through someone in his projects that she was Hector's sister. Serenity supposedly didn't know that he knew. He was to go on to say that he checked into it and found out that Serenity and Hector weren't close, but he still planned on killing her just for being Hectors' sister. If one of the Heads was the snake, then the assumption was Hector would soon contact Serenity in hopes of using her to set Koran up. Four or five days after he passed this information off, if Hector didn't contact her, then Koran would focus on the Heads lieutenants and tell the Heads what he knew. Although he would still be taking a chance, the odds would be in his favor.

If Hector did contact Serenity, Koran hoped to find out who supplied the information. If not, he would kill Hector and still know one of the Heads were behind the plot. One thing was for sure, and it was something that had been on his mind since Emma told him not to chance nothing. He wasn't about to waste time trying to figure out which Head or lieutenant was trying to kill them. If Serenity's plan didn't work, then he would kill the Heads and their lieutenants to eliminate the threat. Whatever guilt he felt afterwards he would deal with it. All he knew is that he would kill a million people if he had to if it meant protecting his family.

U. E. Wynn

Chapter Twenty Four

Koran devoted the next three days to handling his duties as one of the Head M.G.'s. The first two he spent transferring the money and drugs from Emma's apartment to the four stash houses. It was a job that took Serenity's help. He cleared everything out except for one army duffle bag which he planned to keep for himself. The Heads still didn't know the whereabouts of the stash houses and until he found out who was trying to kill them, he wanted to keep it that way. So far no one had asked about it so he didn't volunteer the information.

The third day, which was on Friday when the drugs were passed down and the money was collected, he spent most of the day in traffic. First, he went to Harlem, where he parked his Range Rover in front of Princes' brownstone. He traded the Range out for a Plymouth Voyager, equipped with a large hydraulic powered stash compartment stuffed with drugs.

From Harlem, he drove the minivan back to the Bronx, where he met Joey who won the coin toss. They met up to make a pass off at a Jamaican restaurant on Jackson Avenue. After meeting Joey, he switched vehicles again for a 1938 Pontiac Bonneville. He then drove straight to Joe's Moving Company and dropped the money off so it could be counted.

Feeling like he was about to starve, he returned to the same restaurant he met Joey at and ordered curry chicken, peas and rice, coco bread, and an apple juice to wash it all down. After grubbing, he took a cab back to Harlem to pick up his truck. This was the first and last time he would hand deliver or have any dealings with drugs period.

Once he and Serenity moved to North Carolina he was college bound. Serenity could be the lawyer, his mind was set on business. With millions to work with there was no limit to what he could build. It would be a legal enterprise worth billions.

When Koran made it back to the Bronx thinking his day was almost over, he remembered the stash in Emma's apartment which called for another trip to meet Joey. This added to the trip back to Joe's to pick up the money, then another trip to the stash house.

Finally, at seven o'clock that evening, he made it home tired but happy that he wouldn't have to put up with Jahad's job no more after this week. When he walked in Serenity was in the living room staring at the wall, a pensive expression on her face. Koran knew right away, Hector had contacted her.

"What he say?" he asked without bothering to confirm his thoughts.

Serenity gave him an ominous look. "He wants to meet you."

"What?"

"My mother called me right after you left this morning. My girlfriend Veronica, you probably remember her from Junior High, she was at your apartment wanting to see me."

"Yeah, I remember shorty. She was part of your little clique." Koran pictured the pretty Puerto Rican he had swung a few episodes with in high school. Serenity nodded. "But listen, I get to my mother's expecting a reunion, instead she gives me a phone number telling me Hector said to call him immediately because my life was in danger. Like he really gives a damn." She rolled her eyes. "When I called he told me everything about you and the Heads. That you're supposed to kill me because you found out I was his sister. I played…"

"Where's the shit about him wanting to meet me come in at?" Koran asked, impatiently.

"I'm getting there!" Serenity snapped back. "After he said that, he told me to tell you that he really wasn't your enemy. I asked him what he meant, but he said it was best for you and him to meet. He said you name a place and he'd be there."

Caught off guard, Koran sat down and rubbed a hand over his face. This was the last thing he expected. He just knew Hector would take the bait and try and use Serenity to get to him. Then again, this could be just that.

"You know what this means, right?" Serenity asked, breaking into his thoughts. "It's one of the Heads."

"Yeah, it's good to know, but fucked up just the same. I'm trying to figure out what's up with Hector. What the hell he mean he ain't my enemy?"

"Don't trust him Koran!"

"C'mon Sin, you think I just fell off a banana boat? Call him back. If he's serious about meeting me, he'll come here. If not, I'll have to set up something else. Just in case I do get him here, start packing our shit. I won't rest with him knowing where we rest our Heads at. That's if I don't body him."

Serenity nodded and dialed Hector's number. Once it started ringing, she passed it to Koran.

"Hello?" Hector answered on the second ring.

"Yeah, Hector, this Koran. What up with you wanting to meet me? You know like I know that could be a death sentence for one of us."

"Whether you believe it or not, it's in your best interest that we meet. Trust me."

Koran laughed mockingly. "Trust you? You got jokes, huh? And what's this shit about me killing Sin? You must be getting your information from a crackhead."

"No. My information comes from someone who wants you and Jahad dead."

"And you're coming to my rescue? Yeah, right. Save the bullshit for somebody else."

Hector exhaled a frustrated breath. "I'll level with you. That was my people who tried to kill you and Jahad on story Ave, but my information had to come from someone in your circle. He's too well informed not to be. And truthfully, he's not only a serious threat to you. I feel he may be a serious threat to me also. That's my reason for wanting to meet with you."

"Let me see if I understand this right. You wanna call a truce. You for real?"

"Yes, whoever this person is, he's crazy as hell, but smart. So think about it. It would be best for both of us if we knew his identity."

Koran stayed quiet a moment, his mind working, trying to decide how to proceed. Then something from 'The 48 Laws of Power' struck him. Selective honestly.

"Since you say you're keeping it hands up with me, I'll keep it hands up with you. Only four people had that information to give you, so I half ass believe you. This is how it's going down though. If you wanna meet it's gonna be here at my crib. You can bring two of your people. They stay outside in the hallway while we meet though."

"Now you're being the comedian. You think I'm…"

"Breathe easy Duke and listen," Koran cut in. "I'm bringing you to my crib where I rest my head at. If I body you, then I gotta body your men and most likely that's gonna draw too much damn attention. How can I explain that to Jake?"

"So you're asking me to walk into the lion's den?"

"Listen man, let's cut through the bullshit. There's a muthafucka close to me and my brother trying to kill us. This same nigga will probably body your ass too after he get's us. So it's only common sense that we dead our beef until we find out who this bastard is. After that we can go back at it if you want."

"Now I'm about to give this phone back to Sin so you can tell her where to pick you up from. She'll escort you here and back so you'll have a safe pass." Koran paused. "On a show of good faith, I've been expecting your call. I deliberately fed that information to whoever gave it to you thinking you would try to use Sin to set me up. My plan was to get the information outta you, then body your ass. Your willingness to help even though I know you ain't doing it for me changes things. You never know. This could be the turning point in our beef."

Hector chuckled. "Maybe. And since you put it in plain English, I believe you."

After Hector gave Serenity his information she hung up, grinning. "Damn you slick baby. He went for it."

"Went for what? I'm serious about not killing him here unless he makes me."

"You can't let that bastard live!" she shouted outraged. "He'll only end up trying to kill you when this other stuff is out the way!"

"I said I wasn't gonna kill him here. Before I leave New York that muthafucka gonna be dead! You think I forgot that he bodied my pops? This first meeting will open his trust. The second I'll open his chest!"

Chapter Twenty Five

Koran sat in the kitchen fumbling trying to open a Heineken with his cast hand when he heard the apartment door open. Despite his effort to stay calm his heart began to race. Here he was about to meet Jahad's nemesis. Not to kill him, but to his own disbelief, work with him. Jahad would probably flip when he found out. Placing his beer on the table, he grabbed his gun and held it against his leg just in case Hector tried something slick. There was no way in hell he would let Hector walk right into his apartment and kill him.

"I'm in here," he called out as Serenity and Hector walked passed the kitchen headed to the living room.

A second later, Hector entered the kitchen behind Serenity dressed in a white Arani silk suit with a black silk shirt opened to the middle of his chest exposing a large platinum diamond crusted cross. On his feet were a pair of black Salvatore dress shoes. Koran stared, taken back by the resemblance between the brother and sister. Both had the same exact haunted green eyes and high cheekbones. However, Hector favored Janet more with his sharp straight nose. His wavy black hair was like Serenity's and hung well past his shoulders. He wore his facial hair in a neatly trimmed five o'clock shadowed beard that added definition to his angler shaped face.

Hector sized Koran up with a slight smile, then his eyes lowered to the gun and narrowed suspiciously.

"Nah, Hector, it ain't like that," Koran said, reading his thoughts. "I'm just cautious."

"I understand, but I'm not here under any false pretenses. We both have a mutual enemy, so like you said, let's work together and eliminate our problem."

"You can sit down." Koran nodded towards the chair across from him. He sat the gun on the table beside his beer as Serenity walked around the table to stand beside him. "You say we have the same enemy, but how can you say that when he's trying to help you? Seems like a win-win situation to me."

"That's what I thought until I realized, *The Operator*' as he calls himself, is crazy. He thinks he's playing a chess match and we're the pawns. I'm serious. He also made it known that I could be next. Went so far as to prove it," Hector said bitterly.

"How?"

Hector explained the incident with Melody.

"Oh word!" Stunned, Karon sat back in his chair. Whichever Head was behind the plot, he had put a lot of planning into his twisted game. Why, was the question Koran still asked himself. "This chick, she couldn't tell you nothing about him? Give you a description at least?"

"The worthless bitch claimed she didn't know nothing," Hector spat venomously cutting his eye at Serenity. "Sort of reminds me of another worthless bitch I once knew."

Serenity shot Hector a look of pure hatred, then walked off with her hands bunched into fist. Koran followed her with his eyes without a clue of what was about to happen before turning his attention back to Hector.

"You told me only four people had the information we spoke of," Hector continued. "So it has to be one of the four, right?"

"Three... What you do to her?" he asked, changing the conversation to Serenity.

Hector looked confused until he realized who he was referring to. "Oh, my baby sister doesn't like my honesty. She asked about Janet and I told her the truth. If that puta would have stayed loyal to me, she'd still be alive. She chose Jahad over me and look what it got her."

Koran frowned. "Damn Hector, I thought I was cold hearted, but you the worst. That was your sister man."

"That puta never meant nothing to me." Hector waved his hand dismissively. "Back to what's important. The logical thing for you to do is to call whoever had the information and let me hear their voices. I'll never forget that voice... Never!"

Koran nodded and reached for his cell phone. At the same moment, Serenity entered the kitchen with a look of burning malice in her eyes. Koran was on the verge of asking her what was wrong when she stepped behind Hector and raised her orange box cutter. The words froze on his lips. Without saying a word she snatched Hector's head back by his wavy hair and slashed his throat repeatedly before stepping back. Hectors hands went immediately to his neck just as a stream of warm blood skeeted across the table directly into

Korans face.

"Goddamn, Sin! What you do that stupid shit for?" he roared pushing away from the table. Hector's pitiful eyes locked with Koran's while he tried to stop the blood from gushing, but it was obvious he only had a few more seconds to live. Finally, his life force bled out and his head hit the table with a loud thud.

"I hope you know what the fuck you just did." Koran's voice was deadly calm as he glared at Serenity. "I was so fucking close to finding out who was on the bullshit, then you come along and fuck it up."

"Fuck him!" she yelled spitting on the back of Hector's head. "He killed my damn father and shot my sister. Fuck him!" She turned to walk off, but Koran quickly circled the table and grabbed her by the arm.

"Bring your ass back here!" He roughly turned her around. "I don't give a fuck what he did, you coulda waited. He killed my damn father too, but did I cut his damn throat? Now I got to kill innocent niggas on my own fucking team because of this stupid shit you just did. Did he bring anybody with him?"

His words seemed to sober her up. "Koran, I'm sorry. I…"

"I don't want to hear that sorry shit! Did he bring anyone with him?"

"Two guys. One stayed by the elevator, the other by the staircase door."

Koran muttered a curse under his breath. "Go turn the stereo on and play some music." He looked her up and down forming a strategy. "Take them jeans off too, and put on one of my T-shirts, nothing else. Then tell them two dudes Hector wants to seem them."

"Koran, I…"

"I ain't trying to hear that shit. Now go!"

Silently, Serenity walked off while Koran grabbed his gun off the table. A few minutes later *Dreams, 'Shorty Is a Ten'* came booming from the stereo speakers. He waited by the kitchen entrance, gun by his side, until he saw light spill into the hallway. As the shadows drew closer he took a deep breath, then bent the corner with his gun extended in his left hand. Serenity walked a few steps in front of the two men, one black, the other Puerto Rican. Their eyes were focused on how Serenity's ass jiggled beneath the thin t-shirt. Catching sight of Koran, neither had time to blink before he shot them both in the head from only two yards away. As the two men fell Serenity covered her ears and screamed.

"Shut the fuck up Sin!" Kora shouted in her face. "This is your damn fault! Pull yourself together and clean this shit up. You can start in the kitchen." He turned abruptly and walked off toward the bathroom mumbling curses while Serenity stared after him in shock.

Koran locked himself in the bathroom after taking a quick shower. Serenity had him so mad that at the moment he couldn't stand to be around her. Never once had he ever hit a woman. Never had the urge to. But the way he felt right now made him want to beat the shit out of Serenity. This led to another thought. She had to leave. As soon as he figured out what to do with the three bodies, he was sending her back down south. Tonight!

He was deep in thought an hour later when there was a soft knock at the door. Serenity stood before him when he opened it, sweaty with blood stains on his t-shirt. Her eyes held an empty hollowness that made him want to wrap her in his arms. Instead, he covered his emotions with a cold stare.

"The kitchen and hallway are as clean as I can get them. Koran I..."

"Go take a shower Sin. Get all our bloody clothes together too. Mine is on the bathroom floor. We'll talk about this shit later," he said, then walked into the bedroom before she could respond.

"Forgive me baby," she said quietly to his back.

Koran sat on the edge of the bed with her words ringing in his ears. How could he not forgive her when he understood her rage? Tupac said it best: revenge is the sweetest joy next to getting pussy. Still, it didn't change the fact that she fucked up.

A half hour later she returned wrapped in a large towel holding a large black trash bag. After she dressed, she sat beside Koran and took hold of his hand. For a while they sat without speaking. Koran was staring at the wall while Serenitys' eyes were glued to his face.

"You fucked up Sin," Koran said after a while without looking at her. "You fucked up big time, but I forgive you. I want you outta here, though. Take my truck down south tonight. If something happens to me, I have some dough stashed in Mrs. Harris's apartment. Get it and make sure Kay wants for nothing."

"I'm not leaving!" Serenity stood and backed away from him.

"Yes the fuck you are! This shit is about to get real dangerous and you'll fuck around and get me bodied with that crazy shit you on."

"Please Koran, I…"

"Please my ass! You getting the fuck outta here." He grabbed her by the arm while she tried her best to pull away and dragged her to the front door. "Now leave!"

"Koran don't do this! Please baby, don't push me away!" she cried, clinging to him as he opened the door.

Koran shook his head. "You gotta go, Sin. When this shit is over I'll meet you down south. I promise. Now stop making this harder for me than it already is," he said, pushing her out the door.

Chapter Twenty Six

Right after Serenity left Koran called the Heads and told them to come to his apartment immediately. He called Sha' last with instructions to bring one of the largest suitcases he could find. To his surprise no questions were asked by none of them. Now all he had to do was think of a believable story. He didn't want to involve Serenity, but saw no way around it. He decided to tell parts of the truth and make up the rest. There was a knock at the door an hour later that drew him from his thoughts. When he looked through the peephole all four Heads along with their lieutenants could be seen pacing the hallway impatiently.

"What's up with this urgent shit?" Prince asked as soon as Koran opened the door. "We thought nigga's were trying to get at you."

"Just come in, you'll see." Koran stepped aside holding the door open.

Prince took two steps inside before he noticed the two bodies. "What the fuck!"

"Oh shit! What the hell happened?" Lord asked, looking over Prince's shoulder.

"Come in before somebody walks by and see this shit," Koran snapped before he walked off towards the living room leaving others to follow.

In the living room the Head's and their lieutenants filled the sofa, loveseat, and recliner. Sha' and Crook stayed posted by the doorway with three large brown suitcases. All attention was focused on Koran as they waited for him to speak from where he stood near the window.

"Check it though, the two dudes in the hallway are Hector's people. Hector…"

"What!" Prince interrupted. "How in the hell them niggas end up here?"

"Chill Prince, let me finish. Hector is dead in the kitchen. That's why I called you niggas so y'all can help me get these damn bodies outta here."

The room grew quiet as everyone digested the information, then Star broke the silence. "How in the hell you manage that? Jah been trying to get his ass for years. What he just walked into your hands?"

"Yeah, something like that. I came up with a scheme using Sin. The stupid muthafucka went for it."

Star smirked. "What kind of scheme?"

"That ain't important right now. Let's get these bodies outta here, then I'll put y'all on. You see I ain't in no shape to do this shit by myself."

"Where that bitch Sin at?" Star asked intent on keeping the questions coming.

Koran locked eyes with him before answering. "I got Sin, so don't stress that. What we need to be stressing is these bodies like I said. I'll answer your questions when that's done."

"He's right," said Lord. "Let's get this shit cleaned up first. We'll holla later about this, because this changes a lot of shit."

They all nodded and set off to work. All except for Star who lagged behind until the living room was cleared.

"A yo, I ain't feeling this shit Koran, word up. What you keep moving dolo for? You could have told us what was poppin' off. That's some bullshit with you trying to impress muthafucka's. You won't be satisfied until that shit gets you killed."

"Whatever Star," Koran turned to walk off, but Star snatched him around by his shoulder.

"You think you can't get fucked up nigga?"

"And who the fuck gonna do it, huh? You? Now get the fuck off me!" Koran growled, his face contorted in a snarl as he walked off.

Sha' and Crook was in the process of breaking Hectors legs when Koran entered the kitchen. Lord was stripping the diamond rings off his fingers and sticking them in his pocket. Although Hector had only been dead a little over an hour, rigor mortis had already begun to set in.

"C'mon Lord, stop bullshitting and snap the niggas arms so we can stuff his ass in the suitcase," Sha' said as he grunted while twisting Hector's right leg so that it pressed down flatly against his chest.

Koran laughed, dragging the suitcase beside Hector's body. He shook his head, grinning as Lord pulled the last ring from his fingers. "You Brooklyn nigga's don't miss shit."

Lord grinned up at Koran as he removed Hector's platinum chain. "He won't be needing this shit where he's going. Let me check his pockets too before we zip his ass up. I betcha he's holding a few thousand." Sure enough, he dug in Hector's pockets and came out with two thick rolls of money. "Bingo! Ain't nothing like free money. A yo check them niggas pockets too!" he called out to the hallway.

An hour an a half later all three bodies were tightly stuffed inside the suitcases. The lieutenants left to dispose of them in the body junkyard better known as the Hudson River. The Heads filed back into the living room to hear how Koran managed to lure Hector to his apartment.

Koran stood in the middle of the room and took a deep breath. He let his words spill out telling the half truth he had come up with. "Hector somehow found out I was fucking Sin and tried to send a message to her through this Puerto Rican chick we used to go to Junior high with. It was just my luck I used to fuck the chick back in the day. So she delivered the message to me and gave me his number."

"What was the message?" Star and Sha' asked at the same time.

"That Sin needed to get at him right away. About what she ain't say. Anyway, come to find out Sin don't fuck with Hector like that for real. She thinks he had something to do with her sister's death. So she was all for setting his ass up. Plus, she thinks I'ma marry her. Now this is where the ill shit comes in at," Koran said warming up to his lies. "Sin told Hector I had mad dough stashed in the crib. Said it was so much that she couldn't tote it all by herself. She came up with this shit herself figuring Hector would come personally just to make sure nobody fucked with the money. That shit worked, Son! When they got here I handled my business."

Lord shook his head in wonder. "That's some wild shit, word up."

"What's up with Sin?" Star asked. "Maybe we should wrap her ass up in a suitcase too. I ain't feeling her being mixed up in this shit. Bitches talk too much."

"I thought about that too. I was gonna body her tonight, but I'ma chill and wait until we leave. I'm thinking about taking her to Vegas and leaving her planted in the desert. I wanna beat the pussy up a few more times before I dead her ass," he said with a smile, even though his heart pounded against his chest. Silently, he prayed they would accept his story and didn't suggest that he kill Serenity tonight. If so, he would kill them all right then and there.

"Since Hector is dead I guess we can cancel the shit we had for his spots," Princes said, reaching for the half of blunt Koran had left in the ashtray.

"Nah, let's stick to the plan," Sha' replied glancing at Koran. "Hector is dead, but his people are still in place. Somebody in his clique is bound to step up."

"Yeah," Koran added without caring what they did. All he cared about was that they were off the subject of Serenity.

After the Heads left, Koran sat in the living room smoking blunt after blunt of Cush mixed with Purple Haze. Tony Yayo's album *Thoughts Of A Predicate Felon'* played on the stereo while his thoughts were on how to stay alive without becoming a felon. So far he had a pretty good track record. His body count was well into the teens, his money was right and he had faced death on numerous occasion with only a few scratches. How long would his luck last though, he wondered. A jail cell or head shot could become reality at any time.

As high as he was, his thoughts skipped around like a scratched CD taking him back to the conversation he had earlier with Hector. Another five minutes and he would have known which Head he had to kill. Now he was left with no choice. They all had to die. He wondered how Sha' would feel if he ever found out, then quickly dismissed the thoughts. Sha' needed to be somewhere else when he did it. Koran dozed off with those thought lingering in his mind.

Hours later, around three o'clock that morning, a sound at the apartment door woke him. Alarmed, he snatched his gun off the coffee table thinking one of the Heads had returned to kill him. He entered the hallway cautiously placing his back against the wall in case whoever it was shot through the door. As he drew closer he noticed hat the door was slightly ajar, held together only by the chain lock. The tension automatically seeped from his body when he knelt to peek through the crack and saw the pink and white air max sneakers. Serenity. She stood before him looking like a sad puppy when he opened the door her eyes bloodshot with tear stains on her cheeks.

"Don't get mad, but I'm not leaving unless you come with me," she said looking up at him through pleading eyes. "Don't try to make me leave either. I'll only cause more problems."

Koran sighed in resignation as she walked into his arms. "C'mon in man. And since you wanna be hard headed, we got a lot to talk about."

He secured the door, then led her to the living room and plucked a blunt roach from the ashtray. He fired it up before speaking.

"Before you commit yourself to anything let me tell you what's going on and what's about to pop off. Tonight after you left I gave the Heads a bogus ass story about how I got Hector here. I had to put you in it though. Now they gonna make sure I body you. If I don't, they will. That's if I ain't able to body them first. With that to stress about, I gotta find a way to kill them without Sha' finding out. Before any of that goes down I got a job at the Wedge to do. My chances of coming back are 50/50 being as though I don't know if one of the Heads will have a nigga there waiting on me. If I do make it back, I gotta hit the Heads the same nights. The tricky part will be getting them together without Sha' knowing. Now if I can accomplish all this and still be breathing, we should be good. Now, after hearing all this, you sure you don't wanna bounce?"

"If they kill you, then they better kill me too," Serenity answered with a straight face.

"What about Kay? If something happens to me, you gotta hold him down."

"Jamel has your mother to hold him down if something happens to us."

"A'ight. But until we leave you keep your ass right here in this apartment. Don't even answer the phone. Got me?"

"I got you. Koran, I messed things up and I'm sorry. But I'm not sorry I killed Hector. He..."

Koran put a finger to her lips. "Don't even think about it. In fact, come give me some of what I need so I can take your mind off it."

"I'll be happy to," she said, smiling as she reached for his zipper.

Chapter Twenty Seven

The next morning Jahad sat propped up in bed watching soap operas when Koran entered his room. Over the past couple of days his color had returned and he looked like he had picked up a few pounds. Emma's cooking was doing the trick. Twice a day she snuck in food for him in her large purse and made sure he ate every bit of it.

"I know you ain't in here watching no damn *Days Of Our Lives*," Koran said, laughing. He pulled a chair up beside the bed shaking his head. "Wait until I tell niggas this."

"You better not nigga. I'll fuck you up when I get outta here." He grinned clicking the television off. "What's up?"

Koran flashed a sly grin. "Guess who got sent to hell last night?"

"You got that bastard!"

"Nah. Sin bodied his ass." Koran related what happen.

"Oh word! Shorty gangsta like that, Son? You need a chick like that on your team."

"Yeah, but she fucked up. I didn't get the info I needed from Hector. So you know what I gotta do," Koran said in a flat tone.

Jahad nodded. "That's the way it's gotta be. Just make sure you do it right."

"That's been on my mind like crazy too. I pretty much know how I wanna do it, I just gotta figure out how to get Sha' to be somewhere else though. I'd hate to body him too. If only I could tell him. It would make this shit a lot easier." Frustration showed all over Koran's face.

"Listen lil bruh, nothing we do is easy. That's what makes us who we are. Remember that."

When Koran came home later that afternoon Serenity was in the living room singing along to Destiny's Child, 'Cater To You'. So engrossed with her singing, she didn't notice him walk up behind her until he grabbed her butt. Startled, she spun around holding her chest, her right hand drew back to throw a punch.

Koran laughed. "What, you gonna do, hit me?"

"No. But stop sneaking up on me like that. You scared the hell outta me boy. You know I'm already paranoid." Serenity kissed him on the cheek, then turned the music down.

"I'm sorry sexy. I didn't mean to scare you. Hit that high note again, though."

Serenity arched her eyebrow smiling. "Maybe I'll make you hit a few high notes."

"I can't right now. I got work to do. When I get back we can have our own little concert though."

"What kind of work?"

"Got a little bit of this, little bit of that to do. I'll…"

"Don't give me that shit!" Serenity snapped. "We're in this together, remember."

Koran held up his hands up, grinning. "Well, pardon me, Ma. All I'm gonna do is sit and watch some people for a while."

"You're gonna kill somebody aren't you?"

"Something like that."

"Who? The Heads?"

"Nah. Some other niggas so we can establish our place back in a few spots."

"Why?"

"What's this, twenty fucking questions?" he asked getting annoyed.

"No," Serenity replied calmly. "But if we're leaving, what's the use in killing people over some spots you won't even be running? What you need to be doing is plotting on how we're gonna kill the Heads instead of some people who don't even post a threat."

Koran stared at her a moment, then smiled. She made a good point. What happened after Friday wouldn't be none of his concern. "Listen to you."

"Don't tease me boy," she said, trying not to smile. "So how will we do it?"

"We?"

"Yes, we. Me and you. Serenity and Koran."

"You don't even know how to use a rachet, talking about how we gonna do it."

Sin sucked her teeth. "Yes, I do."

Koran gave her a sly look, then took her hand. "C'mon."

He led her to the bedroom where he pulled a medium sized suitcase from his closet. Inside were all types of clean guns with the serial numbers scratched off. He took out a .25 automatic, checked to make sure it wasn't loaded, then gave it to Serenity.

"Show me that you know how to shoot it."

"Any bullets in it?" she asked, turning the small gun over in her hands.

"Nah, but show me how you would shoot it if it was loaded."

Serenity looked at him like he was crazy, then pointed the gun at the wall and pulled the trigger. "Like that silly."

"Nope. You didn't even cock back. How you gonna shoot it without a bullet in the chamber?"

He took the gun and slid the top half back before handing it back. "Now pull the trigger."

Sin lifted the gun and pointed it towards the wall again. This time when she pulled the trigger, the gun fired with a loud click. "Oh!" she said, surprised. "Do I have to do that every time I want to shoot it?"

"Nah. That's why it's called an automatic. All you gotta do is keep pulling the trigger. This little red button by the trigger is called the safety. When you push it in, it won't shoot. Push it out and you got action."

He went on to show her how to load the clip, cock, and aim. After several practices he felt she had it down pat.

"This is a small caliber gun so the best way to get the job done is up close and personal. A head shot or upper chest. A body shot will only piss a muthafucka off," he said just as his cell phone vibrated. "Yeah, what's up?"

"A yo Koran, this Crook. You seen, Sha'?" Crook asked sounding stressed.

"Nah. Why? What up?"

"Can't nobody find that nigga. None of his Shorty's seen him either. I called the Heads and they said they ain't seen him. He ain't even answering his cell phone."

Koran felt a cold sense of dread. "Maybe he's outta town or something. If he stops by here I'll get at you."

"Yeah, do that. One."

"One." Koran frowned hitting the end button.

"What's wrong?" Serenity asked, grabbing his hand.

"Sha'. Nobody seen him since yesterday and he ain't answering his phone. It may be nothing. I have enough going on with trying to figure out how to do what needs to be done with the Heads. I'll worry about Sha' some other time."

Koran was about to speak when his cell phone vibrated again. "Yeah, what up?"

"A yo some ill shit happened, Son," Prince said sounding out of breath.

Goosebumps broke out on Koran's arms. "What happened?"

"Some M.G's just found Sha's Beamer shot the fuck up on Linder Boulevard near the Pink Houses! Mad blood and shit was on the seats from what niggas tell me."

Koran went numb. Sha' had an assortment of cars, but favored his red 2006 745i B.M.W. "What the fuck is going on! First a muthafucka tries to kill me and Jah. Now Sha'. A yo, word to my moms, if…"

Serenity shook her head to make him conscience of his words.

"Yeah, some ill shit is poppin' off. What's bad is it could be coming from so many different angles. We made a lot of enemies over the years, so I'm saying stay on point."

"Oh, I'm sharp as a fucking ice pick right now, believe that!" Koran hung up fighting the urge to throw his phone.

Chapter Twenty Eight

Thursday rolled around and there was still no with no sign of Sha'. Although no body was found Koran knew he was dead. Especially after the second day had passed and he was still missing. He concluded that Sha' had learned the snake's identity and somehow the snake found out that Sha' knew, and killed him. The idea that all three Heads were in on it began to play on Korans' mind.

The first hits were attempted on him and Jahad, then Sha' get's murdered and they get rid of his body. However, no attempts were made on the other Heads. Prince said it could possibly be one of their many enemies they'd made over the years, which Koran thought was bullshit.

It wasn't possible for anybody to know the M.G's were their enemies? No, Koran thought it had nothing to do with enemies from their past. Before Sha' came up missing he dreaded the thought of killing the Heads. Now he couldn't wait until tomorrow so he could end it all.

Later that afternoon after Koran stopped by the hospital to see Jahad, he drove to Harlem for a meeting to go over the assault plans. When the meeting broke up, he pulled the Heads away from their lieutenants and fed them the bait that would lead to their deaths. Since Sha' was dead, he weaved him into the scheme to make the bait more enticing.

"I don't really wanna speak on it right now because I might be wrong," he said as they all stood in Princes' foyer. "But I think Hector's people might've had something to do with what happened to Sha'."

"How?" Star asked, looking at Lord and Prince. "That muthafucka dead."

"I'm not talking about Hector. I'm saying it could be one of his lieutenants. One of the niggas we gotta merk tomorrow. But like I said, I ain't sure. You remember a while back when Sha' said something about some niggas moving weight around this way? Well the nigga I'm talking about is Hector's lieutenant and he's far from Brownsville. I found this out from Valentino."

"Tomorrow I'ma snatch his ass up. That's if he don't make me kill him. I'll call y'all if I get him. If not, I'll meet y'all back here. Y'all with that?"

The Heads nodded unaware that tomorrow would be their last day breathing.

Before returning home Koran stopped by Joe's Moving Company to see Joey, who was now the new manager. Although Sha' was dead, Koran still planned to cover his tracks. Joey and Kwan were the only two people he knew who could help. Joey was sitting at Jahad's desk when Koran walked in, his forehead wrinkled in concentration as he went through the stack of shipping addresses. He wore a pair of Kenneth Cole bifocals giving him the appearance of a high school student. He had a smooth dark chocolate baby face and razor sharp edge up spinning with waves.

"What's good, Jay?" Koran asked, dropping down on the brown leather loveseat across from the desk.

Joey pushed the papers aside and took off his glasses. "This shit is a headache Koran. I don't see how Jah put up with it all these damn years. I'll be glad when he gets his ass out the hospital so he can come get this shit."

Koran laughed. "Nah, you better get used to it. Joe's is about to be you and Kwan's spot."

Joey screwed up his face. "What the hell you talking about Koran?"

"Before I say anything, I need you to know that this shit stays between us."

"C'mon nigga, look who you talking to."

"I'm serious Joe. Me and Jah's life might depend on it."

Joey studied Koran for a moment and took note of the seriousness surrounding him. "I don't know what the hell you about to tell me, but you of all people should know it won't go no further than this room."

"No doubt. I'ma give you the whole story so you'll know how serious this shit is."

Koran started from the incident in Bronxdale ending with his assumption of what happened to Sha'.

"Why the fuck didn't he tell me sooner!" Joey shouted angrily. "After all the shit me and Jah been through. All the shit he did for my fam and he didn't even tell me! I'ma curse his ass out when I see him."

"It wasn't like that Joey," Koran said, hoping to save Jahad from getting cursed out. "This is what I need from you, though. Tomorrow night around twelve I need for you and Kwan to go up on the roof of my building and clean up my mess. Take what you see up there to the grave."

"You gonna body the Heads right?" Joey asked, his expression unreadable.

Koran nodded, holding Joey's eyes.

"What up, though? You need some help? Shit, a threat to you or Jah is a threat to me and Kwan. Before the M.G's were formed, it was Jah, so he'll always come first. Just like we always came first when it came to outsiders. So what's up?"

"Nah, Joey. I got'em. I'ma need you and Kwan to be with the other M.G's when it goes down so it won't look funny. And whatever you find make it disappear feel me?"

"Say no more. It'll get done."

"Good. Now check this." Koran gave him the key to the apartment in Rosedale. "Swing by Rosedale tomorrow and pick up that dough. That's a going away present for you and Kwan from Jah."

Joey looked down at the key in his hand and what it represented. After this shit was over, Jah and Koran would be leaving. He looked up at Koran and nodded.

"That's love right there."

"True dat," said Koran.

Chapter Twenty Nine

On the way home after making a quick stop by a Chinese restaurant, Koran wondered if the Heads took the bait. His story was believable enough. Then again, he knew he wasn't dealing with no dummies, which led to another thought. If they were on to his scheme could he kill all three before one got him. He had full confidence in his abilities, but at the same time he knew what he was dealing with Star, Prince, and Lord. They were all trained killers like himself. Maybe not as good, but killers just the same. If only his right arm wasn't still in a cast he could kill all three with ease.

Then Serenity came to mind. She had already killed once. She could be his right arm if she was up to it. She was in the kitchen when he walked in packing dishes. She wore one of his tee-shirts and nothing else. He grew hard instantly watching how she bent over exposing her hairy bush every time she grabbed a pot from under the sink. She was unaware that she was tempting him to enter her from behind.

Business before pleasure, he thought, dropping the Chinese food on the dining table.

"What you packing dishes for? I told you I was keeping the apartment."

Serenity wiped beads of sweat from her forehead. "I've been stuck in this apartment for a week. I had to do something or go crazy from boredom."

"Well, take a break. I got some stuff we need to talk about." He pulled out a chair for her to sit in.

"What's up?"

"I didn't want to chance having Sha's lieutenant around when I offed the Heads, so they gonna meet me up on my roof tomorrow night. The thing is I don't know if I made them suspicious."

"Okay... and?"

"I know you said you would die for me. But will you kill for me?" Koran asked, his eyes staring straight into hers.

"Yes." Serenity answered without hesitating. "Who do you want me to kill?" she asked, ready to make moves for her boo.

"After I make the call, we'll go up on the roof and wait. I want you to hide beside the roof exit door. When they walk through, wait until the last man walks out, then come from behind and put two in the back of his head. Think you can handle that?"

Serenity nodded.

"You sure?"

"Yeah, Boo. I'm sure. And after that we leaving, right?"

"Yep. We're outta here."

"Good." She stood and pulled the tee-shirt over her head. "Since this will be our last night here, let's make some memories."

Koran's eyes roamed all over her body and his dick bounced in his jeans.

"Come take my clothes off then."

U. E. Wynn

Chapter Thirty

Friday, September 2nd was the beginning of the end for the M.G's. Or was it? Koran and Serenity spent most of the morning packing and loading his truck. The army bags stuffed with money he was leaving behind. Jahad would bring it when he got out the hospital along with the other duffel bags, with the help of Joey and Kwan in stash equipped vans.

Around two o'clock Koran went to Emma's to tell her he was leaving. He also had a surprise for her. Something he and Jahad had worked out. When he came in she was siting in the living room watching Wheel Of Fortune with a joint burning in the ashtray on her coffee table.

"Don't bankrupt baby, don't bankrupt!" she said coaching a young black lady on the screen. "Okay, baby, now ask for an S... No baby an S!"

Koran laughed. "I don't think she can hear you Mrs. Harris."

Emma turned, grinning. "I reckon she can't. Come on in here and sit down." She patted the seat beside her. "You want something to eat."

"Nah, I'm good. I came to tell you I'm leaving tonight. I'm moving to North Carolina. Jah moving down there too when he gets out the hospital."

"Moving?" Emma stared at him with a blank expression, then her eyes filled with tears. Koran and Jahad were all she had in terms of family. She couldn't imagine not having them around. "You're moving? I thought you didn't like the south."

"I gotta learn to like it. I'm taking your advice and leaving the streets alone. Figured I'd go to college and try my hand at something legal."

Emma wiped her eyes and smiled, although her heart was shattered. "That's good baby. You go down there and make something of your life. But you better not forget about ole Mrs. Harris, you hear? Y'all come back and visit me and bring my baby, Jamel."

Koran smiled. "We won't have to, you're coming with us. I know you ain't think we were leaving you up here and miss out on your good cooking. When Jah gets out the hospital, he's bringing you with him. You can either live with him or me. Or you can have your own house. And before you say anything we ain't taking no for an answer.

"I'm coming with you?" Emma asked softly, confused.

"Yep."

Emma blinked a few times, then wrapped her frail arms around his neck.

"Thank you baby! I don't know what I'd do without my boys."

"We don't know what we'd do without you either Mrs. Harris." Koran smiled and hugged her tightly with his good arm.

The rest of the day crept by at a turtle's pace. To pass the time, Koran and Serenity made memories from the kitchen to the living room. They fucked in the bathroom, the bedroom on the floor, then back to the bathroom where they took a long hot shower. By the time a quarter to ten rolled around they were both lying in bed exhausted and jittery.

Soon it was time for Koran to make the call.

"A yo Prince, I got scrams on my roof right now," Koran said in a rushed tone when Prince answered the phone. "I wanna body his ass right here and now, but I want y'all to hear this shit first."

"What you mean? What duke screaming?"

"Some shit about one of the lieutenants being on some bullshit. Just hurry up man! Call Star and Lord so y'all can come together."

"A'ight give us like an hour. A yo, Son, shit is crazy right now. I know you here the sirens. Bronxdale is a national disaster area! I'm waiting on Star and Lord now to find out what happened with the other shit."

"Well, y'all niggas hurry up man. It's kinda chilly on this damn roof."

"A'ight. One."

"One." Koran nodded at Serenity as he hung up. "It's on now. We got an hour before they get here. You know it's gonna be windy on the roof so wear your jacket. The black one. What's up you ready?"

"Ready as I'll ever be," Serenity replied, with a malicious gleam in her eyes.

The temperature on the roof was right at fifty degrees when they exited the staircase, but with the strong wind it seemed more like forty and brought tears to their eyes.

"Damn baby, it's windy as fuck up here," Serenity said, pulling the hood from her Nylon Nike wind breaker over her head to keep her hair from blowing. "Why didn't you tell them to come to the apartment?"

Koran shook his head. "Nah, this is where it all started for me. Right here on this roof. This where I'ma end it. Go ahead and get in position." He looked down at his watch. "We have about ten minutes before they show up. Make sure you can see with the hood over your head too. Don't fuck around and shoot me."

Serenity giggled. "I won't shoot you, boo. Give me a kiss before I go." She wrapped her arms around his neck and plunged her tongue in his mouth.

"Whoa! C'mon, Sin. We gonna be up here fucking in a minute if you don't chill." He laughed as he broke the kiss. "That shit would be crazy right? They'll walk though the door and I'll have you bent over and shit."

"Shut up," she laughed pecking him on the lips before rushing off.

Koran watched her leave tempted to send her back to the apartment. If he knew it wouldn't be a wasted breath, he would have done just that. But, like himself, Serenity was looking forward to the kill. It showed in her eyes. Five minutes later his back was to the door when it open and he heard the crunch of the footsteps on the small pebbles that layered the roof.

This was it. The finale. Taking a deep breath, he tightened his grip on the gun he held listening as the footsteps grew closer.

"A yo Koran, where the nigga at?" Prince asked from behind him.

"Right here." Without hesitation Koran spun around and raised his gun in one motion. Prince stood no further than six feet away. Lord and Star flanked his sides.

"Koran, what the…"

'Boom! Boom!'

Koran fired two shots into Princes' forehead that lifted him off his feet and sent the New York Yankee's fitted he wore flying through the air with a chunk of his head still inside the cap. Reacting off instinct, Star reached for his gun and had it half way up when Koran squeezed off two more rounds that hit him right between the eyes. The force from the bullet whipped his head back before his body landed on top of Prince's. At the same moment, Serenity ran from beside the exit door and shot Lord, who stared at Koran through perplexed eyes, three times in the back of his head. He fell flat on his face only inches from where Koran stood with tears threatening to fall from his eyes.

Serenity walked over and grabbed him by the arm, but he made no motion to move. Lying dead in front of him was three men he once considered his brothers. He shook his head as the tears fell from his eyes. This is where it ended. After tonight he couldn't see himself killing anymore.

"Come on baby. It's over now," Serenity said leading him to the roof exit door.

Back at the apartment they took a quick shower and changed clothes. The whole time Koran stayed silent, too caught up in his thoughts to speak. It was over. The Heads were dead. Still, he didn't understand why. What was the real reason behind their treachery? Were they in on it together? Greed? Power? It didn't add up when they all had so much money they'd never be able to spend it all. It had to go deeper. It had to. But he guessed he would never find out.

On the way out the apartment with Serenitys' arm looped through his good one, he gave one last look at the living room just as his cell phone rung. Probably Jahad he thought. How wrong he was.

"Yeah, what up?"

"Surprise muthafucka! You thought it was over?" the Operator asked mockingly.

Koran nearly dropped his phone hearing the voice he knew so well.

"Nah, man! It can't be you! It can't be!" he roared, sliding down the wall.

"What is it Koran?" Serenity asked, noticing that his hands were trembling.

Koran ignored her, focused on the voice in his ear. "How? Why? You supposed to be…"

"How?" the Operator laughed. "You wanna know how? You, was how nigga. I tried to use Hector stupid ass to body you an Jah. Then I was gonna sic him on the other Heads, but them damn Puerto Ricans can't do shit right. So I switched up tactics and used you instead. Smart, huh? I knew how to push your buttons. How to make you move and you did exactly what I thought you would do. You and your little bitch killed three birds with one stone, or some shit like that." He laughed again. "Oh, and yeah, I was watching. Saw you cry like a bitch too."

Koran closed his eyes and shook his head. "Why man? You of all fucking people. Why?"

"Ask your brother why, nigga. You lucky I just didn't kill your ass and even the score. I wanted to add some fun to it though. But you still gonna die. It's only right. A brother for a brother. I don't think Jah will be able to answer your question though. I'm bout to body his ass in a few minutes. Oh yeah, before I go. Remember that hit you did on the Polo Grounds? That was Jah's ex-girl you bodied. And yeah, that little bastard Kay, Kay-Kay or whatever it is you call him, that's Jah's son. I set all that up just to see how far you would go. Yeah, you a killer, but you my killer nigga. Now start making funeral arrangements for your brother, you stupid muthafucka!"

The Operator hung up leaving Koran speechless.

"Koran! Koran! What's wrong?" Serenity asked, jerking his arm.

"Goddamnit! I gotta call Jah. It's Sha'!"

COMING SOON
BOSS: Caught Up In The Hustle!

A Whores Conscience

COVER REVEAL SOON!

SEND MONEY ORDER/CHECK TO:

WYNN PUBLICATIONS
P.O, Box 40411
2777 Brentwood RD.
Raleigh, NC 27604

NAME	
ADDRESS	
CITY	
STATE	ZIP
EMAIL	

BOOK TITLE	PRICE EACH	QUANTITY	TOTAL
BEHIND THE MASK	12.00		
FALSE	12.00		
MY BROTHERS KEEPER PT 1	12.00		
MY BROTHERS KEEPER PT 2	12.00		
	TOTAL		
THANK YOU FOR YOUR BUSINESS	SHIPPING & HANDLING	6.00	
	FINAL TOTAL